Ann Barker was born and brought up in Bedfordshire, but currently lives in Norfolk.

For more information about Ann Barker and her books, please visit:
www.annbarker.com

A COUNTRY GENTLEMAN

Lord Thurlby can only ever recall previous visits of Lavinia Muir, his mother's goddaughter, with a shudder. So it is with undisguised horror that he hears she is to come and stay again. Her arrival on the common stage, accompanied by the flirtatious Isobel Macclesfield, does nothing to allay his fears. When he learns that Lavinia has become entangled with the rakish Lord Riseholm, his reservations appear to be justified. However, with the passing of time, perceptions begin to change, and the arrival of Lord Riseholm himself begins to resolve matters once and for all.

Books by Ann Barker
Published by The House of Ulverscroft:

HIS LORDSHIP'S GARDENER
THE GRAND TOUR
DERBYSHIRE DECEPTION
THE SQUIRE AND THE
SCHOOLMISTRESS
THE ADVENTURESS
THE OTHER MISS FROBISHER
LADY OF LINCOLN
CLERKENWELL CONSPIRACY
JILTED
THEODORA IN LOVE

ANN BARKER

A
COUNTRY
GENTLEMAN

Complete and Unabridged

ULVERSCROFT
Leicester

First published in Great Britain in 2011 by
Robert Hale Limited
London

First Large Print Edition
published 2012
by arrangement with
Robert Hale Limited
London

Copyright © 2011 by Ann Barker

British Library CIP Data

Barker, Ann.
  A country gentleman.
  1. Love stories.
  2. Large type books.
  I. Title
  823.9′2–dc23

  ISBN 978–1–4448–1278–7

Published by
F. A. Thorpe (Publishing)
Anstey, Leicestershire

Set by Words & Graphics Ltd.
Anstey, Leicestershire
Printed and bound in Great Britain by
T. J. International Ltd., Padstow, Cornwall

This book is printed on acid-free paper

For Finella and Mario
— happiness always

1

Lord Thurlby took off his spectacles, polished them, and stared across the room and through the window that looked out into the garden. In truth, the prospect was not particularly inviting. The late spring rain which had held off for so long was falling in torrents, drumming musically against the panes, splashing on the paved area outside, and causing little rivulets to form amongst the gravel. The water garden, constructed some fifty years before by his grandfather, would be full to overflowing, he mused. Later he would go and inspect it. Later, when it was fine; but not now.

He put his spectacles down on top of the letter that he had just been reading, pushed back his library chair, and strolled over to the window. It was a grim day, indeed; so unseasonably chilly in fact that even such a hardy individual as the earl had ordered a fire to be lit. He smiled down as Lilly, his brindled greyhound got to her feet, and began prancing about, her tail wagging in anticipation of a walk. Bending, he stroked her head gently, pulling her silky ears and looking down into her trustful, melting brown eyes.

'Not today, girl,' he said, in his rather husky, gravelly voice. Lilly would be making do with a scamper about the hall today. Her walk would have to wait until the weather was better. In truth, she wouldn't really mind. She was a fair-weather dog, only going outside from grim necessity if the weather was bad. Once she had poked her nose out of the door and discovered the realities of the situation, she would willingly return to the fireside rug.

He looked outside again, and frowned briefly as he saw one of his gardeners going doggedly about some task. Walking over to the mantelpiece, he rang the bell, and then kicked the logs in the hearth into some more positive action with his booted foot. When the footman entered, his lordship was in the act of putting two more logs onto the flames.

'Allow me, my lord,' said the footman hastening forward. Dressed immaculately in dark green with fawn trim, the servant, like all his lordship's male staff, wore his own unpowdered hair, tied back in a queue.

'It's done,' the earl replied straightening, brushing his hands together and then wiping them on a handkerchief. 'Fetch me some claret would you, Hewson? Then go and have someone find out what the devil that gardener is doing in the wet, and tell him to stop it. There's no task that I can think of that can't wait until the weather is better. It's not part of my plan to have any of my people contracting pneumonia.'

'Very good, my lord.'

The footman was about to withdraw when the earl said, 'How is your mother, by the way?'

'Much better, my lord. The beef broth you had sent to her has set her up a treat.'

'It wasn't my doing,' Thurlby said dismissively. 'Mrs Campsey packed the basket. Now go and see about that gardener. And don't forget my claret.'

'Yes, my lord. No, my lord.' Knowing that the earl's abrupt manner sprang from his dislike of being thanked, Hewson said no more; but he and every person that served Lord Thurlby knew that their noble master carefully observed the needs of his staff and saw that they were attended to in the most unobtrusive way possible. The cook may have packed the basket, but the earl would have ordered it to be done.

After the footman had left, the earl remained looking down into the flames. Lilly, who was never far from his side, trotted over to where he was standing, and lay down next to him, her head on her front paws. His lordship was still standing in the same place when the footman returned with claret on a tray.

'Jenks was tying up one of the climbing plants, my lord,' he said as he set his burden down on a small table.

'Is he coming in?'

'I believe so, my lord.'

'Not without a protest, I'll warrant. No, don't pour for me. I'll do it myself.'

The earl grinned as he poured himself a glass of the rich red wine. He could well imagine the conversation between Jenks the gardener, and the unlucky soul who had been given the task of summoning him inside. 'I've known Master Victor since before he was ever breeched,' he would have said, quite unimpressed by his employer's rank. 'If he thinks he's going to tell me when I should and shouldn't tie up them roses, then he's got another think coming.'

Jenks was only one of many servants who had known the earl throughout his life. Victor William Carey Scott, sixth Baron Northborough, fourth Earl of Thurlby had been born in this very house just over thirty-four years ago. He had not been destined to be the earl, being the younger of the two sons born to the third earl and his countess. There were no other children, and there had been ten full years between the two boys. Victor, still only a baby when his brother had gone off to Eton, had hardly known him in adult life. A tragic riding accident to the third earl's son and heir had brought about Victor's elevation, first to the position of Viscount Croyland, then upon his father's death, to the earldom itself.

A novelist, he supposed, would have made some piece of drama of that. The gallant older brother, handsome, popular with the ladies, clearly made to occupy a seat in the House of Lords, is sadly cut off in the flower of his manhood. Left to take his place is the less dashing younger son, not so dark, not so handsome, and not so popular. No doubt, too, this fictitious younger son would ingloriously rejoice over the death of his sibling. The truth was far less exciting. The death of Allan had been deeply grieved by all; but his father, although much distressed at Allan's death, had never doubted his younger son's abilities.

As the third earl had lain dying, Victor had been summoned to his bedchamber to make his last farewells. 'God bless you and keep you, my boy,' the dying man had said. 'You'll do your duty. You'll look after your mother. You'll care for our people.' It hadn't been a request for some kind of reassurance. It had been spoken with confidence; a comforting thought for the old earl to dwell upon in his last earthly moments. He had had no doubt that his son would indeed do his duty; that the heavy charge of the earldom with all its responsibilities together with its privileges would be safe in this young man's hands.

For the ten years that had followed his father's death, Victor had faithfully fulfilled the charge laid upon him, and for the most part, his duty was also his pleasure. He loved this place, every bit of it, from the furthest field, to the most sheltered flowerbeds next to the south wall; from the huge ballroom, used only very rarely for great functions, to the schoolroom on the upper floor where he had first learned his letters. He acknowledged that he was unusual amongst men of his class, infinitely preferring country life to town pursuits. He liked the company of his neighbours, finding it as easy to chat with the local farmers and professional men as with the Earl of Burghley, his near neighbour. Looking round at the oak-panelled library, surrounded by the smell of books and leather, he felt at home and at ease with himself.

Needless to say, he had thought more than once that he ought to take a wife. He was not by any means averse to the company of ladies. He had kept a mistress in Stamford for several years, until she had decided to move to London, wanting a taste of city life. Since her departure over a year ago, he had never lacked for female solace when he had a need for it.

As for a countess, he only had to look at his own mother to decide that a lady would have to be very special indeed to take her place. He had not yet found anyone that special, and he was not prepared to settle for second best. There had been a young lady to whom he had been very attracted when he had still been Viscount Croyland. He had dreamed of marrying her and living happily ever after. What a foolish fantasy that had been! Nevertheless despite the heartbreak of the past, he had no wish to see the title die with him, but that was unlikely to happen. He had a distant cousin who would be the one to succeed him, and he knew nothing to the man's discredit. He could afford to look about him at leisure.

He walked back towards his desk and picked up a letter which had come to him that day from London, consulting him about some matter. Lilly raised her head from her paws, thought about following him, then settled back again close to the fire.

There were some of his station who, on receiving such a missive, would immediately have been calling for their bags to be packed so that they might head for the capital without delay. Thurlby was not one of their number. He would not dream of neglecting the request that had been made of him. At the same time, he could not think of any reason why he should be obliged to visit a place that he cared for so little. A thoughtful letter in reply would suffice. If his correspondent wanted more of him, then he could come to the country.

Out of the corner of his eye, Thurlby caught sight of Jenks, soaking wet, making his way across the lawn towards the kitchen. No doubt the old man was sorely tempted to shake his fist at him! He smiled. Someone in the kitchen would make sure that he took off his wet things and had a warm by the fire. After a few moments' thought, the earl picked up the letter again, and put his glasses back on in order to examine it further.

There was a gentle tap upon the door, and a moment later, the countess came in. 'May I join you, dearest?' she asked. 'It is such a depressing day, and I know how cosy this room is.' Her voice, though feminine in pitch, was husky like his own. He could well remember her complaining how many people were prone to ask her if she had a cold. 'I always sound like this,' was her response. 'Had you not noticed?'

Her voice was his only inheritance from

her. She was slim and willowy, her bearing still proud and elegant despite her sixty-odd years. Her once fair hair was now white, and her blue eyes retained some of their youthful sparkle. Dressed fashionably in a gown cut in the new Empire line, she looked like a superbly dressed woman of her own age.

'Of course, Mama,' the earl replied, coming forward to kiss his mother on the cheek, then led her to the hearth where she sat down. Lilly stood up and buried her face in the countess's outstretched hand, her tail waving gently. 'Would you like a glass of claret?'

She raised her brows. 'At this hour?' she asked. 'No, thank you. I have long since discovered that alcohol in the morning does not suit me at all. I should simply end up sleeping for the rest of the day, and I don't want to sleep. I want to talk to you.'

The earl sighed, grinning at the same time. 'Now why should that have such an ominous ring?' he mused, as if talking to himself.

'I haven't a notion,' his mother answered. 'When am I ever anything but reasonable?'

She looked up at him and reflected that here indeed was a son of whom a woman could be proud. Tall, upright and broad, he looked the picture of male health and vigour. His plentiful dark-brown hair was swept back from his broad, intelligent brow, and his hazel

9

eyes, rimmed with green, were exactly like his father's. His chin was square and manly, and gave the impression of one who would not easily be swayed from his chosen course. It was true that he was not as conventionally handsome as his elder brother had been, and was inclined to deprecate his own looks. A severe expression did not bring out the best in him, but when amused and at his ease, he could truthfully be described as an attractive man. He could easily have married e'er now, had he not been so picky.

'Strange,' murmured the earl, narrowing his eyes, 'but as soon as you start to talk about how reasonable you are, I begin to scent danger.'

The countess's expression softened. 'Sometimes, Victor, you are so like your father,' she said.

He grinned wryly. 'Then you'll recall that I dislike flummery as much as did he. What is it, madam?'

'Nothing to which you would take exception,' she replied. She stopped stroking Lilly, then resumed caressing her on being butted with a wet, insistent nose. 'It is only that I have invited Lavinia to stay.'

'Lavinia Muir!' exclaimed the earl, looking horror-struck. 'Oh my God!'

'Victor!' exclaimed the countess reproachfully. 'There is no need to blaspheme when all

I have done is issue an invitation to my goddaughter.'

'I beg your pardon, Mama,' Thurlby responded. 'It is simply that I cannot forget what happened last time.'

Miss Lavinia Muir was the daughter of Lady Thurlby's oldest friend, so much so that Miss Muir was accustomed to refer to her ladyship as 'Aunt Phyllis'. Lavinia's mother, Miss Beatrice Harris as she then was, and the Honourable Phyllis Camberwell had met when they had made their come-out, and had kept in close contact ever since. Lavinia's parents had married for love, and while they had been very happy, there had never been much money to go round. Perhaps in those circumstances it was as well that they had only been granted one child, the little daughter to whom the countess and her husband and another friend had acted as godparents.

They had not lived nearby; indeed, the Muirs had spent a large part of their married life abroad, where Richard Muir had been employed at various embassies as a minor functionary. Once Lavinia was old enough, she had been sent to school in England, and the headmistress had been prepared, on payment of a fee, to keep the child at school during the holidays if necessary. Needless to

11

say, if an invitation was ever issued for her to stay with friends, then she was encouraged to accept it.

On one disastrous occasion five years before, when she was fifteen years old, she had spent the summer holidays at Thurlby Hall. Lady Thurlby's soft heart had meant that she had acceded to Lavinia's request that she might be permitted to bring her friend Isobel Macclesfield with her. The countess had regretted her kindness almost from the first, for Miss Macclesfield had been spoiled, selfish and a little on the insolent side, and her hosts had been obliged to administer more than one reproof.

Between them, the girls had managed to release the bull from his field, kill the gardener's prized pineapples, lose the fish from the pond, almost ruin Lady Thurlby's best Turkey carpet, and narrowly escape being shot by their host, all within the course of the first few days.

The girls had declared themselves contrite, although Thurlby had suspected that Miss Macclesfield was only just able to prevent herself from giggling, even while his lordship was raking them down for their folly.

No other day had gone as badly after that. Nevertheless, the earl had quite understandably been on tenterhooks for the rest of the visit, and had been heartily glad to see the back of the two young visitors. Regrettably, Miss Macclesfield had not seemed to think it necessary to send Lady Thurlby a letter of apology. Lavinia had done so, however, and from then onwards, a regular correspondence had enlivened the existence of both ladies.

The following year had brought dreadful news. Lavinia had been at school in Bath when tidings had been received that the vessel carrying her parents to Portugal had sunk, with the loss of all on board.

It had been a devastating blow. In the absence of the necessary elements for a proper funeral, the earl had arranged for there to be a memorial service in the parish church at Thurlby. He could still recall Lavinia's small, upright, dignified figure, all in black, standing at the front of the church. Although only sixteen years of age at the time, she had insisted upon attending the service, in company with her maternal aunt and uncle, with whom she was to reside at their home in London.

Mindful of the charge that his father had placed upon him, Thurlby had attended the funeral, prepared to offer what help he could. The news that she was to be given a home by someone else had come as a great relief to him. He would have been the last person to try to wriggle out of doing his duty, but he was glad that this had not meant that he would be obliged to give her houseroom.

Her aunt and uncle had no children of their own, and were willing to take the girl in. He had thought that she would be engaged or even married in two or three years and had supposed, perhaps naively, that his responsibilities, nominal though they might have been, would be over. His mother's request would appear to indicate otherwise. Her next words confirmed his suspicions.

'The most shocking mischance! Mrs Stancross — Lavinia's aunt, you know — has suffered a severe stroke.'

'Brought on by what?' asked the earl, his tone ominous.

'Victor!' exclaimed his mother reproachfully. 'That was quite uncalled for.'

'I beg your pardon, Mama. You were saying?'

'She is unlikely to regain her former health. Mr Stancross is very anxious, and the last thing they want — '

' — Is a wilful young miss in the house,' the earl concluded.

'Is a young lady in need of chaperonage, I was going to say,' corrected his mother in dignified tones. 'Mr Stancross wants to take his wife to the sea. Life with an invalid aunt and her anxious husband will be quite inappropriate for Lavinia.' She paused. 'We may have her, may we not, dearest? I should like it so much.'

The earl glanced at her in surprise. Surely he was not so formidable a domestic tyrant that his mother was wary of making such a request? At once, he smiled reassuringly. 'Of course we may,' he assured her. 'This is your home. You may have whomsoever you please to stay. She will be very welcome.'

He could not see how they could refuse. What was more, he could see the very real pleasure on the countess's face at the prospect of entertaining Lavinia. He had never doubted his mother's love, but he had always known that she would have liked to have had a daughter. When his father and his brother had been alive, it must have seemed to the countess at times that the house was full of men's talk. To have Lavinia's company would make a welcome change for her, and give her some company when he was out overseeing his estate.

With an effort, he suppressed a sigh, regretting the disruption to his peaceful existence. Nevertheless, he could not help saying, 'There had better be some improvement in her behaviour this time. She very nearly drove me to drink, I can tell you.'

'And me,' his mother agreed ruefully. 'But what else can we do? The poor child has no one else. Besides, she is several years older. She will have outgrown the follies of youth, surely. In any case, I do not see that we can honourably do anything other than have her here.'

'Yes, I know that,' her son replied. 'I can quite see that we have no alternative. There is just one stipulation: Miss Isobel Macclesfield is not to be allowed within one hundred miles of this place.'

'I quite agree,' said his mother, barely repressing a shudder.

2

The entire Stancross household had been cast into complete confusion by the stroke suffered by Lavinia's aunt. This was not really surprising. Neither Uncle Seth nor Aunt Betty was a decisive person to begin with. A situation such as this tended to bring out the worst in them. It had been Lavinia who had ordered that Mrs Stancross should be carried up to bed, and who had insisted that nothing should be spooned down her throat until the doctor had been. Even the summoning of the doctor had been a challenge to Lavinia's ingenuity, for neither her uncle nor her aunt had suffered a day's illness for years. Before a doctor could be consulted, therefore, it was necessary to find the names of some to whom she might apply.

After the nature of Aunt Betty's complaint had been determined, it had been Lavinia who had suggested that Uncle Seth should take his wife away to Lyme Regis in order to recuperate. The doctor had agreed whole-heartedly with this suggestion.

'Lyme will set her up for sure,' her uncle had said, his eyes unhappy and hunted as they had darted first this way and then that. 'I have known the sea air do wonders.'

'I am sure she will benefit from it,' Lavinia had agreed. Impossible to say that she could not see how even Lyme could effect healing for Mrs Stancross's pitifully lifeless limbs, stumbling speech, and crooked face.

'She will, she will,' Mr Stancross had replied, clearly grasping at straws. 'She will be back on her feet in no time, you'll see.'

It had only remained for him to write to Lord and Lady Thurlby, begging their kindness on Lavinia's behalf. He had done so, and soon afterwards, the expected reassurance had come that she would be welcome at Thurlby Hall.

She grimaced. She was doubtful as to whether they actually meant it as she had behaved very badly; but that had been years ago, and she had grown up a good deal since then. What was more, she would not have Isobel Macclesfield to egg her on this time. She blushed when she recalled some of the activities that they had got up to during that memorable visit. She could only hope that the earl and his mother had forgotten most of them.

Perhaps it was not surprising that with all his anxieties directed towards his wife, her uncle failed to confirm the travel arrangements for his niece. Lavinia saw Mr and Mrs

Stancross off to Lyme, and then waited patiently for her own hired conveyance. It never came. An enquiry sent by one of the few servants left behind revealed that no carriage had been hired.

'Then I shall go on the mail,' Lavinia told the caretaker, who had been left behind to lock up the house. This confident pronouncement met with a set-back when she realized that she only had a few shillings to her name. She was by no means penniless, but, as she was still under twenty-one, she was dependent upon her uncle drawing money on her behalf. She had been due for some when Aunt had had her stroke, and then, of course, everything else had been forgotten. After he had left, she had gone to his desk in search for funds, and had found a letter that he had begun writing to his bank on her behalf. He had neither completed nor signed it.

'I've not got much, miss, but you're welcome to it,' the caretaker said, when she had explained her situation.

'That is very good of you,' she said with real gratitude. 'I will go to my uncle's banker first. Perhaps he might let me have something on the strength of this letter.' Lavinia knew where her uncle's banker conducted his business. Without very much hope, she put the unfinished letter into her reticule and went to visit him in his chambers. She came away feeling that she had not been taken even remotely seriously. There was only one thing for it; she would have to go on the stage.

Lavinia had never travelled on the stage, but she knew that it was much cheaper than travelling by the mail. She made her way to the Bull and Mouth, therefore, in order to make enquiries. But when she got there, she found that she did not even have enough to pay for a seat on the stage. She did toy with asking for a loan from some of her acquaintance in London, but thanks to the quiet way in which her aunt and uncle had always lived, she knew very few people in Town, and those that she did know had left the city for the country. She did not want to ask for help from people she barely knew.

It was while she was deep in thought, contemplating this awkward predicament, that she became aware that someone was hailing her, and, looking round, she saw her schoolfriend, Isobel Macclesfield, on the arm of a very rakish-looking man, perhaps as much as twice her age. Lavinia had never been introduced to him, but she had had him pointed out to her, and knew that he was Lord Riseholm, often referred to as 'his rakeship'.

Vernon James Murray Hawkfield, third

Earl of Riseholm was tall, lean and handsome. His jet-black hair was straight, and usually tied at the back of his neck in a queue. There were lines riven between his nose and his mouth, and around the corners of his charcoal-grey eyes, which often held a world-weary, cynical expression, as if he had seen everything that the season could ever offer and found it wanting.

He had been married, but his wife had died some ten years before, and he had shown no inclination to repeat the experiment, choosing instead to enjoy more temporary arrangements with actresses and the like. Clearly, ladies in society found him charming.

Lavinia was glad of the distraction from her troubles, and she allowed Isobel to present her to Lord Riseholm, who, after one or two remarks uttered in a caressing manner which Lavinia did not care for at all, took his leave.

'Is he not heavenly?' murmured Isobel, tucking her hand into Lavinia's arm. 'But he'll be my ruination, I fear.'

Had Lavinia been asked to ascribe some kind of supernatural quality to Lord Riseholm, heavenly was not the one that she would have chosen, but she did not say so, simply murmuring something non-committal as she glanced around. She could not see the slightest vestige of a chaperon. 'I thought you would have left Town by now,' Lavinia remarked.

'No,' Isobel replied in an airy tone. After the girls had left school, they had not met frequently, although they had kept up a desultory correspondence, and were always pleased to see one another. 'I am living with Mrs Wilbraham while my father is in Portugal. She is fixed in Town, and there is nowhere else for me to go, I'm pleased to say. After all, Town has its attractions.' She glanced briefly in the direction in which Riseholm had gone. 'And what of you?'

Lavinia explained about Mrs Stancross's stroke, and how the anxious couple had left London without making any provision for her. 'I have an invitation to go to Thurlby Hall to stay with my godmother, but no means of getting there,' she explained. She paused briefly. 'I don't suppose you . . . ?'

'Oh yes, yes, of course,' Isobel responded hastily, and with a slight air of abstraction. 'You must come to Mrs Wilbraham's with me, and I will sort everything out. Indeed, my sweet life, you might even prove to be my salvation.'

She began to look about her for a hackney and Lavinia, glad of a reprieve from thinking about her own concerns, lent her aid. They were in St Martin's-le-Grand in the shadow of St Paul's, only a stone's throw from Newgate gaol. It was hardly the place for a fashionable young lady to promenade.

'Come on,' said Isobel, a hackney having most fortuitously become available when a young clergyman had stepped down from it and shown himself delighted to help two young ladies to get in. 'You don't want to linger in this part of Town, do you?'

'No, I don't,' Lavinia answered when they were both seated inside the hackney. 'Why exactly were *you* here, come to think of it? I have the excuse of enquiring about the stage, but what of you? What were you doing, Izzy?'

Isobel's eyes met hers briefly before glancing away. 'Oh, this and that,' she answered carelessly. 'Nothing to interest you. But fancy your having to deal with that lady falling ill, you poor thing. Was she ill before? Did you get to see anything much of the season, or were you shut inside all the while?'

'I did get to one or two events,' Lavinia answered, rightly concluding that Isobel would not tell her what she had been up to in this part of Town. 'I was at Vauxhall a few weeks ago — on the night of the masquerade ball.'

'Oh really?' replied Isobel. 'I was there too; with a party, you know.'

Lavinia did not answer. She had enjoyed

her visit to Vauxhall, escorted by Mr and Mrs Stancross on one of the last outings that they had had together before Mrs Stancross had been taken ill. Her aunt and uncle were very kind, but their party had been a sedate one, and she had looked about her with a certain amount of envy, wishing that she was with a livelier group.

She had caught sight of a young woman whose appearance had seemed familiar, and she now suspected that it might have been Isobel. The young lady had been in company with a gentleman who had boldly slid his arm around her waist, and had appeared to receive no rebuke for his effrontery. Lavinia was now almost certain that the gentleman to whom she had just been introduced and the man who had been with the young woman at the masquerade were one and the same.

'Have you known Lord Riseholm for long?' Lavinia asked, then wanted to snatch the question back because she feared that it almost betrayed that she had noticed Isobel and the earl at Vauxhall, if indeed it had been they.

'Lord yes,' Isobel answered with a laugh. 'I don't take him seriously, of course. No woman does; or should.'

'No, I've heard that,' Lavinia answered. Every woman in London knew that his rakeship was a man to be avoided if one's reputation was to be kept intact. Clearly, Isobel had been playing fast and loose with her reputation. Did Mrs Wilbraham know?

The street to which the hackney took them was a fashionable one not far from Hyde Park. Lavinia noticed how hastily Isobel climbed down and paid the driver, glancing surreptitiously about her as she did so. Evidently, she did not want it to be known that she had returned in such a vehicle. Lavinia's suspicion was confirmed when, instead of entering the house that was nearest to them, Isobel tucked her hand into Lavinia's arm. 'Come on,' she said. 'It's such a lovely day that I thought we could have a little stroll before going in.'

Lavinia glanced up at the leaden coloured sky. There had not been a hint of sunshine all morning. 'Don't try to pull the wool over my eyes, Izzy,' she said. 'Does anyone know you went out in a hackney today?'

'I didn't go out in a hackney,' Isobel replied defensively, 'I came home in one.'

'Then how did you get as far as St Martin's-le-Grand?' Lavinia asked reasonably. 'Don't tell me you walked because I won't believe you.'

'I don't care what you believe,' answered Isobel with a flash of temper.

'Well in that case, you won't worry whether I 'prove to be your salvation' or not, will you?'

'And you won't worry about not having enough money to get to Thurlby.'

They stood glaring at one another on the pavement, until Isobel caught hold of her friend's arm. 'Oh, come on, Lavvy. All right, I took the opportunity of having a little flirtation with Riseholm, but no one need know about it. There's no harm done.'

Lavinia allowed herself to be pulled along, but in truth, she was starting to feel an uneasiness that was all too familiar. She very well remembered more than one occasion when she had been pressed into service in order to cover Isobel's tracks in the past.

At the age of fourteen, Lavinia had been sent to a select school in Bath where Isobel, a wealthy heiress and already flirtatious at the age of fifteen, reigned over an admiring court. Lavinia's arrival had occasioned very little remark. She was a pretty girl, fair-haired and with a neat figure, but no prettier than any other girl there. Her fortune was too small to attract attention, but not so small as to make her that most despised of females, a poor relation. She was good enough at her lessons to keep pace with the others, but not so clever that she made them feel stupid. She had no fixed home to miss, but she regretted leaving her parents, and was beginning to feel lonely.

It happened one day, when the girls were enjoying some leisure time, that a chance remark made by Lavinia had revealed to Isobel that her parents were in the diplomatic service. As Isobel's own father was abroad for the same reason, her mother having died some years before, and as no other girls at the school were in that position, a connection was established and Isobel had allowed Lavinia to become part of her court.

After this, loneliness had been at an end, as Lavinia was invited to take part in all kinds of expeditions which included shopping, visits to friends, and even, when the girls were judged to be old enough, the occasional card party.

This had been Lavinia's downfall. Invited to the house of a friend of Isobel's, with the approval of Miss Hackett, the headmistress, she had never had any intention of playing cards. But everyone else was doing so and, when she kept refusing, she had begun to feel that she was in some way being a spoilsport, and preventing other people's fun.

At last, she had accepted and had sat down at one of the tables. She had soon found that those present were very ready to instruct her in the game. She had learned quickly, agreed that they could now play 'seriously', and had been delighted to find herself a winner. Encouraged by this piece of good fortune, she had played and won again. A change in luck had not deterred her, for by then she had been caught up in the excitement of the game.

Strangely enough, it had been Isobel who had brought her to her senses. 'How are you getting on?' she had asked, her own game over.

As Lavinia had glanced up at her friend, she had seen the avid expressions of those around her, looking at the cards as if their lives depended upon how they turned. She had finished her game, and had been horror struck to realize that she owed over one hundred pounds. How could she ever find such a sum? She had got up from the table, knowing that she must pay her debts, but unable to imagine how it might be done.

Then she had heard Isobel speak. 'It's all right,' she had said. 'Had you forgotten, Lavinia, that you entrusted your purse to me for safe keeping? Here it is.'

Later, after paying her debt with the money that Isobel had given her, Lavinia had attempted to stammer her thanks, but Isobel had dismissed the matter with a wave of her hand. 'Look, I've told you not to worry,' she had said reassuringly. 'It really doesn't matter.

I'd only just won some of that myself. You can pay me back in other ways. I'm sure I shall want all kinds of favours doing.'

She had spoken with a twinkle in her eye, but Lavinia had soon found that the other girl had spoken no less than the truth.

On more than one occasion, Isobel had wanted to go out alone at night to meet a young man, a thing that was, needless to say, strictly against the rules of the school. Lavinia had been given the task of covering her tracks by pretending that her friend was in bed with a severe headache. She had been obliged to sneak downstairs much later at a given signal to let her back into school.

Then there had been the time when Miss Hackett had escorted the older young ladies to the theatre to see a production of Shakespeare. The enterprising Isobel had arranged to meet the same young man during the interval, and when the girls were given permission to walk about in twos, Lavinia had been obliged to make herself scarce whilst Isobel had indulged in an agreeable flirtation.

And then there were the bets. Isobel had been one of a group of friends who had dared each other to perform all kinds of bits of mischief for their own amusement. Some of them had involved stealing handkerchiefs from people's pockets, or small items from houses that they visited. Others had entailed tampering with the merchandise in a shop, such as turning all the books upside down on a shelf at one of the local bookshops, or unravelling a whole roll of ribbon at the haberdasher's.

When Isobel had indulged in one of her escapades, however, Lavinia had only been expected to act as lookout; and whilst she might have disapproved of the other girl's behaviour, she had not been able to see how she could refuse. She was never expected to perform any of these deeds herself. Indeed, had Isobel even so much as suggested such a thing, she would have braced herself to go to Miss Hackett immediately and confess the whole, even though it might have meant that she would have been sent away in disgrace.

Then, of course, there were the copious notes which Isobel had needed passing on to whichever swain was enjoying her favour at the time. Lavinia had often objected and tried very hard to extricate herself from these schemes. But Isobel had been very persuasive, and her requests always couched in such terms that Lavinia had felt she was making a silly fuss even to mention it.

'I only want to spend five minutes with him,' she would say. 'Is that such a lot to ask — in view of our friendship?' 'It's just a little note. I would do the same for you; you know I would.' Lavinia had known that this was not just an idle promise. Isobel would indeed have done the same for her; but there had been no one whom Lavinia wanted to meet; no one to whom she had wanted to send a note. The young men with whom Isobel seemed to want to spend her time always appeared to her to be tiresomely juvenile, and certainly not worth the risk of expulsion.

Although she paid off what she could of her debt to Isobel, her allowance was small, and the total seemed to go down with agonizing slowness. And always, Isobel kept saying that it didn't matter; that she could pay in other ways. The trouble with these kinds of 'other ways' was that one never knew when the paying would be finished!

Relief had come when, on her next birthday, she had received a most generous gift of £20 from Lady Thurlby. Together with £10 from Mr and Mrs Stancross, another gift from her parents and her quarterly allowance, she had found herself the possessor of exactly £100. She had thought regretfully of a shawl that she had seen in a shop window in Milsom Street. She had coveted it quite desperately; but the longing to be free of Isobel's demands had been much stronger than her desire for the shawl. Before she could change her mind, she had gone to Isobel with the money in her hands, together with a note which she had carefully composed. 'The bank may not let me have all this quarter's allowance at once,' she had said. 'But I have written a note of promise to you, to say that it is yours, as payment of my debt.'

'You've just been sent this money for your birthday?' said Isobel curiously, taking the note and glancing down at it. The money was still in Lavinia's outstretched hand.

'That's right.'

'And you want to give it all to me?'

'To pay off my debt.'

Isobel looked at her in silence for a long moment before slowly tearing up the paper in her hand. 'Keep your money,' she said, 'and consider the debt now paid.'

'Isobel, I won't keep watch or take notes or . . . or do any of those other things any more,' said Lavinia anxiously, still holding out the money.

'No, no, it's all right,' the other girl had replied, hugging her. 'Call it a birthday present from me. How much do you have now? Over fifty pounds? Shall we go and look at that shawl that you were admiring the other day?'

They had remained friends, but Lavinia

had not made the mistake of thinking that Isobel had changed her ways. Later, when she had seen a new girl going on an errand for Isobel, she knew that the other girl had found another lookout.

Now, meeting Isobel again in London, memories of school, happy for the most part, had come flooding back. Mr and Mrs Stancross knew very few fashionable people and life in their house could be very lonely. It was rather agreeable to meet up again with a friend of her own age.

When they were about halfway down the street, Isobel said 'This is it.' They walked up the steps to the front door and she rang the bell. She was just saying 'You won't tell, will you, Lavvy? Promise me . . . ' when the door was opened by the butler.

No sooner were they inside than a woman's voice was heard coming powerfully from the back of the hall. As its owner came into view, Lavinia saw a stout female of between forty and fifty, dressed fashionably, if not becomingly, in a pale-pink gown, with her light brown hair frizzed and caught up with a ribbon. 'So there you are, miss. I warned you about sneaking off, did I not? I would like to know — ' She stopped speaking abruptly, as she caught sight of Lavinia. 'Oh,' she added blankly, looking at her visitor.

'Good morning,' said Lavinia politely, curtsying.

'Oh Mrs Wilbraham, this is my school-friend, Lavinia Muir,' said Isobel. There was a slight note of tension in her voice. 'Lavinia, this is my kind guardian, Mrs Wilbraham.'

'Good day, Miss Muir,' said Mrs Wilbraham, eyeing the newcomer in a measuring way. Lavinia was dressed fashionably and with modesty. Her demeanour, more restrained than Isobel's, which sometimes had a tendency towards ebullience, earned Mrs Wilbraham's approval. This newcomer did not appear to be the kind of young woman who would tempt her charge into wrong-doing.

'Lavinia has been telling me all about the visit that she will be paying to her godmother, the Countess of Thurlby,' Isobel went on. 'Such a lovely morning we have had, have we not, Lavinia?'

'Yes; yes, we have,' Lavinia agreed. It was not a lie after all, even if Isobel had made it sound as though they had spent far more time together than had actually been the case.

'A friend of mine called upon me just half an hour ago and told me that she had caught a glimpse of you with Riseholm,' said Mrs Wilbraham suspiciously.

'How odd,' replied Isobel, achieving an airy tone. 'She must have been mistaken, because

I was with Lavvy. Perhaps your friend does not know me very well.'

'It was Mrs Craig and I think she knows you well enough,' answered Mrs Wilbraham. 'But she did say it was only a glimpse after all, and in any case we must not argue in front of a guest.' She ushered them into the drawing room and invited Lavinia to be seated. 'Where are you residing in London, Miss Muir? Is it near here?'

'I have been residing in Harley Street with my uncle and aunt,' Lavinia replied, 'but — '

'But they are to go to Lyme Regis quite soon, for Mrs Stancross's health, and Lavinia is to go to her godmother in Lincolnshire,' Isobel put in hastily. 'Just fancy, she has suggested that I might go with her. What do you think? May I?'

Fortunately, their hostess was turning to give an instruction to her butler to bring refreshments, so she did not see Lavinia's dumbfounded expression. 'Go to Thurlby?' said Mrs Wilbraham, the order for ratafia having been given.

'I have been there before,' said Isobel. 'The dowager countess and her son, the earl, were very welcoming.' This was true enough. The fact that they were also very heartily glad to see her go was not something that Isobel chose to mention.

It was now that Mrs Wilbraham turned her gaze upon Lavinia. 'Hmm. Harley Street, you say.'

'Yes, ma'am.' A really truthful person would now say that Mr and Mrs Stancross had already gone to Lyme, and that the invitation from Thurlby was only for one, but Lavinia could not bring herself to expose her friend in this way. Besides, there was something about Mrs Wilbraham that Lavinia could not like. She looked as if she could almost be brutal, given sufficient cause. Suddenly, Lavinia remembered the air of tension in her friend's voice. Mrs Wilbraham might deem Isobel's deceit to be cause enough.

Mrs Wilbraham looked carefully at Lavinia again. The Harley Street address, although unfashionable, and sometimes despised by members of the ton, suggested respectability. There was also her connection with the earldom of Thurlby to be considered.

Although Thurlby and his mother might seldom come to London, eschewing the fashionable scene, their name was an old and honourable one, and their coffers were very well able to afford the luxury of regular visits to the capital. Lady Thurlby might never choose to go to Almack's, but she could have obtained vouchers without difficulty; and although Lord Thurlby was rarely seen at White's, he was certainly a member. What was more, he was young, unmarried and, as far as anyone knew, unattached. This was a connection worth cultivating.

Miss Macclesfield's father was paying her a handsome sum to sponsor her in London and make sure that she made suitable connections. An alliance with Lord Thurlby would certainly meet with his approval and doubtless earn a very welcome bonus for the young lady's diligent chaperon.

'Well, we shall see,' said Mrs Wilbraham, not allowing her face to betray any of these thoughts. She gave a small smile. 'Do you have time to stay for nuncheon, Miss Muir? We should be more than happy to entertain you.'

Lavinia thanked her and accepted. She had been a little concerned as to how to feed herself whilst she was still in London. She would not have that to worry about, for today at least.

3

Lavinia decided to stay on at Harley Street for the time being. She could not think what else to do. The caretaker was very kind, but he made the situation plain. 'I'm to close the house at the end of the week, miss,' he said. 'You can stay until then if you like, but I haven't the means to keep it open for longer. Master didn't leave me any extra, or you could have it and welcome. Would you like me to make enquiries at the market to see if there's a cart going to Lincolnshire? There's all sorts of fruit and vegetables comes down from there, I believe. Someone might be going back and be able to give you a ride.'

Lavinia thanked him gratefully. She did not really want to appear at Thurlby Hall on the back of a vegetable cart, but at least it would be a solution to her problem.

Before she had left Mrs Wilbraham's, Isobel had whispered to her not to leave London. Chance would be a fine thing, she had thought to herself. She did not have the means to get beyond Barnet. It was true that Isobel had offered to help her with funds, but she had not mentioned the matter again, and

Lavinia had not found a moment to remind her, as Mrs Wilbraham had not left them alone. To her relief, the chaperon had not questioned her further about her meeting with Isobel, but she had asked her about Lord and Lady Thurlby. Lavinia had welcomed this topic because she had been able to talk about the earl and his mother without any deceit whatsoever.

The morning after their meeting, Lavinia was just getting up from the kitchen table after a modest breakfast of toast and marmalade, which she had prepared herself, when the caretaker came in with a note. 'P'raps it'll be better news, miss,' he said. He had already been to the market but had not yet had any luck in finding a cart to take her to Lincolnshire.

'Lets hope so,' she replied, opening the note. It was from Isobel.

Dearest Lavvy,

Absolute disaster! Mrs Craig, damn her, was not the only one to see me with Riseholm, and the game's up! At least I managed to convince Willy that you had no notion of what I was about, having met me later, and Willy's crony swore that I was alone with him. (My dear, he's so gorgeous, it was worth every minute of the risk!)

Willy has threatened me with bread and

water, followed by immediate despatch to my grandmother in Harrogate, and I just couldn't bear it! I managed to persuade her to consider allowing me to travel to Thurlby with you, and she is coming to your house, to speak to your aunt and uncle! Help me — please! I'll be so good, I promise!

Your devoted Isobel

Lavinia's first instinct was to go round to Mrs Wilbraham's house and wring Isobel's neck. How dare she involve another in her machinations in this way? She thought ruefully of how her friend had embroiled her in schemes in the past. Maddening though her behaviour might be, it was certainly consistent.

Slowly, she began to grasp the implications of what was said in the letter. Mrs Wilbraham was coming to Harley Street to consult with Mr and Mrs Stancross. Those good people were no longer there. What was she to do? What could she say that would not embroil Isobel and herself in more trouble? Quickly, she hurried to find the caretaker.

'A Mrs Wilbraham will be calling today,' she said. 'She will ask for my uncle or aunt.'

'They're not here, miss,' he said, as if speaking to one who was not aware of the fact.

Nobly forbearing from criticizing him for stating the obvious, she said, 'Yes, that's right. But do you think you could refrain from saying that? When Mrs Wilbraham is here, I mean.'

'I can't tell lies, miss,' said the caretaker, straightening. 'Couldn't face the others in my class meeting if I did.'

Knowing that the man was a devout Methodist who never missed his midweek meeting, Lavinia said, 'Yes, I understand. Do you think you could just not reply when she asks? Say 'This way, madam', or something like that. I'll tell her that you're deaf.'

'All right, miss,' he said, with some reluctance. 'As long as I don't have to lie.'

One room — the morning room — had been left for her occupation, whilst the rest of the public rooms had been shrouded with Holland covers. It was to this room, therefore, that she went, in order to make her preparations. Some cards had been left with compliments, and these she placed on the mantelpiece in full view. A copy of *The Gentleman's Magazine* had arrived just before her uncle had left for Lyme, and this she placed folded open on an inside page on a small table, with an old pair of her uncle's spectacles on the top. Then she opened her aunt's workbox and took out some sewing, a

41

piece of embroidery of which her aunt had been very proud. Poor Aunt, she thought to herself. She will not be completing it now. Suddenly, the tears that she had held back, first of all not to distress her uncle, and then not to embarrass the caretaker who could do nothing to help, would not be denied any more. So it was that when Mrs Wilbraham was announced, it was to discover her hostess quite genuinely dabbing at her eyes with her handkerchief.

'This is a fine welcome,' Mrs Wilbraham declared, distracted by Lavinia's tears from the speech that she had planned to make. 'Whatever is the matter?'

Unable to think of anything but the truth, Lavinia said simply, 'Aunt is ill.'

In common with some other robust-looking people, Mrs Wilbraham had a dread of illness. She took an involuntary step back. 'Nothing infectious, I hope.'

'I hope not, indeed,' replied Lavinia, beginning to see a way forward.

'What is to be done?' asked the visitor in an agitated tone.

'It is imperative that I should leave this house as soon as possible,' said Lavinia, priding herself on being able to speak with perfect truth.

'Have . . . have you been in contact with your aunt since the illness began?'

'Yes, I fear that I have,' answered Lavinia, feeling a little ashamed of making use of her aunt's misfortune in this way.

Now, her visitor was thrown onto the horns of a dilemma. Common courtesy, as well as the laws of hospitality, dictated that she should invite this unfortunate young woman to stay. In welcoming her, however, she might also be opening her home to some unknown, perhaps virulent, possibly even fatal disease.

After a moment or two, her eyes brightened. 'I have a solution,' she said. 'Isobel shall come round to bear you company, then she may go with you to Thurlby as you both wished.' Her face became serious as she recalled the reason for her visit. 'There are reasons why it is necessary for her to leave London at this time,' she said. 'I fear that she has not behaved well. You, on the other hand, are clearly a well-behaved, sensitive, compassionate young lady and, I am sure that she will benefit extremely from your example. How are you to travel? By hired vehicle?'

Lavinia, knowing that to say 'by carrier's cart on top of a sack of potatoes' would not make the right impression, murmured something inaudible.

'I shall send half the cost with Isobel. It is only fair that she should pay for her own share.'

Lavinia nodded. It was one of the few things that Mrs Wilbraham had said with which she felt able to agree whole-heartedly.

★ ★ ★

'Is this not fun?' said Isobel, her eyes sparkling, her dark curls bouncing. 'Far better than going on your own.'

'Far more *possible* than going on my own,' Lavinia corrected, as they waited for the York-bound stage. 'I did not even have enough money for my own fare.'

'Instead of which, we will be travelling together! What an adventure!'

Isobel had arrived the previous day, full of verve and vigour, and clearly delighted at having escaped retribution at the hands of Mrs Wilbraham. 'I dare say you may not believe it, because she was exceedingly agreeable to you, but she can be the most fearful woman,' she had declared after they had greeted one another. 'She really has put me on bread and water before now, you know — I was not making that up. And she thinks that she can withhold my allowance from me; *my* money, notice, not hers at all, but mine from my father! She has even kept all my jewels in London under lock and key; all, that is, except for the pearls which belonged to

Mama. The last straw was when she threatened to write to Papa, and then send me to my grandmother in Harrogate. Grandmother doesn't like to be bothered with me and she would have been furious at having all her plans spoiled.'

This had seemed to Lavinia to be the saddest thing that she had ever heard. She could not remember her father's mother, but her grandmother on her mother's side had been kindly and affectionate, and had spoiled her at every opportunity until her death when Lavinia was seven.

She had heard about Isobel's grandmother before, and what she had heard she did not like. She well remembered an occasion when Isobel had come back from Harrogate having paid a visit to her father's mother. As they had sat talking in the room they had shared with four other girls, Isobel had adjusted her shawl, and Lavinia had been convinced that she had caught a glimpse of bruises on her friend's upper arms. Isobel had said nothing about being beaten, but Lavinia could not think of any other explanation.

Isobel had brought her share of the money for the hiring of a vehicle, but it soon became clear that Lavinia could not find sufficient to cover the rest. It was then that Isobel had had yet another splendid idea. 'We could go on

45

the stage,' she had said. 'I could easily pay for both of our tickets with my share, then you would have all of your money for something else, and I would have something to keep me going until my allowance comes next month.'

'The stage,' Lavinia had murmured. 'Would it not be very shocking?' She had tried and failed to imagine what the earl and the countess would think of her travelling cheek by jowl with any chance met person.

'Not so shocking as sitting in the back of a vegetable cart with cabbages and potatoes,' Isobel had pointed out, Lavinia having told her to what straits she had almost been driven. 'Besides, no one need know. In any case, we will be chaperoning each other. Stay, though,' she had continued, looking even more excited, were that possible. 'Do you still have your mourning things left over from when . . . when . . . you know?'

'From when my parents died? Yes, I do.'

'Then you could pose as a widow,' Isobel had said.

'A widow? No, I could not,' Lavinia had replied, shrinking from the very notion. 'Every proper feeling would be offended.'

'Yes, you could. Just think how advantageous it would be. No one would bother you, or expect you to say anything much, and if they did, you could just get your handkerchief out and dab at your eyes. I could be a friend bearing you company. You have been saying how shocking it would be to travel on the stage. I ask you, what could be more respectable than a widow? As a matter of fact, your widowed state could even explain why you were obliged to travel on the stage anyway; a reverse in fortune, sudden discovery of debts, an entail, perhaps.'

Defeated by this barrage of reasons, Lavinia had laughingly capitulated. There was, after all, some logic in what Isobel had said. 'But we must resume our real characters before Lord and Lady Thurlby meet us,' she had warned. 'I would not have them involved in such deceit for the world.'

Since Lavinia had already been to the Bull and Mouth and made enquiries about the stage, it was she who had sent the caretaker back there again with money and instructions to book the tickets. She was not aware, however, that Isobel had caught the man before he left, and had given him a note to be delivered to a certain house in Berkeley Square. Isobel had smiled to herself. She and Riseholm had spent a delicious hour together in a private parlour in a little known inn. Whilst not wanting to appear as if she was chasing him, she had decided that it would do no harm to let him know where she was going, when, and by what conveyance. She knew that he had a nephew with property in Lincolnshire. Perhaps he might choose to pay his relative a long overdue visit. That would indeed be a feather in her cap!

By dint of arriving early and also, Lavinia suspected, some fluttering of eyelashes from Isobel, they were lucky enough to secure the forward facing seats. Lavinia was in the corner, dressed in black as agreed, and Isobel sat in the centre. Next to her on the other side was a soberly dressed man who looked to be in his fifties. He had his eyes fixed upon a heavy tome, from which he occasionally looked up, his eyes closed, his lips moving as if he were memorizing some passage.

Sitting with their backs to the horses were two women who were obviously mother and daughter. From their conversation, it seemed as though they had had little chance to chat recently, for they appeared to spend much of their time engaged in exchanges where one offered some piece of information, and the other in response exclaimed something like 'Well I never!' or 'Who'd've thought it?' generally with an expression of wide-eyed amazement. After a brief time, it became so predictable that Lavinia found herself longing to join in, and bit her lip to hide her amusement.

Glancing at Isobel, she could see that her friend had been seized by exactly the same thought. Knowing that the girl could easily draw unwelcome attention to them both by actually putting in the next interjection, she said, 'Don't you dare!' a phrase that so surprised the other occupants of the stage that for a brief moment, silence fell on the whole company. Even the man with the scholarly tome looked up with a startled expression on his face.

'No, ma'am,' said Isobel meekly, the incongruity of the remark nearly making Lavinia laugh out loud. Whatever anyone might say about Isobel, at least her company was not dull!

As the journey proceeded, they soon discovered that the stagecoach was by no means as well sprung as a private conveyance, and Lavinia began to think that she would be lucky to retain a single tooth in her head. Mercifully, quite soon the stagecoach stopped at Barnet so that the horses could be changed.

The two gossiping women got down from their seats and were met by a man who looked to be a farmer, probably the husband of the one and the father of the other.

'Thank goodness,' said Isobel with feeling. 'What did she have in that basket? Onions? I swear that if I had had to smell them for very much longer, I should have been quite ill.'

'Yes, but their owners were very entertaining,' Lavinia pointed out. 'What shall we have to laugh about and help pass the time away now?'

There was only a brief interval for them to swallow down some lemonade before the next horses were put to. When they left Barnet, they found that the scholarly man had also got down. They were joined by a young man in his twenties, making only three passengers inside.

The coach-master peered in at them all before recommencing the journey. 'Hmm. Could do with being full,' he said doubtfully. Lavinia said nothing in response, but almost felt like apologizing for being only one person.

The young man, clearly not similarly constrained, said cheerfully, 'Ain't our fault.' Then he added, smiling at his fellow passengers, 'Benjamin Twizzle's the name.'

His clothing was in good order, and plain for the most part, but with a touch of flashiness that denoted someone not quite a gentleman. His fair, curly hair was surmounted by a beaver hat, which he wore tilted at a rakish angle. He sat with his hands in his pockets, his legs spread wide apart.

Lavinia glanced a little concernedly at Isobel, for the newcomer seemed to be just the sort of unsuitable young man with whom her friend might decide to get up a flirtation. Isobel however, dressed very properly for travelling in a rather severe, plainly cut blue costume, inclined her head graciously, in the manner of a dowager.

Lavinia wondered whether Isobel knew any more than she did if it was proper to strike up a conversation with a stranger in this way. What *was* the etiquette in these circumstances? Did one simply introduce oneself, in defiance of all custom, or did one keep silent?

'It's all right,' he said, almost as if he had heard her thoughts. 'It's perfectly in order to introduce yourself on journeys such as this, particularly if you're travelling alone. Who else is to do the job, damn it? Anyway, I'm a parson's son, so what could be more respectable? Could hardly be more trustworthy if I were a parson myself, what?'

'I have known some strangely unreliable people emerge from parsonages,' said Isobel, her tone matching her manner to perfection. 'To be a parson's son is not in itself a recommendation, young man.' She then turned to Lavinia. 'Had it been the case, then poor Mrs Hedges would have been spared a good deal of wretchedness, would you not, my dear?'

51

Horror stricken at being thus appealed to and completely unable to think of anything in response, Lavinia took out her black-edged handkerchief and dabbed at her eyes.

'There, you see,' said Isobel looking at the young man reproachfully. 'Your foolish chatter has distressed her. We will be silent, if you please.'

To Lavinia's relief, the young man seemed to take this in good part, and after yawning, tilted his hat over his eyes and appeared to fall asleep.

'I wish I could do that,' Lavinia whispered to Isobel.

'I should be too afraid of being shaken off my seat,' Isobel replied. 'How long till we get to Thurlby?'

'I think we shall have to spend two nights on the road,' Lavinia replied. 'When we arrive at the George in Stamford, the earl will come for us. For goodness' sake, don't let him know about our deception.'

'There is not the least need for him to do so,' Isobel answered. 'We will not be staying the night there after all, so Mrs Hedges and her companion may become Miss Muir and Miss Macclesfield once again. Thank God Willie Wilbraham has no idea what we've done! What a lark!' She began to laugh.

'Hush,' said Lavinia quickly, glancing at

Benjamin Twizzle, who had not moved.

Had they not glanced away at that moment, they might have seen him smile slightly. So the two young ladies were both single after all, were they? He had not come across Miss Muir's name before, but he had heard of Miss Macclesfield, a young lady of some fortune who had acquired rather a fast reputation in London. He also knew Mrs Wilbraham slightly, and could well imagine that the young lady did not want her exploits to come to the ears of that formidable dame.

As his Christian name might indicate, Benjamin was the youngest son of his family, indulged by his mother, whilst his rather ascetic clergyman father closed his eyes to his imperfections. Early on in his life, Benjamin had developed the notion that his existence was meant to be a pleasure, and that those who surrounded him therefore had a responsibility to ensure that it was as agreeable as possible. Twizzle lived by his wits. His wits told him that there might be some profit, as well as some entertainment, in keeping an eye on these two.

4

The first night of the journey was to be spent at Hatfield, and when the coach swept into the inn yard, the ladies were both heartily glad to be able to get down and stretch their limbs.

Mr Twizzle leaped out ahead of them and claimed the privilege of handing them down from the coach. 'Mrs Hedges,' he said respectfully. 'And Mrs . . . Miss . . . ?' He paused, wondering what name she would make up.

Isobel managed to side-step this situation by simply ignoring him and helping Lavinia solicitously. She was not to be so fortunate once they reached the inn, however. The landlord stepped forward, beaming, and standing next to him was a maidservant with a huge bouquet in her arms.

'Welcome ladies,' said the landlord. 'May I ask if one of you is Miss Macclesfield? I was told to expect you both. These flowers come with the compliments of Lord Riseholm.'

Mr Twizzle was just behind them. Lavinia could almost feel his avid interest. She could certainly see the consternation on Isobel's face. What upon earth could they do? She might have guessed that her friend would not be at a loss for long. Isobel straightened her back. 'For shame,' she declared, turning to Lavinia. 'My poor friend! One would have supposed that your widowhood would have been sufficient to protect you from his advances!'

Lavinia looked at Isobel with a shocked expression on her face. Fortunately, this was probably what any onlooker would have expected.

'Put them in the public rooms,' Isobel continued. 'As for Mrs Hedges and I, we will share a bedchamber.'

'Of course, ladies,' said the landlord beaming. 'I have a very good room available for you. It must be my business to oblige any . . . er . . . friends of his lordship.'

Mr Twizzle smiled as he watched them go upstairs. So either Miss Macclesfield or the bogus Mrs Hedges, alias Miss Muir, was entangled with Lord Riseholm! Of the two, he suspected that it must be Miss Macclesfield — she who had tried to give him a set-down in that coach. He stored the information away to be used at a later date.

'Flowers from Lord Riseholm!' exclaimed Lavinia, as soon as they were in their room — a very superior one, no doubt due to the aristocratic connections of its temporary occupants. 'How ever did he know where to find you? Izzy?'

'Well . . . I may just have let it slip,' Isobel replied, trying to sound careless but blushing nevertheless.

'Let it slip? When?' Lavinia demanded.

'I . . . wrote him a tiny note.'

Lavinia gasped. 'You have been writing notes to Lord Riseholm?'

'What if I have?' Isobel answered defiantly, turning away her head so not to meet her friend's gaze. 'It's got us better accommodation, hasn't it? And better treatment.'

'Yes, but at what cost?' Lavinia pointed out. 'Thanks to your encouragement of Riseholm, everyone here thinks that *I* am the one who has attracted his attentions! Those flowers are for you and not for me.'

'We could not have said that it was I,' said Isobel in a reasonable tone. 'I am single, whereas you are a widow. We are not so far from London. Gossip could easily spread from here, and that Twizzle fellow looks just the kind of man to spread it.'

'Yes, and he will be spreading it about me,' said Lavinia in an agitated tone. 'Izzy, that landlord looked at me as if I was some sort of . . . sort of . . . '

'Oh, what does it matter?' Isobel interrupted.

'Nobody here knows us. We won't be coming back again and we won't be seeing that Twizzle creature either. Honestly! Twizzle! What a name!'

'Yes, and another thing,' Lavinia interrupted, remembering anther grievance. '*You* are travelling under your own name, whilst *I* am the one who has been saddled with a pseudonym when it was your idea.'

'Lucky for you,' Isobel retorted. 'At least nobody knows who you are, do they? There is no such a person as Mrs Hedges, is there? Thanks to a wretched mischance, my real name is known; but I do not mean to cry over spilt milk. How much would you wager that Twizzle is not *his* real name either? Depend upon it, he will no more want to disclose the circumstances of this meeting than do we.'

Since nothing could be done at present, Lavinia said no more on the subject, but this did not stop her from feeling profoundly uneasy. Masquerading as a widow had seemed quite harmless at first and almost a wise precaution to protect their reputations, given the necessity of travelling on the public stage. Now, she wished with all her heart that she had simply retained her own identity and travelled as unobtrusively as possible.

The problem was that Isobel was not very good at being unobtrusive. What was more, she was the kind of young lady to whom things tended to happen. Sometimes, of course, this could make for a more exciting life. Lavinia could only wish that it could have been a little duller on this occasion.

To Lavinia's relief, Isobel was quite happy to dine upstairs in their own room. 'We don't want to talk to that Twizzle fellow any more than we must,' she said. A further cause of thankfulness was that Isobel seemed to accept the necessity of eating very modestly, given their limited means. The landlady's thick home-made soup together with a plentiful supply of fresh crusty bread left them both feeling very well satisfied.

Their room, as well as being a good size, contained a very large bed, so that each young lady would be able to have a half to herself without feeling at all cramped. As they lay together in the darkness, Isobel said, 'Lavvy? Are you asleep?'

In truth, Lavinia had been on the point of drifting off. 'No,' she replied, resigned to a conversation. She had not forgotten how much Isobel liked to talk into the night, whilst she herself preferred early rising.

'I was just wondering — had you ever thought about Lord Thurlby?'

'Thought about him?' said Lavinia blankly, taken by surprise. Of course she had thought about him from time to time. She had no memory of a settled home, for her time with her parents had been spent in embassy accommodation, or in hotels or hired houses. When on their native soil, they took the opportunity of staying with friends. One of Lavinia's early memories was of coming to Thurlby as a child aged eight, and peeping from behind her mother's skirts at a very grown-up looking young man, the Honourable Victor Scott who, at twenty-two, and newly returned from Oxford, was giving assistance to his father on the estate.

When she was younger, she had been childishly infatuated with the Earl of Thurlby who was fourteen years her senior. He had always been kind to her, except when he had been very angry, as he had been frequently when she and Isobel had visited last time. No doubt he had regarded her in the light of something between a little sister and a tiresome responsibility. For her part, she had never forgotten his unsentimental kindness to her after her parents' death.

After the funeral service, everyone had gone back to Thurlby Hall for refreshments. It had been a small gathering, since many of those who knew Mr and Mrs Muir well were themselves serving overseas at foreign embassies. The conversation had ranged over a variety of topics, and Lavinia, younger than everyone else by several years, had felt like a small girl who had been allowed to attend an occasion that was not really relevant to her. She had slipped out of the house and gone back to the church where she had sat in one of the pews at the front, thinking about her parents. Inevitably, the tears had begun to flow.

She had not been aware of anyone else entering the church, but all at once, she was conscious of a gentleman sitting next to her, and a large handkerchief being placed in her hand.

'You didn't have to come,' she had said, after she had dried her tears. 'You have guests.'

'They can manage very well without me,' Thurlby had answered.

'And me.' She was silent for a moment, then said angrily, 'They were just talking and laughing, as if nothing had happened.'

'It's how some people protect themselves from unpleasant things,' he answered. 'Remember that many of your parents' closest friends could not be here today.'

'How is it that you understand?' she asked him curiously, after a short silence.

'I remember when my brother died,' he answered. 'After the service was over, people were slapping me on the back and telling me that I was Croyland now.'

'Did you want to hit them in the face?' Lavinia asked him.

'Is that how you feel?' he said. 'Pray don't hit my guests. I should find it so embarrassing.' She had responded with a watery chuckle.

Shortly afterwards, they had returned to the house and he had stayed by her side until the last mourner had left. She had kept his handkerchief, not under her pillow, as that would be far too foolish, but in the drawer with her special things, like the last letter that Mama had sent, and a drawing of the dog she had had when she was younger.

She was certainly not going to tell Isobel about any of that! 'No, not really,' she said eventually.

'I only wondered whether perhaps your parents — and his, even — might have had him in mind for you.'

'For me?' Again, Lavinia could not think what Isobel was talking about.

'As a husband, silly,' Isobel answered, her voice sounding impatient in the darkness.

The idea had never occurred to her. 'Good heavens, no,' she said quickly. 'I don't think such a notion ever entered their heads.'

Isobel laughed. 'In that case, I might set my cap at him. I'm sure that Willie is expecting me to do so. Indeed, I more than half hinted that I would in order to persuade her to let me come to Thurlby.' She thought for a moment. 'If I married him then I could be your aunt. Wouldn't that be entertaining?'

Lavinia laughed as well. 'Silly! I'm not even related to him. His mother was my mother's friend, that's all.'

Long after Isobel's breathing had evened out into sleep, she lay thinking about what had been said. How old would Lord Thurlby be? Thirty-four? Thirty-five? She was twenty. There were not as many years between them as there were between Isobel and Lord Riseholm, who could not be much less than forty, and with whom Isobel had clearly had some sort of a fling.

Unlike Riseholm, Thurlby was a good man, and he did not deserve to have a wife as flighty as Isobel. He deserved someone . . . someone . . . She was still pondering this matter when she fell asleep.

5

'This letter is worse than useless,' the Earl of Thurlby complained, waving a sheet of paper at his mother. They were sitting at the breakfast table, each having enjoyed that meal in the way that pleased them best. His lordship had downed a plateful of bacon and eggs and two slices of toast, a hearty enough breakfast for a man who has walked three or four miles before nine o'clock. Her ladyship, a later riser, had sampled just a roll and some coffee. Now they were engaged upon examining their correspondence.

'I take it the letter is from Stancross,' his mother remarked. 'Coffee, dear?'

'No, I'll stick to ale, thank you. Yes, it's from Stancross, confirming that your goddaughter is coming, but giving us no idea of how, or whether we are to meet her, and if so, when.'

'Give it to me,' said his mother. He handed the letter across the table and she examined it carefully. 'Yes, you are right,' she said. 'I suppose one cannot blame the man for being flustered, when one considers what he has endured. All the same, this is most awkward. Do you think that perhaps you ought to ride into Stamford and pay a visit to the George?'

He pursed his lips. 'Yes, it might be wise,' he agreed. 'Any conveyance bringing her from London will be most unlikely to avoid Stamford. I can leave instructions with the landlord to keep her there until he sends word to me.' He got up from his place. 'Just to be safe, I'll send a servant to Peterborough as well.'

'Pray heaven the poor girl won't have got herself into any kind of difficulty,' said her ladyship.

'Would you care to wager a small sum on the chance?' the earl asked ironically.

'You are very unlikely to arrive at the George at exactly the same time as Lavinia,' his mother pointed out, ignoring his last remark. 'After you have left a message there, you can go and have a glass of wine with Sir Richard Wallis.'

The earl laughed. 'You sound exactly like my tutor, who used to promise me all manner of treats if I finished my Latin exercise. But it would be good to visit Richard. It must be several weeks since we last saw one another.'

'He has been to London for the season,' her ladyship replied. 'It would do *you* good to go.'

'It would be more likely to drive me mad,' he answered frankly.

The journey from Thurlby to Stamford was a very familiar one to the earl. When escorting his mother in the barouche, they took the road which led them through Market Deeping. Today, on horseback, he was able to take some short cuts across the fields, mostly on his own land. Mercifully, the day was a sunny one, unlike that on which he and his mother had discussed Lavinia's arrival in his library.

The dinner club of which he was a member met at the George on the third Sunday of the month, so his lordship was well known there and, as a consequence, was greeted with the utmost cordiality by the landlord. He took the man on one side and confided his errand.

'I'll certainly look out for the young lady,' the landlord said, eager to oblige one who, although not so influential with regard to his fate as Lord Burghley, was nevertheless a valuable customer. 'Do you know in what kind of conveyance she'll be coming, my lord?'

The earl grinned ruefully. 'That's the worst of it,' he replied. 'I don't know when, or in what she'll be making the journey. The whole matter has been very foolishly arranged.'

'You can count on me to do the best I can, my lord.'

'I'm obliged. Now, will you add to your kindness by bringing me a pint of home-brewed?'

'At once, my lord.'

Thurlby wandered into the inn yard, and stood holding his tankard, his broad shoulders propping up the door frame. It was true that he was not fond of London, but he liked the bustle and liveliness of this place. It would not be too much of a hardship to stand in the inn yard of the George with a pint in his hand, and watch the arrivals.

He had almost drained his glass when he heard the sound of rattling wheels, jingling harness and the clopping of hoofs, and shortly afterwards, the London stage swept round the corner and into the yard. There were two male passengers on the roof, looking as if they were very well satisfied with their lot. Had it been the middle of winter, the earl reflected, it would have been a different story.

The stage pulled to a halt and two lads ran forward from the stables to take charge of the cattle. Thurlby eyed the horses with casual interest. They seemed to be a reasonably well-matched team. Such was not always the case with the stage, as opposed to the mail coach, which invariably took the cream of what was available.

He turned from his observation of the horses to see that the door of the stage had been opened and a young man had jumped down and was turning to help some other passengers. 'Benjamin Twizzle,' Thurlby said to himself with a wry grin. 'I'll wager there's a woman in the case.'

He was acquainted with Twizzle's father, a clergyman in a parish not far distant from Thurlby, and knew that the young man was the bane of his father's life. They had met at various functions where Benjamin's conversation tended to be a little too racy for provincial tastes, and his manner with ladies rather more familiar than was pleasing to most of them.

On one occasion, the earl had been attending a dinner with a few friends at Peterborough, when their quiet, sociable evening had been disturbed by a noisy group of young men in the public rooms. 'We'll not come here again,' an older member of the party had said. 'This sort of thing wouldn't happen at the George.'

Whilst agreeing with the view expressed, the earl, twenty-five years younger and, moreover, remembering his own youth, had been inclined to be more tolerant. Eventually, however, after the noise had continued unabated, he had gone out to make an objection, and had found the young men, Benjamin Twizzle included, behaving disrespectfully to the landlord. He had given them all a good dressing down.

A little later, the dinner over, the earl had seen an acquaintance of his in the public rooms and had stopped to have a conversation. On leaving the hotel after the rest of his party, he had heard screams from one of the upstairs windows. It transpired that two elderly ladies had been looking out of the window at the night sky, when Benjamin Twizzle, out of sheer devilment, had taken down his breeches and bared his backside at them. The earl had given chase, but Twizzle, laughing, had managed to slip away in the dark.

Now, Thurlby's grin broadened, as the glimpse of a dark-blue skirt and a bonnet in profile confirmed his opinion that Twizzle must be in pursuit of a woman.

'Allow me to assist you,' the young man said solicitously. Then, as a smaller, black-clad figure emerged, he said, 'And you too, Mrs Hedges.'

Thurlby was conscious of a sudden stab of attraction. This young woman, fair-haired, petite, but with an excellent figure, was exactly the kind of female that he most admired. Struck by sudden guilt by his disrespect towards a lady who was clearly in deep mourning, he was on the point of turning away when, quite unexpectedly, something about her struck a chord of recognition. As if aware of his scrutiny, 'Mrs Hedges' turned her head, and his lordship found his eyes locking with those of a young lady whom he knew to be Miss Lavinia Muir. At once, the smile disappeared from his face.

'Take that,' he said, handing his tankard to a passing servant before striding forward. It was then that he had his second shock of the morning, for the lady in blue turned at his advent, and he found himself face to face with Isobel Macclesfield.

The earl was not gifted in dissembling and, with no opportunity for giving any thought to how he should react, he simply stood still and exclaimed, 'Oh my God!'

Benjamin Twizzle, after a brief 'Good day, my lord', and a touch of his hat, prudently slipped out of sight.

'Good day, Twizzle,' replied Thurlby automatically, before turning to Lavinia and Isobel. 'And now, *ladies*,' he went on, with gritted teeth, 'if you will be so good as to accompany me into the inn, I shall make arrangements for your next journey.' He extended his arm courteously to Lavinia, but she saw a dire warning in his gaze. 'Mrs

Hedges?' he said, his brow darkening. He turned to Isobel. 'If you will follow us, ma'am?'

'Too kind,' Lavinia murmured in failing tones, wishing that she did not feel as faint as she sounded. She laid her hand on his extended arm. Beneath the fabric of his coat, his muscles felt as hard and unyielding as the expression on his face.

Thurlby ushered his charges into the inn, where the landlord was waiting to attend them. 'A private parlour at once, if you please,' said his lordship, speaking rather more haughtily than was his wont. 'And have the goodness to arrange for a conveyance to be prepared to take these ladies back to Thurlby Hall.'

'At once, my lord,' replied the landlord. 'Shall I bring tea?'

'Tea?' exclaimed the earl, for all the world as if the man had suggested bringing them a pint of gin each.

'That would be delightful,' said Isobel, smiling sweetly at the landlord. 'I am parched and I am sure that Lavinia must be too.' Lavinia glanced warily at the nobleman, his face rigid with disapproval as he held the parlour door open, but said nothing.

'And now,' said the earl, speaking into the ominous silence which had fallen after the door had closed. 'Perhaps one of you will have the goodness to explain to me what the *devil* is going on. Why are the two of you travelling on the common stage? How have you managed to become acquainted with someone like Benjamin Twizzle? And why the . . . ' He bit back the expletive that had been on his lips. 'Why upon earth are you masquerading as someone else, Miss Muir?'

The two young ladies glanced at one another. Lavinia knew that as Lady Thurlby's goddaughter, she ought to be the one to speak, but the story was so complicated that she could not think where to begin. Before she could say anything, the door opened and the tea tray was brought in and set down. The earl shook his head dismissively when offered a cup. Isobel sat down to pour for herself and Lavinia, carefully keeping her eyes on the tray.

'Well?' said the earl, after the servant had closed the door behind her.

'Well, I . . . I . . . ' Lavinia began.

She was saved by a knock at the door. The earl approached it with hasty strides, threw it open and demanded, '*Now what?*'

An enormous bouquet of flowers appeared to enter on its own. It was not until it had come right into the room that the servant carrying it could be seen. 'Pardon me, my lord,' she said, 'but these came for the young lady.'

'For which young lady?' Thurlby asked ominously.

'Mr Twizzle, the young gentleman what was in the yard, said that they would be for Mrs Hedges, my lord,' the girl replied. Lavinia's heart sank right down into her boots.

'He did, did he?' said Thurlby, looking ominously at his mother's goddaughter. 'And what would he know of the matter?'

'He just said that they would be for her, like all the others,' answered the maid, blithely unaware of the violent thoughts that Lavinia was directing towards her and Mr Twizzle. The girl laid them down on a side table, curtsied, and hurried out.

'From an admirer?' said the earl, his tone deceptively mild as he wandered over to the table that held the flowers. ' 'Like all the others', presumably.'

Lavinia glanced at Isobel, who looked up at her from her place behind the teapot, an unmistakable appeal for help in her eyes. Lavinia understood all too well. Thurlby could not possibly refuse to take in his mother's goddaughter. Another young lady, uninvited and engaged in misbehaviour, however, could be sent back from whence she

72

came without delay or compunction.

Lavinia squared her shoulders, a not unbecoming flush staining her cheeks. 'A lady cannot determine who admires her and who does not,' she said. Isobel handed her her tea, which she took with hands that trembled so much that she was afraid that she would slop it all over the floor.

'Possibly,' his lordship agreed. He looked down at the card, and his expression darkened. 'Especially when a man is so experienced at expressing his admiration as Lord Riseholm. Fortunately, my gardens at Thurlby are quite adequate to furnish flowers for any rooms that may need them. You will kindly inform Lord Riseholm that his additional ah . . . decorations are not required at Thurlby Hall, and any further tributes will be returned to him. Is that quite clear?'

'My lord — ' Lavinia murmured.

'I said, is that quite clear?' he barked.

'Lord Thurlby, Lord Riseholm is a single gentleman,' Isobel ventured, 'and perhaps — '

'Lord Riseholm may be as single as you please, but he is a rake and a libertine and he will not be practising his wiles upon any young woman under my protection,' the earl replied. 'By the way, Miss Macclesfield, am I to assume that I am to have the honour of entertaining you at my house?'

'I beg pardon, my lord,' said Lavinia, 'but — '

'You will be silent,' said his lordship. 'I would prefer not to converse with you again until I am in command of my temper.'

'Well, I would prefer it too,' answered Lavinia, greatly daring, 'for I do not like being shouted at.'

At this unfortunate moment, there was another knock on the door. 'God in heaven, what now?' bellowed the earl, throwing the door open. 'Boxes of sweetmeats and palomino ponies from his lordship?'

The servant who had knocked on the door stared at him blankly. 'No, my lord. Just the carriage you wanted. But if you was wishful for sweetmeats, I'm sure that — '

'Never mind, never mind,' snapped the earl, thrusting his charges' bonnets at them and almost dragging them to the door, so that Lavinia even had to hand her tea cup to the servant who was standing there.

A hired carriage was waiting in the yard by the time that they emerged from the inn. 'In there with you,' said Thurlby, bundling the two ladies into the carriage with the same haste with which he had hurried them out of the room. He slammed the door behind them, and mounted his own horse.

'Thank goodness he isn't riding inside with

us,' said Isobel, once the carriage had got moving. 'I quite thought that he was going to explode.'

'He was in a fearful temper, wasn't he?' Lavinia agreed.

'Heaven only knows what he would have said had he realized that the flowers were really for me. Thank you, Lavvy. You saved me.'

'Yes, I did, and now I am in more disgrace than you are. Oh, why did he have to be standing there at that moment? Just five minutes later and Twizzle would have gone.'

'I must say, I have quite changed my mind about making a play for him,' said Isobel. 'Did you see how his brows drew together when he was angry? I really do not think that I could marry a man who could be as cross as that.'

'I am just wondering what I can say to Aunt Phyllis,' said Lavinia.

'Why tell her anything?' Isobel asked. 'What's done's done, I say.'

Lavinia thought for a moment. 'I think that I shall have to tell her the truth,' she said eventually.

'The truth!' Isobel exclaimed, horrified. 'You can't possibly do that. I would be sent back to London in disgrace, and Willie would pack me off to Harrogate and then what would I do?' The memory of the bruises on Isobel's arms hovered between them.

'I don't mean the truth about everything,' Lavinia replied reassuringly. 'I mean about having to catch the stage, and you lending me some money, and deciding to change identities because we had to stay the night.'

'What about Riseholm?' said Isobel cautiously.

'I think the less said about him the better.'

For his part, the earl, riding beside the hired coach, his face like thunder, was remembering a letter that he had received from an acquaintance in London only the day before.

I was sorry to see your mother's goddaughter with that minx Isobel Macclesfield, and the two of them consorting with Riseholm in the open street. I only hope they do not set the whole of London by the ears, the pair of them.

He thought about Lavinia as she had stood in the inn parlour, her face pale, but her back straight as he had confronted her about Lord Riseholm. As he had looked at the black-clad figure, he had been reminded of that occasion when she had been told where she should go following the death of her parents. Perhaps losing sight of the fact that she was now a young woman, rather than the child that she had been then, he had spoken with less than courtesy. He remembered how her upright posture had shown off her excellent figure. The recollection that he had felt strongly attracted to her did nothing to improve his temper.

The chief cause of his anger, however, was Lavinia's entanglement with Lord Riseholm. Strangely, he would have thought that it would have been more like Isobel to behave thus. He knew Riseholm. They belonged to the same clubs and had even played cards together, but the notorious rake was not the sort of man whose company he would seek, or whom he would allow within hailing distance of any young woman for whom he was responsible. Yet that very man had obviously been dancing attendance on Miss Lavinia Muir — his mother's goddaughter — no doubt whilst Miss Macclesfield conspired to promote the whole affair! 'Those two minxes are not going to set *me* by the ears,' he muttered under his breath.

They drew within sight of Thurlby Hall, entered the gates and travelled up the drive, which curved gracefully and was lined with well-kept trees. 'I had forgotten that your godmother lived in such style,' said Isobel, as she gazed at the house through the carriage window. It was indeed an impressive sight, being a fine Palladian building which had been constructed nearly fifty years before. It had replaced the old manor house which had been considered too out-moded to be a suitable residence for the then earl and his family.

'Yes, it is very fine,' Lavinia replied with a sigh. She was remembering the kindness with which she had been treated by Lady Thurlby and her son after the death of her parents. Her ladyship had been motherly and comforting. The earl had been hospitable, gentlemanly, very kind and surprisingly understanding.

Even when her parents were alive, she had not really felt that she had a home. Since their death, Mr and Mrs Stancross had been kindly enough, but she did not feel as if she belonged in their home either. Yet when she looked at Thurlby Hall she felt a tug at her heart-strings, as if this might be a place where she could belong. Perhaps because of the death of her parents, it felt like the place to be for life's major crises. How she wished that she could have arrived here without all of the masquerade, subterfuge and lies with which she and Isobel had surrounded themselves. How happy she would have been then! She glanced at Isobel and prayed that her friend would not do or say anything too outrageous whilst she was here.

As the carriage drew up outside Thurlby Hall, the earl, who had already dismounted, came himself to help them down. Looking hopefully into his face, Lavinia could still see anger written across his features. She looked away hurriedly. She could only hope that Lady Thurlby would be more understanding.

'You will be escorted to your rooms as soon as we get inside,' he said. Lavinia thought that it sounded as though he was giving orders for some wardress to come and march them to their prison cells. 'After you have put off your bonnets, you will come downstairs immediately and explain yourselves.' Exactly like a magistrate, Lavinia concluded, and began to feel angry. He might speak of hearing their explanation, but he had clearly judged them already.

'When I have put off my bonnet, I shall wash my hands and face, brush my hair, and change my gown. After that, I shall come downstairs,' she said, forcing herself to hold his gaze. Her voice, she was pleased to note, hardly trembled at all. 'Then, if I think that there is the smallest likelihood of your listening, I shall give you the explanation that you have asked for.' A spark flew between them that must surely have been one of anger. What else could it be?

He drew a deep breath, but before he could say anything, Lady Thurlby came hurrying into the hall, a letter in her hand and an unmistakable expression of distress upon her face.

'What is it, Mama?' asked the earl, his anger forgotten as he became aware of his mother's anxiety.

'I have received a letter from Thomas Jacklyn, the son of my dear friend Clarice. It appears that Clarice is very ill and not expected to live.' Her voice choked on a sob.

Lavinia hurried forward with quick sympathy, her hands held out. 'Oh dear, God-mama, I am so sorry,' she said.

Lady Thurlby gave her hands a little squeeze and, swallowing her sob, smiled mistily at the younger woman. The earl who had reached his mother's side just after her goddaughter, laid a hand on her shoulder. He looked down at Lavinia. For the very first time, there was something in his eyes which might have been approval.

'Thank you, my dear. I am so very distressed that I am obliged to welcome you in this kind of way. It is not what I had intended at all.'

'Please do not worry, Aunt Phyllis,' said

Lavinia. 'You have far more pressing matters to consider.'

'Indeed, I cannot seem to be able to think of anything else,' her ladyship agreed. 'Victor — '

'You want me to take you to her,' said the earl. 'Of course. How soon can you be ready to travel?'

'I am packed already,' confessed her ladyship. 'I was confident that you would make such an offer.'

'I trust you will not have to make too long a journey,' said Lavinia anxiously.

'Some thirty miles,' replied her ladyship. 'I must confess that my one fear was that I should be obliged to leave you alone, but by a happy chance, you have brought Miss Macclesfield with you.'

'Happy indeed,' murmured the earl sardonically.

Isobel, showing more discretion than might have been expected from one of her temperament, had remained in the background until now, when she made her curtsy. 'Thank you for your welcome, Lady Thurlby,' she said. 'I am so sorry to hear about your friend.'

'I shall only be away for two or three nights at the most,' the earl resumed, a slight frown between his brows, 'but I can hardly entertain two young ladies here without a chaperon.'

'I have sent for Miss Wheatman,' said Lady Thurlby. She turned to Lavinia and Isobel. 'Miss Wheatman is our late vicar's sister,' she explained. 'She is at something of a loose end since her brother passed away twelve months ago. Although her little cottage is comfortable enough, I think she will be glad of a change.' Hearing the earl mutter under his breath, she added, 'Did you say something, my dear?'

'Nothing of consequence, Mama,' he replied innocently. 'I merely observed that it would be an ideal solution.'

Lady Thurlby turned to Isobel and Lavinia. 'I am so sorry about this, not just for you both, but selfishly for myself as well. I had been looking forward to outings and going shopping, you see.'

'All of that can easily wait,' said Lavinia. 'Isobel and I will keep each other very well amused, you may be sure.'

Her ladyship agreed with a nod, and turned away to deal with some matter that had just come to her mind.

The earl caught hold of Lavinia's arm. 'Yes, that may be so,' he said in an undertone. 'But if you get up to anything — *anything* untoward in your efforts to amuse yourselves, I will make you wish that you had never been born. Do you understand me?'

Lavinia stared back at him, her expression as stony as his. 'Yes, I understand you,' she responded. But, she added to herself, I don't think that *you* understand *me* at all.

6

'We must escape,' said Isobel the following morning. They were not sharing a room, but they had been placed next door to one another, and Isobel had padded through to Lavinia's room in her dressing-gown. 'I do not have the slightest intention of collecting grasses to please that silly old woman.'

'I do not see how we can avoid it,' Lavinia replied.

Miss Wheatman had been admitted by his lordship's butler at the same time as Lavinia and Isobel had descended the stairs the previous day, their bonnets discarded. Lavinia had also put off her mourning attire, to her great relief, and was dressed much more becomingly in a gown of pale yellow, with bunches of primroses embroidered above the frill near the hem, on the cuffs of the puffed sleeves and at the neckline. Lord Thurlby, glancing up the stairs, had seen her, looked away, and then looked again. She had looked pretty enough in black. This particular shade complemented her colouring, bringing out golden tints in her soft, light-brown hair, and the style of the gown emphasized her excellent figure. His mother's goddaughter had blossomed into a very pretty, exceedingly desirable young woman. Forcing this idea to the back of his mind, he had reminded himself of all the things that she had done wrong. What a pity she is so giddy and thoughtless, he had said to himself, before stepping back to avoid being noticed.

Miss Wheatman had beamed at the sight of the two young ladies, professing herself to be delighted to be of service, if in such unfortunate circumstances.

'You are very good,' Lady Thurlby had said, after she had formally introduced the newcomer to her guests, and conducted them all into the drawing room, the earl strolling in behind. By that time the countess must surely have been longing to be gone, but she had given no indication of it. 'I am sure that Isobel and Lavinia will benefit extremely from your company.'

'I have all kinds of schemes for our entertainment,' Miss Wheatman had said, adding after a moment's consideration, 'I have always thought botany an unexceptionable study for a young woman. It seems to me that there are many different kinds of grasses to be found in any ordinary meadow in England. It would be a charming project to go out into the fields and see how many different types we might find. We could even have a little competition to discover who could find the most; perhaps with a little prize. What say you, my lord?' Miss Wheatman smiled at the earl, and then at the two young ladies, who were looking decidedly unimpressed at this idea.

'A splendid notion,' the earl had answered blandly. 'Make sure you choose a sizeable meadow.'

'Ah, but the size of the meadow is not necessarily the most significant factor,' Miss Wheatman had responded, holding up an admonishing finger, then remembering to whom she was speaking and hastily putting the finger down again. 'The age of the meadow is by far the more important determining feature in matters of this kind.'

The two young ladies had listened to Lord Thurlby enduring a lecture from the diminutive grey-haired, rosy-cheeked spinster, and had tried not to giggle. Lavinia had been more successful than Isobel, for she had found herself watching the earl, rather than his interlocutrice. How patient he had looked, as he had sat, his head tilted to one side as he had listened to this string of information which must surely interest him not at all! Why could he not show the same patience with me, she had wondered?

'Well what do you say, ladies?' Miss Wheatman had said eventually. 'How exciting it will be to find our grasses, and stick them into a book. I shall award a pretty handkerchief to which ever of you can collect the most. In fact, my lord, I have another splendid idea.'

'Not another one,' the earl had answered, trying to sound pleased and impressed.

'Yes, indeed. We could have an additional prize for whichever young lady makes the most attractive arrangement in her book! You could award that on your return, my lord. It will be something for you to look forward to.'

'Undoubtedly,' Lady Thurlby had agreed, carefully avoiding her son's eye.

'If it is fine, we could start tomorrow, could we not, ladies?' Miss Wheatman had beamed, quite unconscious of the torture that she was inflicting. 'And if it is wet, I have an alternative plan, you may be sure; but do not expect me to tell you what it is straight away! I want it to be a delightful surprise!'

'We *must* find a way to avoid that woman,' Isobel had said fervently when they had gone upstairs to change for dinner. 'I vow and declare that if I have to suffer very much of her company, she will drive me stark-staring mad!'

Lavinia was in agreement with this

sentiment but, as she said the following morning, she could not see how Miss Wheatman and her schemes could be avoided. 'We will just have to make the best of it,' she sighed. She was still sitting up in bed, sipping chocolate in her room, whence Isobel had come, having risen much earlier than usual in order to plan their campaign. 'Remember that she said she would be waiting downstairs for us in the breakfast parlour,' Lavinia went on. 'If we want to have any breakfast, we will have to go down there, and then we will be caught.'

'Not necessarily,' Isobel replied. 'Ring your bell.' Lavinia did so. When the maid came, Isobel said, 'Miss Lavinia would like her breakfast in bed today. Bring mine up here as well, and we'll have it together.'

Lavinia did not really like the way in which Isobel had given the order in her name. Furthermore, she knew that breakfast in bed was frowned upon at Thurlby Hall. 'The staff have plenty to do without us making them trail food up to the bedrooms,' her ladyship always said. The only exception to this rule was if someone was ill.

Isobel wrinkled her nose on being reminded of this custom. 'Oh pooh, who's to know?' she said. 'Lord and Lady Thurlby are both from home.' Lavinia was as reluctant to spend the morning looking at grasses as was the other girl, so she said no more on the matter, and soon they were sharing toast and coffee, leaving Miss Wheatman to a solitary repast in the breakfast parlour.

After the two friends had helped each other dress, they crept downstairs, trying not to giggle, and escaped out of a side door.

'Now where?' Isobel asked. 'You know this place best.'

Lavinia thought. 'We could always go to the church,' she suggested. 'It has some interesting brasses.'

Isobel cast her eyes heavenwards. 'Now you are beginning to sound like Maisy Daisy,' she said. They had discovered the night before that Miss Wheatman's Christian name was Daisy, so Isobel, making a play on her name in the way in which she had been so adept at school, had nicknamed her Maisy Daisy.

'I'm sorry,' said Lavinia apologetically. 'There isn't a lot to do around here. Perhaps you would have been better off staying in London after all.' Then she remembered Mrs Wilbraham and the threat of Harrogate and instantly wanted to bite back her words.

Isobel gave no sign of distress but simply tucked her hand into her friend's arm and gave it a little squeeze. 'But then I wouldn't have had your company, would I? Lead on, then. The church it must be.'

The walk to the church was about a mile in length, but the day was sunny, and the time passed pleasantly enough in conversation about some of their acquaintance in London. Yet again, Lavinia noticed the curious phenomenon of Isobel blushing at the mention of Lord Riseholm's name.

In a moment of impulse she said, 'Isobel, are you in love with Lord Riseholm?'

Again, Isobel blushed, but quickly recovered herself. 'In love with him? Good heavens! He is an amusing rake, that is all, and far more entertaining than some of the insipid youths that one meets — or than stuffy country gentlemen without a sense of humour.'

Lavinia made no reply to this, but she recalled Lord Thurlby's wry expression when Miss Wheatman had been outlining her schemes, and decided that he certainly did have a sense of humour, although at times it might be rather well hidden. She also noted with interest that Isobel had not actually denied being in love with Lord Riseholm.

The parish church was a fine example of Norman architecture, with a charming lych gate, under which many a newly married couple had paused to exchange a kiss before embarking upon their new life together.

Lavinia had a fondness for the place. She remembered attending services there with her parents, when she had visited her godmother years ago. The present Lord Thurlby's father and brother had still been alive then, and he himself had been newly home from Oxford. She also recalled how later Thurlby had found her there after her parents' death. The quiet serenity of the ancient church had offered her comfort when she had needed it most. She did hope that Isobel would not say anything mocking about it.

In the event, however, they did not go inside the church immediately, for as they strolled through the cemetery, a young man opened the gate on the other side of the graveyard, and began to walk towards them.

'Oh my goodness, who is that?' exclaimed Isobel in an admiring tone.

'It looks as if it might be the vicar, by his dress,' Lavinia replied.

'Suddenly, I am starting to feel rather pious,' murmured Isobel, her eyes sparkling. In her experience, clergymen were often elderly, nearly always married, and very seldom the answer to love's young dream. This young man, on the other hand, was of medium height, with lustrous brown, wavy hair swept back from a broad brow. His complexion was healthy, his eyes clear, and without doubt he would count as a handsome man in any company.

He smiled at them, showing an excellent set of teeth. 'Ladies,' he said, bowing politely. 'Timothy Ames at your service. I am the vicar of this parish. Are you hoping to visit the church?'

Both ladies curtsied in response. 'I am Lavinia Muir, and this is my friend Isobel Macclesfield,' said Lavinia. 'We are visiting Thurlby Hall. Lady Thurlby is my godmother.'

'We have come out for a walk, but we would love to see round the church, if you are not too busy,' Isobel added. 'We love old churches, do we not, Lavinia?'

Refraining from contradicting this astonishing assertion, Lavinia simply nodded her head.

'Then I would be delighted to escort you,' the young man responded. 'Please come this way. The church is very old, as you see. It was begun in the year 987, but not completed until a hundred years later. Notice the dog tooth design around the round arch in the porch. This is very characteristic of the time.'

Both young ladies looked and admired; but it has to be said that although Lavinia was dutifully admiring the stonework, Isobel was more interested in the man who had drawn it to their attention.

Once inside, they all paused for a few minutes to allow their eyes to adjust, for the interior was quite dim. That done, they looked about them. 'Here is the font,' Mr Ames said, pointing to a venerable stone object which stood near the door. 'It is probably as old as the earliest part of the building.'

'Have you baptized any babies in it as yet?' Isobel asked. 'Even your own, for instance? Or is a vicar not permitted to baptize his own children?'

Lavinia blushed at this — to her ears at least — blatant piece of probing, but the vicar did not appear to take exception to her words. 'Yes, indeed I have, but not my own. I am unmarried as yet. But a vicar is certainly allowed to baptize his own children.'

Isobel smiled saucily at Lavinia. 'I hope you haven't dropped any,' she said. 'I'm sure I should be terrified.'

Ames laughed. 'Then it is fortunate that it does not fall to your lot,' he said. 'No, I have never dropped a baby, but I must confess that I was a little nervous at my first few baptisms. Now, allow me to show you something else.'

'I do trust you will show us the brasses for which I believe this church is famous,' said Isobel, shamelessly quoting the piece of information that Lavinia had let slip earlier.

'You have been well informed,' said the vicar. 'Yes indeed, come this way, ladies. They are well worth a journey by themselves.'

Some half-a-dozen brasses were set into the floor in the chancel, and the girls stood looking down at them. 'Were they all people of this parish?' Lavinia asked.

'Yes indeed. This one' — and here the vicar led them over to the one at the far end, depicting a gentleman in elaborate courtly robes of the medieval period — 'was Sir Carey Scott, who was — '

'One of the ancestors of the Earls of Thurlby,' Lavinia put in.

'Yes, that's right,' said the vicar. 'Have you been in this church before, Miss Muir?'

'Yes, but not for several years,' she replied. She looked around and realized that she was standing next to the very pew where she had been sitting when Lord Thurlby had comforted her. She ran her hand over the carved end, before turning her attention once more to the brasses.

Isobel strolled from one brass to another, whilst Lavinia stood looking down at Sir Carey, trying to detect a likeness to the earl.

'I can tell you a certain amount about these, but there is someone in the parish who knows far more than I do,' Mr Ames told them. 'I would be happy to introduce . . . '

As if on cue, the door of the church opened, and a lady came in. She paused for a moment to accustom herself to the change in light just as they had done, so they had the advantage of being able to observe her for a while before she could see them properly. She was a little older than Isobel and Lavinia, probably about twenty-four or five. Dressed neatly but plainly, and not in the height of fashion, she looked as if she might be a governess or a companion. Her gown was fawn and her bonnet a plain straw, tied with a brown ribbon. Her brown hair was neatly, even severely tied back, and her round face with its unremarkable nose could not have been described as anything other than plain. But as she came forward, she smiled sweetly. If she was a governess, then she would be a humane and gentle one.

'Ah, Miss Tasker,' said the vicar, a delighted smile on his face. 'In a good hour! These young ladies are visitors to the area, and are interested in the brasses. I have told them all I can, but you are a much more knowledgeable authority than I. Miss Muir, Miss Macclesfield, allow me to present to you Miss Tasker, our esteemed village school-mistress, and my betrothed.'

Eventually, after Miss Tasker had spoken informatively about the brasses for some time, the vicar said, 'I think that we all deserve some refreshment. Ladies, do you have leisure to adjourn to the vicarage and join us for some lemonade and biscuits?'

Lavinia accepted on her and Isobel's behalf, and they strolled along the little path, Isobel making sure that she was walking with the vicar, leaving Lavinia to bring up the rear with Miss Tasker.

'For how long have you been engaged?' Lavinia asked her.

'For six months,' the young woman replied, smiling. 'We are to be married in the autumn.'

'And will you be married here?'

'Oh no, we will be married in a parish to the north of here, where my father is the rector,' was the answer. 'That was where we met, when Timothy was Father's curate. I was appointed to the post of village school-mistress here a year ago, and Timothy came to be the vicar here a few weeks later.'

The vicarage was a handsome brick-built house, with a fine, square hall and a charming drawing room at the back, decorated in shades of blue. Over the hearth was a portrait of a lady and gentleman, which looked to have been done quite recently. 'Are they relatives of yours, Mr Ames?' Lavinia asked him.

'My uncle and aunt, Lord and Lady Smilie,' he answered. 'They have always been very good to me.'

The lemonade proved to be excellent, as were the biscuits. 'Caroline makes these,' said the vicar, smiling at Miss Tasker. 'You must take care not to make too many when we are married, my dear, or I shall become too fat for my cassock!'

'I shall be careful only to make them once a week,' Miss Tasker replied with mock severity.

Lavinia and Isobel left after a correct half-hour, but, to Lavinia's surprise, Isobel expressed a desire to continue the friendship. 'We do not want to be a bother to Lord Thurlby, especially when his mother is away,' she said. 'It would be delightful to spend some time with friends in the village.'

Miss Tasker's plain little face lit up with pleasure. 'That would be lovely!' she said. 'Simply lovely. There are lots of places where we can go, are there not, Timothy?'

'There are indeed,' he replied. 'Are you fond of ruins, ladies?'

'Ruins with hidden rooms and dark corners?' asked Isobel with a saucy look at the vicar. 'Oh yes, beyond anything.'

'Then we shall have to see what we can do to arrange such a visit, will we not, my dear?' he said to his betrothed.

'What a waste! What a terrible waste!' Isobel exclaimed, as she and Lavinia walked back to Thurlby Hall. 'He's handsome, he has a sense of humour, and he is obviously quite well-to-pass. And it is all to be thrown away on that plain little pudding!'

'In that case, I cannot imagine why you want to pursue the acquaintance,' Lavinia said frankly. 'Miss Tasker is not at all the kind of person you normally befriend — although I have to say that I thought her quite agreeable — and as for the vicar, well, he may be as handsome as you say, but he is already spoken for.' She glanced at her friend then said quite involuntarily, 'Oh no.'

'Now Lavinia, don't spoil-sport,' said Isobel. 'To think that he should be the nephew of Lord and Lady Smilie!'

'Well, what of that?'

'Only that I have met them in town. They have no children and are very comfortably off. I have actually heard them say that they intend to leave everything that they have to their nephew who is a parson. That makes his prospects very good indeed. In fact, now I come to think of it, he may be in line for the title as well.'

'That may very well be so, but I do not see how that would benefit you,' said Lavinia.

'I have already said that he is quite wasted

on her. As for her, she is obviously a born schoolmistress. No doubt she is wedded to her profession. I doubt if it would distress her at all if he were to turn from her to someone else. She would probably be delighted to have the excuse to remain with her pupils. Some people are not meant to be married.'

'Isobel, you wouldn't,' said Lavinia reproachfully. All she could see in her mind's eye was Miss Tasker's plain but happy face.

'Wouldn't I just? Do say you'll help me.'

'Help you to break an engagement? By no means.'

'You don't have to do much. You've said yourself that you like Miss Tasker's company. You can keep her amused while I steal away her fiancé.'

Lavinia stared at Isobel. She had not had many friends in her life. She had often envied young ladies whom she had seen walking along, their heads together, obviously sharing secrets. When Isobel had befriended her, she had enjoyed the feeling that she could join the ranks of those with close friends in whom they could confide.

She had always known that her friend enjoyed the power that her beauty seemed to enable her to exert over men. Five years ago, she had been able to regard Isobel's 'conquests' as something of a joke. Now however she had discovered that this was a side of Isobel that she could neither like nor approve.

Isobel, seeing her friend's shocked face said quickly, 'I'm only teasing, silly. But a little flirtation will do no harm, surely? It can't possibly be a love match. Just look at how dissimilar they are. Besides, it will be something with which to torment Riseholm. When I write to him, I shall tell him about the handsome vicar and tease him with the idea that he might be losing his looks.'

'You are planning to write to Lord Riseholm!' exclaimed Lavinia, shocked.

'It is only courtesy to thank him for the flowers that he sent,' said Isobel, her careless shrug concealing her annoyance with herself at the slip she had made. 'Besides, all kinds of people write to one another every day. If it were Mr Walpole whom I was writing to, you would not turn a hair.'

'Lord Riseholm is half Mr Walpole's age and a rake into the bargain,' Lavinia pointed out. 'Oh pray, Isobel, do not do such a shocking thing! I could not bear it if you did so and Lord Thurlby found out.'

Isobel's face took on a serious expression. 'No, that would never do,' she replied.

'I am so glad that you have thought better of it,' Lavinia exclaimed thankfully. 'I hate being on bad terms with Lord Thurlby, and am anxious to get back into his good graces.'

Isobel eyed her keenly but made no comment upon her words. 'You may be quite easy,' she said. 'After all, I could hardly ask our host to frank letters from me to 'his rakeship', could I now?'

Lavinia smiled in relief and the subject was dropped; but Isobel had not abandoned the idea of communicating with Riseholm; only the notion of letting anyone else, even Lavinia, know what she was about. It was obviously vital to employ a way of writing to him which did not involve any of the inhabitants of Thurlby Hall. As they walked through the village, something that she saw gave her an idea as to how to go about this, but naturally she did not say anything to Lavinia.

They were now walking through a meadow, with the Hall in sight. That was not the only thing that they spotted, however. Walking a little way ahead of them, glasses on her nose, a book in one hand and a bunch of grasses in the other, was Miss Wheatman.

'Oh Lord, it's Maisy Daisy,' whispered Isobel urgently. 'Duck!' They both crouched down, then crept through the long grass, giggling. Lavinia smiled at her friend, the recent *contretemps* forgotten.

'Oh Timothy, I fear that you have turned her head,' said Miss Tasker in a tone of mock reproach, as the two young ladies from Thurlby Hall disappeared from sight.

'As long as you do not imagine that she has turned mine,' the vicar replied, catching hold of his fiancée around the waist as soon as the visitors were safely out of sight. He glanced about him to make sure that his housekeeper was not within the immediate vicinity, and pressed a kiss upon Miss Tasker's lips. 'You are the only woman who has turned my head, my love.'

'I can't imagine why,' she answered frankly, smoothing his hair back from his brow.

To Rev'd Timothy Ames, the beauty of Caroline Tasker's character had always made her a very acceptable helpmeet for a clergyman. He was well aware that a good many people were inclined to compare them, wondering why such a handsome man should be attracted to a woman whom many condemned as being rather plain. He blushed now when he remembered that there had been a time when he had been almost as superficial in his judgements of her as those who went upon appearance alone.

He had always known that as a country

clergyman, it would be a very desirable thing to be married. Not long after his appointment as vicar, the bishop had spoken to him about that very matter, reminding him that a handsome clergyman would always be a source of temptation to single young ladies in his parish.

He had met Caroline when he had served as her father's curate, and had always regarded her highly. Needing a wife as soon as possible, he had looked at Caroline, seen an ordinary looking woman, capable, practical, and sensible, and used to life in a country vicarage, and had decided that that would be sufficient for her to make him a conformable wife. He would need nothing more. Very properly, he had proposed, and had been accepted at once. Caroline was too down-to-earth to keep a man dangling if she had already made up her mind.

Then, one stormy night, a few weeks after the engagement had been announced, he had been on his way home from visiting a parishioner, and he had noticed that the schoolmistress's house had appeared to be in darkness. A little concerned, for he could not think of any reason why she should be from home, he had knocked at the door to enquire whether all was well. She had answered his summons looking a little flustered and somewhat dishevelled. She had told him that she had fallen asleep in her chair earlier on. His knock had woken her up. Now, she needed to light the fire, and could not find a candle.

He had gone inside to help her. They had both been hunting for candles when a flash of lightning had lit up the sky. Caroline had given a little shriek and hurled herself into his arms. It was then that The Rev'd Timothy Ames had discovered that his sensible, down-to-earth fiancée was frightened of thunderstorms. When he had arrived, far from being tranquilly asleep, she had in fact been huddled on the sofa with her face under a cushion.

Very touched by this demonstration of weakness, Ames had said, 'There, there, my dear. Don't be alarmed. I think that I saw a candle when the last flash of lightning came. I'll light that, then get the fire going and close the curtains.'

'Don't leave me,' she had said urgently, clinging to him, her voice not quite steady.

'I won't,' he had promised. Briefly he had hesitated, wondering how he could light the candle then the fire without letting go of her hand, for she was holding tightly onto him in her panic. Eventually, he had sighed, before sitting down on the sofa, and pulling her onto his knee. There they had remained, while the storm had continued its vigour unabated. She had tucked her head into his neck, and he had stroked her hair, murmuring soothingly.

After several more flashes of lightning and ominous rumbles of thunder, the storm had begun to die down, and she had lifted her head. 'Thank you,' she had whispered. He ought to have released her then; instead, he had drawn her against him and kissed her. It was the first time that he had kissed her on her mouth, and he had felt her quiver. Thinking that he had shocked, perhaps even disgusted her, he had made as if to draw away, saying 'Forgive me'. Her response had been to cradle his head with her hands and kiss him in return. After that, the kissing had gone on for some considerable time. When eventually the vicar had left the school-mistress's cottage, it had been with a very different notion of what his marriage would be like; and a new excitement when he contemplated the idea of his wedding night!

Now, he smiled tenderly down at her. 'It is because you are you,' he answered, which reply Miss Tasker found so satisfactory that she was obliged to pull his head down so that they could kiss again.

7

At about the same time as Lavinia and Isobel had been making their way to the village, Lord Thurlby had arrived at his home. Making use of a team of fast horses, he had escorted his mother to see her dying friend and they had made good time on the road. They had arrived at the Jacklyn residence on the evening of the day when they had left Thurlby Hall and had found the house shrouded in gloom. The earl had been offered a bed for the night, but he did not know the family well, and had no wish to intrude at such a time. He had therefore bade his mother a fond farewell, and had set off immediately for home, making the most of some good moonlight, then staying the night at Colsterworth and setting off early the following day.

He did not want to leave Miss Wheatman alone with her charges for too long. Goodness only knew what they might be up to, or what gifts from Lord Riseholm might have arrived for Lavinia in his absence. He wished he did not feel as he imagined how his old headmaster at Eton must have felt when confronted with a wayward pupil.

He smiled at the idea of the young ladies spending the morning in collecting grasses. That would certainly teach them to behave themselves!

He rode round to the stables in his carriage, stopped to have a word with his stable staff, gave notice that he wanted to ride later, then strolled to the house and into the hall, where he encountered Miss Wheatman looking rather forlorn, a book in her hand.

'Miss Wheatman,' he said, 'were you not intending to explore the meadows today?'

'Why yes indeed,' she replied. 'It is such a fine day for it, as you see, but the young ladies have gone out without me.'

'Really?' he said, frowning. 'I thought that a definite arrangement had been made.'

'So did I,' she agreed. 'I waited for them at breakfast but they did not appear. I suppose I must have been mistaken. Perhaps they will come and find me later.'

'I shall be sure to tell them to come and find you when I see them,' he promised. A truly gallant man would offer to go and collect grasses in their place, he supposed. Clearly, he could not be very gallant. Salving his conscience with the thought that he had much estate business to be getting on with, he went thoughtfully to his study. Encountering his butler on the way, he paused briefly to make a discreet enquiry as to where his two young guests had consumed breakfast. The answer that he received made him a little tight-lipped as he opened his correspondence.

No doubt there were many of his milieu who would have thought it strange to make such a thing of breakfasting downstairs. To ask for breakfast in bed was not a grave solecism, certainly. At the beginning of a visit, however, such a deliberate disregard for the known customs of the household did not augur a very helpful attitude.

He recalled that he had not yet spoken his mind either with regard to their mode of travel on the day of their arrival, or concerning Lavinia's masquerade. He would have more than one thing with which to tax them when they deigned to return. He had no intention of running off looking for them. No doubt there was nothing that two such bold young ladies would like better.

★ ★ ★

On their arrival back at Thurlby Hall, Isobel declared that she wanted to go to her room to lie down. 'All those tedious church brasses have given me a headache,' she said.

She did not sound very ill, and Lavinia wondered whether she was making an excuse to be alone so that she could think about Lord Riseholm. Undesirable though this might be, it would probably be preferable to making plans for the seduction of the vicar.

It was perhaps just as well that Lavinia could not see what her friend was up to, for she would have discovered her speculations to be disturbingly accurate.

Isobel had no intention of allowing Lord Riseholm to forget her whilst she was out of London. He should be made to remember how desirable she was and, if possible, he should hear of her triumphs with other members of his sex. Timothy Ames would no doubt soon fall victim to her charms, whilst Lord Thurlby, though a tougher nut to crack, could probably be coaxed out of his ill humour. Riseholm would not know if she exaggerated her conquests a little.

She had thought carefully about how to continue her clandestine correspondence with him. On their visit to the village, she had noted an inn, the Horseshoe, and had guessed that mail was probably distributed from there. She decided that the best way to proceed would be to send her letters directly from there, and pick them up from the same place. She knew perfectly well that Lord Thurlby would frank any letters that she sent to respectable sources. She also knew that correspondence directed to Lord Riseholm from a single young lady could not be included under this heading. What was more, if the earl caught her sending anything to the notorious rake, he would instantly guess that she had been the object of his attentions all along. Then she would be sent back to Mrs Wilbraham in disgrace. There could be only one consequence of that; Mrs Wilbraham would pack her off to Harrogate to stay with her grandmother.

This aged relative had very firm ideas on how a disobedient granddaughter should be brought to heel. These included walking a horrible, bad-tempered smelly dog, sitting day after day in a cold house, and listening to a tirade of criticism, occasionally punctuated by a few blows with a switch wielded by the old lady, whose arm was much stronger than someone of that age had any right to expect. If Grandmother was in an exceptionally good mood, then she, Isobel, might be permitted to be a fourth at one of the interminable whist parties attended by her aged relative. She would rather die than go to Harrogate, but she could not give up Riseholm.

With this in mind, she made her way up to her room with deceptive casualness, then waited for Lavinia to come upstairs afterwards. After waiting for a while without hearing her friend's footsteps in the passage, she crossed to the window and by great good fortune, spotted Lavinia crossing the lawn. Quickly, she put her bonnet back on and hurried down the stairs and out of the house, taking care not to be seen. Should Lavinia catch sight of her, she had an excuse prepared — a lost handkerchief which she feared she had dropped earlier. She walked back to the village and once there, she made her way to the Horseshoe, and asked if she might speak to the landlord.

'How may I be of service, miss?' the landlord asked her, wiping his hands on his apron as he came to attend her.

'It is simply that I would like to bring some letters here to be sent to London, from time to time. I am also expecting letters to arrive. Could you hold them safely for me, until I can come and fetch them?'

'I'll do better than that, miss,' the landlord replied beaming. 'I'll make sure they're brought up to the Hall with the rest of the mail. You are from the Hall, aren't you?'

Inwardly, Isobel cursed the inquisitive nature of village society. No doubt the servants at the Hall were related to half the village. 'That is very good of you, but I would prefer to collect them myself,' said Isobel, keeping her manner calm so as to not arouse attention. 'Mrs Hedges, my friend whose correspondence it is, is a very retiring lady, and has particularly asked that only I should collect her letters.'

If the landlord thought that this was a trifle odd, he did not say so. 'Very well, miss,' he answered, smiling even more broadly when she handed over some coins.

'For your trouble,' she said graciously. 'And for your discretion.' She gave him her first letter, which instructed Riseholm to send his correspondence to Mrs Hedges. 'I'll be in here regularly to deliver and collect her letters,' she concluded. Her expression as she returned to Thurlby Hall would have instantly told Lavinia that she was up to mischief, but Lavinia was elsewhere and did not see her.

★　★　★

Benjamin Twizzle had been sharing a jar or two with an acquaintance in the tap room of the Horseshoe. He had been on the point of leaving the inn, when Isobel had appeared, and asked to speak to the landlord.

Although a hedonistic young man, he was not essentially greedy, and providing for the future was not something that had ever occurred to him. As long as he had money in his pocket to spend on the needs of today, the requirements of the morrow concerned him not at all.

Recently however, his sunny existence had become overshadowed by a cloud. His father, displaying an optimistic streak somewhat at variance with his generally gloomy cast of mind, had always hoped that his youngest son would follow in his footsteps and, eventually, take Holy Orders. This would at least be a means of making his way in the world and also, as Rev'd Josiah Twizzle had admitted to himself somewhat guiltily, a way of removing from the vicarage a presence which the clergyman found very disturbing.

When at last the vicar had accepted that this would not happen, he had given his son an ultimatum; he would continue to pay him an allowance until he was twenty-five. After that, young Mr Twizzle would be obliged to fend for himself.

Benjamin had put these warnings to the back of his mind. It had therefore come as quite a surprise on his twenty-fifth birthday when his father, as a birthday gift, had presented him with a full year's allowance. With it was a copy of the letter which he had sent to his bank, terminating the regular quarterly payment from then onward.

The money itself had been very welcome,

and Benjamin, thinking as usual only of the present, had simply seen that in his hand he had four times as much as usual. He had therefore set about spending it four times as quickly.

Part of this spending had involved joining a select group who played cards together at one of the less salubrious establishments in Peterborough. The table had been presided over by one Cyrus Nightshade, who had been impressed by Benjamin's well-turned-out person and apparently affluent circumstances. Carried away by the excitement of the game, Benjamin had signed numerous IOUs, and by the end of the evening, he had found himself owing a large sum of money that he had no way of paying. When he had first met Lavinia and Isobel, he had been attempting to hide from Mr Nightshade, whilst at the same time, trying to decide which of his relatives might be good for a trifling loan.

The reason why he had been on the stage was that he had been visiting his eldest sister, who resided in Huntingdon with her husband, an impecunious army officer with a weakness for cards. Esther was the most sympathetic of his siblings, and he had been hoping that she would help him out, but to no avail.

'We haven't sixpence to scratch together,' she had said frankly. 'Tom is on half pay and I'm increasing again. And if you try to persuade Tom to gamble with you, I'll skin you alive.'

Vigorously denying any such intention, he had decided to set out for home and apply to his father. Asking any other of his siblings for money was simply not possible. One of his brothers was in the navy and at sea, whilst another was a curate living in lodgings. A third was serving in the army overseas, and a fourth was a tutor, escorting his charge around Europe on the Grand Tour. Another sister was married to the meanest man on the planet, whilst another was visiting her husband's family somewhere in Scotland. Then just before he had left Esther's house, she had scuppered his plans completely.

'Father and Mother are visiting an old university friend of Father's,' she had told him. 'Mother told me in her last letter that they would be away for some weeks.'

This news had effectively cut off his last source of money. On hearing the name of Miss Isobel Macclesfield, however, he had felt an immediate surge of optimism, for he knew that she was a considerable heiress. He had not been able to decide how to make use of this knowledge to begin with, particularly since he was *persona non grata* at Thurlby Hall.

Since making a strategic retreat from the inn yard of the George, therefore, he had resolved to drop in at the Horseshoe in Thurlby to find out what he could about the activities of his two travelling companions. He had been on one previous occasion, but had discovered nothing. This time, he could not believe his luck.

He kept out of sight, and managed to hear what had been said. Knowing better than to approach the landlord himself, he beckoned to a waiter and gave the man a coin, after first making sure that the man could read.

'Send me word whenever letters pass through this place either for or from Mrs Hedges,' he said. 'And tell me who is her correspondent.'

He would wager that the latter would prove to be Lord Riseholm, otherwise why not have the letters sent directly to Thurlby Hall? And what might the young lady not be prepared to pay to ensure that her host did not discover to whom she was writing? The whole business gave every evidence of being profitable enough to extract him from his immediate difficulties.

Had anyone challenged him on the morality of this plan, he would have defended himself stoutly. His motive was not greed; it was sheer survival, and his involvement of Miss Macclesfield would enable her to perform a noble act of charity, which would no doubt be good for her soul.

Mr Twizzle's extremely pliable conscience having thus been assured of the merit of his enterprise, he left the inn, an angelic smile on his countenance.

★　★　★

As soon as Isobel had gone to her room, Lavinia began to think about Miss Wheatman, and soon started to feel guilty. On an impulse, she put her bonnet back on, collected a basket from the kitchen and headed for the meadow where they had last seen Miss Wheatman. Sure enough, she was still standing with her book in one hand and grasses in the other. Had Lavinia not noticed the position of the Hall with relation to that lady, she might have supposed that the spinster had not moved since they had last seen her.

'Miss Wheatman,' she called. 'Have you found many? I have brought a trug basket for your specimens.'

Miss Wheatman looked up, her face alight with pleasure, and for a moment, Lavinia

117

thought that she looked a little like Miss Tasker. 'That is kind,' she said, all at once making Lavinia feel guilty. 'Where have you young ladies been? I thought that I made our plans quite clear yesterday, but you did not appear at breakfast or afterwards either.'

Lavinia made a sudden decision. 'We did not like the idea of a competition, Miss Wheatman,' she said placatingly. 'Remember that we have come from London where ladies are for ever competing over who has the best bonnet or gown. What's more, during the season one's every activity runs to a timetable. We want to be a little more relaxed in the country. I hope you don't mind.'

'No, no,' answered the other lady with a relieved smile. 'I had the silliest notion that perhaps you were avoiding me.'

'Not at all,' replied Lavinia hastily, if not with perfect truth. 'I had not realized that you wanted to set off straight after breakfast; but I am here now, although sadly, Miss Macclesfield is not feeling well. Pray tell me, how is it that there are so many kinds of grass? I had thought that grass was just grass, but evidently that is not so.'

'No indeed,' replied Miss Wheatman. 'Now look at this one.'

To her surprise, Lavinia found her interest captured, as much by Miss Wheatman's enthusiasm as by the topic itself. Yet again, as the older lady compared two different kinds of grass, Lavinia was reminded of the time in the church that morning when Miss Tasker had drawn their attention to the different kinds of work on the brasses set in the church floor.

On impulse, she said, 'Are you related to Miss Tasker, by any chance?'

'She is my niece,' replied Miss Wheatman, smiling delightedly. 'Her mother is my sister. Now how did you guess that?'

'We made her acquaintance when we called in at the church this morning,' Lavinia explained. 'There is a great likeness between you when you are absorbed in something that interests you.'

'She is a dear girl,' said Miss Wheatman, as they stood up, and began to assemble their specimens in the trug. 'I am so happy that she is to marry Mr Ames. I must say, I had not thought that she ever would marry. She loves her work at the school, you see. But I am sure that she will enjoy the responsibilities that will come to her lot as the parson's wife just as much.'

As Lavinia went inside thoughtfully, she decided that she would not share this conversation with Isobel. The other girl would only take it as proof that Miss Tasker would be just as happy continuing as the village school-mistress as she would be marrying Mr Ames, and Lavinia was by no means convinced that this would be the case.

Whilst they had been at the vicarage having tea, Mr Ames had reached out for another biscuit and Miss Tasker had leaned over to smack his hand. Mr Ames had looked at his bride with an arrogant expression and reached out for a biscuit once more. Isobel had given Lavinia a knowing look before strolling over to the window. Lavinia had paused before following her a moment or two later and had thus seen something out of the corner of her eye that Isobel had missed. Having taken the biscuit, Ames had looked at Miss Tasker again, broken it in two, compared the pieces and given her the bigger one. The tiny incident had been over in a flash, but it had almost had the appearance of a sacrament. It had made Lavinia wonder whether perhaps the attachment between Miss Tasker and Mr Ames was deeper than anyone suspected.

Isobel may have spoken in fun about taking the vicar for herself, but Lavinia decided that she would do all that she could to make sure that her flirtatious friend did not destroy the plain little schoolmistress's romance. Miss Isobel Macclesfield, with her looks and her

120

more than adequate dowry, could attract a large number of men with very little difficulty. Miss Tasker only had one, and she would keep him, if Lavinia had any influence in the matter!

After they had returned to the house, Miss Wheatman took charge of the grass specimens. 'We may perhaps lay them out together when Miss Macclesfield is feeling better,' she said, as she went up the stairs. 'I will take them up to the schoolroom where we will have plenty of room.'

'Very well,' agreed Lavinia. She was about to go upstairs when her eye was caught by a picture which was hanging in the hall. It was of Vauxhall Gardens. For a time, she stood looking up at it, trying to reconcile the artist's view with what she recollected from her visit there. At last deciding that there must have been quite a degree of artistic licence used, she turned to go up the stairs herself in order to put off her bonnet.

'Miss Muir.' She turned to find that the Earl of Thurlby was standing at the other end of the hall, looking rather grim. 'A word, if you please.'

It was the first time that she had seen him since his departure the previous day, and she had had no notion that he would be returning so soon. Her heart gave a little lurch at the sight of him and she could feel herself blushing, for no accountable reason.

To hide her confusion, she hurried over to him, laying a hand on his arm. 'My lord, you are back,' she said. 'You look disturbed. How have you left my godmother? How did she withstand the journey? I do trust that she managed to reach her friend's side in time.'

He inclined his head gravely. 'My mother stood up very well to the rigours of the journey,' he replied. 'Her friend continues to be seriously ill. Judging that I would be very much in the way, I set off for home last night.' He paused briefly. 'If you would come with me, I would be grateful for the favour of a word with you in private.' He gestured towards his study. She entered the room and he followed her, very correctly leaving the door a little open.

'My lord?'

He directed her to a chair, and when she had taken her place, he walked over to the window, his hands clasped behind his back. He was silent for a time, her sympathy having rather taken the wind out of his sails. 'In the absence of my mother, I feel it incumbent upon me to say something about your behaviour,' he said eventually.

'My behaviour?' Lavinia echoed.

'I wish that it was not necessary, but you

have made it so. To begin with, I feel that I must take issue with you concerning your conduct towards Miss Wheatman. I found her standing in the hall this morning, waiting for you and Miss Macclesfield, when there had certainly been an arrangement for you to collect grasses together. You may not find Miss Wheatman the most congenial of companions, but she is my guest and I must insist that you treat her with greater courtesy in my home.'

Lavinia could not think what to say. On the one hand, while she had certainly not wanted to collect grasses any more than had Isobel, it had been the other girl's idea to sneak off elsewhere. On the other hand, she did not want to tell tales about her friend. She opened her mouth to say that she had just come back from the meadow but Lord Thurlby held up his hand.

'If that were the only thing, I might hold my peace. To speak plainly, however, I am obliged to say to you that other actions of yours have ensured that my opinion of your conduct is not very high.'

Lavinia straightened her shoulders. 'Indeed, my lord?' she said, with a touch of hauteur. 'I am at a loss as to know what I have done to merit your low opinion.'

'I am staggered that you even need to ask,'

answered the earl. 'Needless to say, you are welcome to bring a guest with you, but I find it extraordinary that you took it upon yourself to invite Miss Macclesfield without first making application to my mother.'

Lavinia blinked. That had indeed been a solecism, but she had quite forgotten about it with all that had gone on besides. 'I realize that I was remiss,' she began.

'You astound me,' he interrupted.

'But I needed a travelling companion,' she finished more spiritedly.

'Undoubtedly,' the earl replied. 'Particularly since you chose to come on the common stage.'

'My lord, there were reasons,' Lavinia began.

'I have no doubt that there were,' he agreed. 'Your use of a pseudonym tells me what they were, too. You were clearly engaged upon a vulgar, unladylike frolic.'

'No indeed,' Lavinia protested. 'It was not unladylike. It — '

'And how else would you describe your behaviour when you were clearly observed to be on terms of intimacy with a rogue such as Benjamin Twizzle?'

'I was not on terms of intimacy with him,' Lavinia responded indignantly.

'And then,' he went on regardless, 'added

to every other folly, you have wilfully encouraged the attentions of Rake Riseholm.'

Lavinia opened her mouth to protest that she had done no such thing. Before she could do so, she realized that to say anything would be to incriminate Isobel. The wisdom of this thought was confirmed when Thurlby spoke again.

'Unfortunately, for my mother's sake, I cannot send you packing as I should very much like to do. Apart from anything else, Mrs Stancross's frail state of health means that there is nowhere to send you. Indeed, I am forced to wonder whether the seizure she suffered had anything to do with you.' No sooner were the words out of his mouth than he realized how unreasonable they were. Even his own mother had taken him to task for expressing this very sentiment in jest.

To Lavinia, his words were not only shocking, but cruel as well. Everything else that he had said to her could have been excused by the misleading appearance of events. This last comment, however, was utterly unfair. What was more, it brought back to Lavinia's mind all the upset of those last few days, when Aunt had been so ill, and Uncle had turned to her, even though she did not know what to do any more than had he. During this last speech, Thurlby had walked towards her. Now, utterly frustrated by his refusal to listen, as well as hurt by his assumptions, she slapped him across the face.

'How dare you!' she exclaimed, her eyes filled with tears that were as much from anger as from distress. 'You know nothing about the circumstances prevailing in my uncle's household, or about my reasons for taking the stage. Nor do you know anything about the degree of my . . . my acquaintance with Lord Riseholm. You know nothing at all, and you will not even listen!'

She whirled around and, ignoring his voice calling her back, she ran to the door, threw it open, and hurried up the stairs to her room, her vision so blurred by angry tears that she could hardly see where she was going.

8

It was in a mood that was a strange combination of anger, apprehension, injured innocence and defiance that Lavinia went downstairs that evening, accompanied by Isobel. After she had fled the earl's presence and attained the sanctuary of her room, she had sat on her bed, half expecting that despite what he had said about not turning her out, a servant would arrive at any moment and tell her to pack her bags. The message never came and eventually, she came to the conclusion that his retribution would fall upon her in some other way.

Over and over again, she told herself that he should have been prepared to listen. She had had good reasons for acting as she had done. It was quite unfair of him to condemn her unheard. Unfortunately, every time she came to that conclusion, she heard again the whack that her hand had made as she had struck him. Her palm had still been tingling when she had got to her room. How must his cheek have felt?

Isobel came to find her, yawning after a restful sleep, and, seeing her friend's stormy expression, demanded to know what had happened. Lavinia made no mention of Lord Riseholm, or of Thurlby's reference to Isobel. She certainly said nothing of the slap, judging that her friend would merely find this entertaining. She simply told her about how his lordship had expected them to have gone collecting grasses with Miss Wheatman. She also said how angry he had been about their travelling on the stage in disguise, and mixing with the likes of Benjamin Twizzle.

'He is the most infuriating man in the world,' Lavinia concluded. 'He makes such sweeping judgements and does not even bother to listen.'

'It comes of being stuck in the country all year round,' Isobel replied, making a sweeping judgement of her own. 'People who live in the country tend to be very stuffy and old-fashioned, and are inclined to think that they know best about everything.'

'I know I did wrong, but he should not have condemned me unheard,' said Lavinia. Again she heard the sound of her hand against his cheek, and she coloured slightly.

'I do not see that you did wrong at all,' Isobel declared. 'To assume another identity on the stage was a wise precaution.' A wicked look came into her eye. 'Shall I make him fall in love with me just to teach him a lesson?'

she asked. 'I'm sure I could.'

'I really don't care what you do,' answered Lavinia. 'If you want, you could make him pine away until he's as . . . as skinny as Benjamin Twizzle,' she added, which notion made them both laugh.

In preparation for her next meeting with Lord Thurlby, Lavinia armoured herself by dressing very becomingly in primrose silk. As she studied her reflection in the mirror, she found herself considering a very curious circumstance. She knew that she was not as bold or as adventurous as Isobel, but after an initial moment of surprise, Lord Thurlby's anger had not frightened her at all. It had made her want to square her shoulders and face up to him. What was more, it had occurred to her that when he *was* angry, he looked particularly manly and vigorous. When he had drawn a deep breath to try and keep his temper, for instance, it had been impossible to ignore the breadth of his chest. She remembered observing him from the window of the carriage on their way to the Hall. He had certainly cut a fine figure on horseback.

It came as something of an anticlimax to discover when they got downstairs that his lordship would not be joining them. 'He begs our pardon, but he is engaged to dine with some gentlemen this evening,' said Miss Wheatman, in the tone of one who feared that she was inflicting some grave disappointment upon her auditors.

'Indeed,' replied Lavinia, her voice as glacial as might have been expected from one of the patronesses of Almack's had the earl turned up at its hallowed portals in top boots and a riding coat.

'He was all for calling off his engagement,' Miss Wheatman hastened to explain. 'I told him that that must not be thought of. It is a regular thing, you know, and what with your arriving unexpectedly and then his mother having to rush away, he did not have the opportunity to send word that he would not be coming. Indeed, he looked very disconcerted about the matter,' she went on. 'Although that might have had something to do with the door.'

'The door?' echoed Lavinia. Isobel, having lost interest in the conversation, had wandered over to look out of the window.

'Yes, he walked into his dressing-room door, apparently,' replied Miss Wheatman. 'His cheek was quite reddened.'

'Oh dear,' said Lavinia, momentarily conscience-stricken. Then, recalling his unkindness earlier, she added callously, 'I dare say he was drunk, in which case, serve him right.' Ignoring Miss

Wheatman's gasp of shock she went on, 'Shall we go in to dinner?'

★ ★ ★

The moment of meeting the earl could only be postponed, not cancelled indefinitely, and so Lavinia decided that whatever Isobel wanted to do, she herself would go down to breakfast. This decision had nothing to do with not antagonizing his lordship further by going against the customs of the house, of course. It was simply that she wanted to get an unpleasant encounter over as soon as possible.

Lavinia was a little afraid that Isobel might refuse to go down with her, but to her surprise, the other girl was quite ready to do so. 'I want to further my plans to entice the vicar,' she explained. 'Let's make an arrangement to visit some of those ruins that we were talking about.'

'I thought that you had decided to make Lord Thurlby fall in love with you,' said Lavinia, a little puzzled after the previous evening's conversation.

'There's safety in numbers,' Isobel replied airily. 'Shall we go down?'

All four members of the party were present at the breakfast table that morning. Lavinia had been a little apprehensive about having to confront Lord Thurlby if he was still sporting his reddened cheek. Fortunately the mark had faded away completely. If she had hoped that the subject would not be mentioned, however, she was to be disappointed.

'I am glad to see that your face is better, my lord,' said Miss Wheatman. Lavinia, who had just taken a mouthful of coffee, narrowly avoided choking, and thereby drawing attention to herself.

'You are very good to enquire,' the earl answered blandly.

'You must take great care not to do such a thing again,' Miss Wheatman went on.

'You may be sure that I will be on my guard on another occasion,' he responded, glancing at Lavinia, with whom he had only exchanged the briefest of greetings.

'I hope your head is feeling better too, my lord,' Lavinia said sweetly.

'My head?' he asked, frowning.

'I quite thought that your head might have been hurting you after — ' she began, then broke off, as if aware that she had over-stepped the mark. 'That is to say, gentlemen do sometimes have bad heads in the morning, do they not?'

'Really, Miss Muir,' said Miss Wheatman in shocked tones. 'I told you last night that I was convinced his lordship never overindulged in such a way.'

'Oh. I did not know,' said Lavinia innocently.

'Then you would do well to say nothing on the subject,' he replied.

'Should we all therefore avoid speaking about matters we know nothing about?' she enquired swiftly.

Miss Wheatman, sunnily unaware of the tense atmosphere, offered the earl more ale before he could make a reply, and the moment passed.

When the meal was over, the earl got to his feet, excusing himself as he had some estate business to see to.

'What are your plans for today, ladies? Will you hunt for the grasses that you did not collect yesterday?'

'Oh no indeed,' responded Miss Wheatman. 'We found plenty later on, did we not, Miss Muir?'

'Really?' said the earl, raising his brows as he looked at Lavinia. 'I was not aware of that.'

'You did not give me an opportunity to tell you,' she answered, lifting her chin.

He flushed.

'It only remains to identify them, which in some ways is the most exciting part,' Miss Wheatman continued happily, once more unaware of the unspoken communication that was taking place under her nose.

'Thrilling,' Isobel murmured as she stirred sugar into her coffee.

'I am glad to hear that you are looking forward to it,' said the earl ironically, inclining his head.

Isobel looked up at him through her lashes. 'I can think of many more exciting ways of passing the time,' she said saucily.

'I make no doubt,' he answered, narrowing his eyes. Her flirtatious manner caused his mind to clutch fleetingly at a notion somewhere at the back of his mind, but there was not time for him to grasp what it might be. He turned again to Lavinia. 'Miss Muir, I would value a conversation with you later on, when you are at leisure.'

'A conversation is an interchange when both have an opportunity to speak, my lord,' Lavinia replied with dignity, looking him straight in the eye.

'I am aware of that,' he answered, bowing to the ladies before leaving the room.

'Shall we perhaps walk into the village?' Miss Wheatman suggested.

Both the other ladies agreed and they parted company with Miss Wheatman in order to make their preparations. 'We can make sure that we look in at the vicarage,'

Isobel said, as they were putting on their bonnets. 'I want to establish my personality in the vicar's mind. By the end of the week, he will not be able to think of anyone but me.'

Lavinia made no response. As they came down the stairs, they heard the sound of voices in the hall, and reached the bottom step to see the back of an unknown gentleman as he was admitted into the drawing room. Glancing at each other, they took off their bonnets and laid them on a table by the window before following him.

Lord Thurlby and Miss Wheatman were already in the room, conversing with two young men. 'Ah, ladies,' said Thurlby, inclining his head to Lavinia and Isobel. 'You must allow me to present to you Mr Hawkfield and Mr Laver.' He did not look particularly pleased. The two young gentlemen made their bows.

'Mr Hawkfield,' said Isobel in an interested tone. 'I have heard that name before.'

'I am the nephew of the Earl of Riseholm, ma'am,' replied the young man. He was a little like Riseholm in looks, but his countenance was not lined, his face was rounder and he was not quite so tall. There was in addition a twinkle in his eye which seemed to indicate that he had a far from serious disposition. Mr Laver was a much slighter man, with hair of a distinct shade of ginger, and a rather foxy expression to match.

'To what do I owe this pleasure?' Lord Thurlby asked. He had no real need to ask the question. He knew perfectly well why the visitors were there. They had obviously heard about the arrival of two young ladies in the district, and had come to investigate.

The men in question were about ten years younger than himself, and although Laver was a near neighbour, living just the other side of the village, he had never called before. The other was not known to him, but one look convinced him that Mr Hawkfield was cut from the same cloth as his rakish relative. Maybe Lord Riseholm had even informed them about his, Thurlby's, two female visitors.

Mr Laver blushed, his heightened complexion, together with his bright hair, making him look like some kind of living beacon. 'As to that, sir, er . . . my lord, it has occurred to me that . . . um . . . ' He put his fingers inside his neckcloth and pulled at it as if it were too tight. He glanced at Lord Thurlby, who returned his look with a bland expression. 'We are . . . are nearly neighbours, after all,' he went on. 'Just . . . just paying my respects, don't ye know?'

'That is very civil of you,' Lord Thurlby

replied. 'No doubt you thought to find me alone here, and came to . . . ah . . . succour me in my solitude.'

'Oh, ah . . . exactly,' responded Laver, sounding relieved.

Hawkfield laughed. 'I can see that you understand perfectly, my lord,' he said impishly.

Thurlby inclined his head. On the whole, he liked Hawkfield's roguish honesty better than Laver's disingenuous deceit, but he would have preferred to give neither gentleman house-room. Nevertheless, mindful of his duties as a host, he sent for refreshments, and soon they were all enjoying a glass of wine, and discussing the beauties of the Lincolnshire scene.

'I have a small hunting box to the north of the county,' Mr Hawkfield was saying. 'My uncle's principal seat is in Berkshire.'

'You must mean Riseholm Halt,' Isobel remarked. 'It is said to be very impressive.'

'You have not visited it then,' observed Mr Hawkfield.

'Not as yet,' Isobel admitted, lowering her eyelashes. Thurlby, exchanging remarks with Miss Wheatman, did not overhear this exchange.

After they had finished their refreshments, the two young men rose to take their leave.

'We were about to walk into the village,' said Isobel. 'So I suppose that we had better bid you *adieu*.'

The gentlemen glanced at one another. 'How delightful that sounds, does it not, Laver?' said Hawkfield. 'It so happens that we have no other calls upon our time this morning. May we accompany you?'

'Indeed you may,' put in Miss Wheatman.

Thurlby thought of the business that he needed to transact, and one or two tasks that ought not to be left for too long, and sighed inwardly, sensing an end to peace. Perhaps naively, he had hoped that with Miss Wheatman on the premises, he would be able to get on with his usual concerns, leaving the young ladies in safe hands, and largely forgetting about their presence, except at mealtimes. He now perceived that he would have to take a more active role in proceedings. 'It sounds such a refreshing prospect that I believe I will come as well,' he said, mindful of his responsibility.

It was therefore as a party of six that they set off for the village a short time later. 'We can take refreshments at the Horseshoe,' said Thurlby. 'They do a tolerable cheese platter.'

It was about half-a-mile's walk to the village, and they made a cheerful party. Isobel, with two young men to charm, was in high gig, and soon set about playing one off against the other. This left Lavinia to walk with Miss Wheatman and Lord Thurlby.

'Such a lovely time we had yesterday, did we not, Miss Muir?' said Miss Wheatman. 'See, my lord,' she went on, pointing, 'that was the very meadow in which we found our grasses.'

'Really?' said the earl, looking attentively towards where she was pointing. 'I had never thought about grass having different varieties.'

'And yet you must be used to different crops,' Lavinia pointed out. 'Wheat, barley, corn, and so on.'

'True enough,' the earl agreed, looking at her with an arrested expression on his face. 'I had not supposed that you would know anything about crops, Miss Muir.'

'Yes I do,' she replied. 'Do you not remember that you told me about them when I stayed here before?'

'I confess that I do not recall,' he answered. 'I have too many memories about the bull, and almost shooting you.'

'Oh dear,' she replied. 'What a charge I was.' There was a brief, telling silence. 'You are thinking that I still am, I suppose,' she added, her tone regretful.

He was saved from replying by Miss

Wheatman, who asked him a question about the ownership of the land around the church.

On arriving outside the vicarage, Isobel said, 'Do let us call in. The vicar may want to join us for lunch.'

'And my niece, of course,' Miss Wheatman put in. 'We must not forget her.'

'No, indeed,' Lavinia agreed, throwing Isobel a meaningful look.

And so, in the end, there were eight around the large round table which the landlord of the Horseshoe prepared for them in a private room. Isobel somehow managed to manipulate the situation so that she ended up sitting next to the vicar, whilst Miss Tasker took a place on the other side of the table.

Lavinia found herself next to Mr Hawkfield, whilst Lord Thurlby was at her other side, with Miss Tasker to his left. That lady did not appear to be at all disturbed that her fiancé was being charmed by another woman. Instead, she devoted herself to her conversation with his lordship. She seemed to keep him very well entertained, for he smiled a good deal, and Lavinia noticed that he was listening attentively to what she was saying, often nodding in agreement.

'My uncle was disappointed when a certain lady left London,' said Mr Hawkfield to Lavinia under his breath.

'I am surprised that he noticed the loss of one young lady among so many,' she replied, very conscious of Thurlby on the other side of her.

Hawkfield laughed. 'My uncle is well known for his excellent taste in the female sex,' he replied.

When he turned to speak to Isobel, who was on his other side, and slightly balked of her prey because Miss Wheatman was intent upon talking to the vicar about parish business, Thurlby said to Lavinia, 'I believe I have already warned you not to have too much to do with Lord Riseholm. He is not a proper associate for young ladies.'

A little annoyed by this proprietary attitude, Lavinia said provocatively, if not with perfect truth, 'Nevertheless he is exceedingly amusing.'

'One cannot spend one's whole life being amused,' he answered her.

'No, but it would be agreeable to spend some of it thus,' she responded spiritedly before turning back to Hawkfield. To Thurlby's great annoyance, she then seemed to find a great deal to amuse her in the rake's nephew's conversation, so he turned to Miss Tasker.

'I fear I have been somewhat remiss recently,' he said in an apologetic tone. 'I have neglected the school.'

Miss Tasker smiled, her expression making her face look less plain. 'Your mother has been more than kind,' she replied. 'What is more, I cannot tell you how grateful we have been for the gifts of pencils, paper, chalks and books from the Hall; and I know that the funds for those gifts have been granted by you. I would not call that neglect.'

'Perhaps; but I have failed to look in on you in person. How are things going? Do you have plenty of pupils? Are the local people prepared to send them?'

'We have over twenty children,' she replied. 'Their ages range from five to fifteen and they are mostly from the village. Some are from the outlying farms, but there are not as many as I could wish.'

'Would you like me to mention the school to the farmers as I go round?'

'I would be very grateful, my lord,' answered Miss Tasker. 'Part of the difficulty is that if someone is needed to bring a child, then that person is taken away from his own tasks.'

'Maybe some kind of transport could be put in place to collect the children,' the earl suggested. 'One of my people could drive a wagon round, perhaps. Then no other person would miss his work.'

'I would be obliged, my lord,' she said gratefully.

'I'll look into it,' he promised. 'I hope that you don't find that you are over-burdened. Do you teach them all? That must be difficult.'

'The older ones help the younger ones,' she replied.

'Which is as it should be. Well, let me know whether you need anything more.'

Miss Tasker then turned to speak to Mr Laver, leaving the earl free to turn his attention to Lavinia and raise a subject that had been a little on his mind.

'Why did you not tell me that you had gone hunting for grasses after all?' he asked her in a low tone. She hesitated. 'You need not worry about sparing my feelings,' he went on.

'I was very annoyed that you had thought the worst of me, and decided that you might as well continue in error,' she replied, looking straight at him.

'Well that's frank,' observed the earl, picking up his wine glass.

'You told me not to spare your feelings,' she said. 'I thought that you wanted me to be honest.'

'I should have preferred it if you had been honest before.'

She coloured. 'I did not like it when you

judged me with so little evidence.'

'No, I don't suppose you did. I shouldn't have done so in your place. I was too hasty.'

'Yes, you were,' she agreed.

'It's a failing of mine, I fear. May we start again, do you think?'

She said nothing, but merely nodded. 'Was it terribly dull, collecting grasses?' he asked her after a short pause.

'Not as dull as I had expected,' she told him.

A trill of laughter betrayed the fact that Isobel was finding Mr Hawkfield very amusing; or, at any rate, that she wanted others to believe that to be the case. Perhaps, Lavinia wondered, she might transfer her interest to Mr Hawkfield. Or perhaps this was another ploy to attract the vicar's notice.

In fact it was Lord Thurlby who directed a long look at the young lady in question, but his comment to Lavinia would not have been particularly pleasing to Isobel. 'Miss Macclesfield did not help you in your search for grasses, I take it.'

'She . . . she suffers from hay fever,' answered Lavinia hurriedly.

'You are very charitable,' he replied. 'More charitable than she deserves, I suspect.'

Before the party had broken up, Isobel was suggesting another expedition. 'Did you not

144

say, Miss Tasker, that there were ruins to be visited in the vicinity? Would it not be agreeable to form a party and explore them?'

Miss Tasker confirmed that she had indeed made such a comment. 'There is a castle perhaps a dozen miles the other side of Bourne — at Folkingham, I believe,' she said.

'There certainly is,' Thurlby agreed. 'It belonged to the barons of Folkingham before the line died out some two hundred years ago. The castle was left untended, those in need plundered it for stone and lead, and it soon fell into disrepair. But there is plenty to see. We could take a picnic. I'm sure that Mrs Campsey would oblige.'

'Then let us go by all means,' said Mr Hawkfield gaily. 'I cannot wait to tell my uncle that I have been visiting ruins in company with a bevy of beauty.' Isobel fluttered her eyelashes, hoping that the young man would mention her name when he did so. Lavinia inclined her head gracefully, and Miss Tasker glanced at the vicar and smiled slightly. Lord Thurlby pressed his lips together in a thin line.

Care was taken to choose a day when the duties of both the vicar and of the schoolmistress would permit them to come. Lord Thurlby, of course, had duties too, but could arrange them to suit himself. 'All we have to do now is to pray for a fine day,' said Isobel. 'But,' she added, looking meltingly at the vicar, 'I think that we may safely leave that to you.'

He smiled politely in response, but did not say anything.

9

Isobel had enjoyed the outing to the Horseshoe Inn. As a child, she had been enchantingly pretty, and had learned at a very young age that her smiles, frowns and pouts could conjure precisely the response she wanted from the male species. A gathering such as the one that had taken place at the inn, therefore, had been very much to her taste. The admiration of Mr Hawkfield and Mr Laver had been open and very flattering. Lord Thurlby had been the perfect gentleman, dividing his attention very courteously between all those present. Nevertheless, Isobel had been able to detect his eyes fixed upon her in a very meaningful way on more than one occasion. Mr Ames, too, had not been unaware of her attractions. It had all been most satisfactory.

To add to her enjoyment, the landlord had nodded to her very particularly as she had arrived, and she had concluded that there was a letter for her. As her party was preparing to leave, therefore, she slipped out of the room, murmuring something about pinning a hem. A waiter appeared and indicated that her letter was in the parlour, so seeing that the door of the room was open, she went in.

As soon as she was inside, the door closed behind her, making her jump. 'Looking for this?' said Benjamin Twizzle, grinning. He was leaning negligently against the door, her letter swinging between his fingers.

He had dropped in to the Horseshoe by chance and, on discovering that the large party being served in the dining room was hosted by Lord Thurlby, had decided to stay out of sight. The waiter whom he had bribed before had revealed that there was a letter for 'Mrs Hedges'. Knowing that Isobel would want to claim it as soon as possible, he had handed over a few more coins, taken possession of the letter and laid his trap.

Isobel gave a little gasp. As she had told Lavinia, she had never expected to see Benjamin Twizzle again. He had kept very much to himself for the remainder of the journey to Stamford. His appearance now, and with her letter in his hand, was a very unwelcome surprise. 'What are you doing?' Isobel asked indignantly. 'Hand over my letter at once.'

'Your letter? I think not,' said Mr Twizzle.

'Of course it's mine,' she declared, reaching out for it as he dangled it before her, then lifted it out of reach.

'Now who's telling fibs?' he said archly. 'You see, this letter is directed to' — he paused artistically to glance at the superscription — 'to one Mrs Hedges, and I know for a fact that you are not Mrs Hedges, you are Miss Macclesfield.'

Isobel took a deep breath. 'The fact remains that for the purposes of collection, this letter is mine, even if it is directed to someone else,' she said, desperately trying to retrieve the situation. 'Anyway, it certainly is not yours.'

'Mrs Hedges, I believe, is in the other room,' Twizzle went on, almost as if she had not spoken. 'I should be happy to renew my acquaintance with her. So why do I not take it to her immediately? It would be only courteous.'

'No, it would not,' said Isobel, a touch of desperation in her voice. She paused. It was not yet clear what this young man was up to, but whatever his purposes, she needed all the weapons in her armoury. 'Mr Twizzle,' she said with one of her most charming smiles, 'I am sure that you have come upon that letter as a result of a misunderstanding. You extended to us the hand of friendship on the journey. Surely I can now presume upon that friendship and reclaim my letter?'

'Now that's much better,' he replied. 'If

you are prepared to be accommodating, I am sure that we can come to some . . . arrangement.'

She stared at him measuringly. 'What do you want?' she asked him. She was conscious that with every minute that passed by, she might be missed by the rest of her party.

'Oh, nothing out of your power,' he replied. 'You are an heiress after all.' He paused. 'Shall we say a hundred?'

Isobel gasped. 'Where upon earth would I find that amount of money?' she asked.

He shrugged. 'That isn't my problem, is it? Or shall we just take the letter into the other room? I'm sure that Lord Thurlby would be glad to pass this on to its rightful owner.'

'No!' she cried. Then she added, in calmer tones, 'No, that would not do at all. I may be able to let you have twenty pounds.' He laughed derisively. 'It is of no use laughing,' she went on. 'I do not carry large sums of money on me, and I am limited in how much I can lay my hands on. I spent most of my allowance before I left London.'

'I don't believe you,' Twizzle protested.

'You can believe what you like,' Isobel replied haughtily, 'but it is perfectly true. You can have twenty, and do not say that you will go through with the letter instead, because if you do that, you will get nothing at all.'

For the first time he looked faintly annoyed. 'Twenty, then. I heard your party planning a trip to Folkingham. Bring it when you go there. I'll appear as if by chance.'

'All right, but that will be the end of it. Now give me my letter.'

He handed it over, but after she had gone he remained for a little while in thought. Twenty pounds would be sufficient to hold Nightshade off for a time; but for how long? He would just have to hope that Lord Riseholm wrote again very soon.

★ ★ ★

The following day dawned bright and clear, and Lavinia, waking early, decided to make the most of the beautiful morning by strolling in the grounds before breakfast. She arrived downstairs to find Lilly lying sphinx-like in the hall. The dog got to her feet, yawning and stretching, first her forelegs, then her back legs. Then she wandered over to Lavinia, sniffing her skirts and wagging her tail gently, as if to say, 'Well, you're not the person I was hoping for, but you might do for an hour or so.'

'Where is your master?' Lavinia asked, bending to scratch behind the dog's ears. She headed for the door, and soon found that

Lilly intended to accompany her. She looked around doubtfully. She had no desire to spend the best part of the day playing hunt the greyhound across the earl's acres, and wondered whether there was a lead that she could use. Fortunately, the butler came into the hall and she was able to ask him whether taking the dog out would be advisable.

'Oh yes, miss,' the man answered readily. 'She's very obedient and will come when you call. I'd take a couple of biscuits, though, just to make sure. Dogs always come for food.'

Taking his advice to heart, Lavinia procured two biscuits, and went out into the garden with Lilly trotting along, first beside her, then lingering behind to investigate a particularly interesting smell, then dancing ahead, very light on her dainty feet.

'I wonder, will you play?' Lavinia said to the dog, after they had walked for a little time. 'If I throw a stick, will you fetch it?' Lilly looked at her in such an intelligent manner, tilting her head to one side, that Lavinia was convinced that the dog understood every word that she was saying.

The girl looked around for a stick, then threw it. Lilly galloped after it with great enthusiasm, but as soon as it fell to the ground, she stood staring at it with her ears pricked, as if wondering what it might do next. Lavinia called her over and did the same thing again, but with exactly the same result.

'You silly dog,' she said, laughing.

'I'm afraid she never will retrieve anything,' said the earl apologetically, as he strode towards her across the grass. He was in his riding dress. 'I saw you out here with Lilly as I rode home. May I walk with you for a little while?' On catching sight of Thurlby, Lilly pranced towards him wagging a tail with the demeanour of a dog who had bade farewell to her master months, if not years, before, without the expectation of ever seeing him again.

Lavinia signified her assent with a gesture. 'The day was so beautiful that I thought I would enjoy the garden before breakfast. I hope you don't mind that I brought Lilly. Grant said that I might.'

'No, you're very welcome,' he answered. 'You like dogs?'

She nodded. 'We had a dog when I was a girl — a golden retriever. He was very beautiful but not very clever, I'm afraid.'

'Like my dog, in fact,' smiled the earl.

'Oh, I beg your pardon,' said Lavinia, with a conscience-stricken expression. 'I called her silly.'

'And so she is,' answered the earl. Lilly had rolled over onto her back, and was now lying blissfully contented as her master scratched her tummy. 'Very silly, and very beautiful. I seem to recall now that you had a dog. What happened to him?'

'Oh, he got old, and died when I was fourteen,' she answered. 'I wasn't even there. I was at school, my parents were abroad and Brandy was with them. I found it so hard to accept. Why do dogs age so much more quickly than people do?'

Thurlby recalled that it could only have been a short time after that that she had lost her parents as well. 'Poor little girl,' he said, still crouching next to the dog. Their eyes met in sudden sympathy, and there was a faint frisson of feeling between them.

He straightened and they walked on for a time in silence. 'Tell me, why did you travel on the common stage?' he asked her eventually, his tone even.

'I had no money,' she said simply. 'Mr Stancross was so anxious to set out for Lyme that he forgot to leave me the wherewithal to hire a conveyance. I did not even have enough for the stage until I met Isobel.' Deciding to say nothing about the other girl's machinations, she simply concluded, 'We pooled our resources and together we had enough to pay for us both to travel on the stage.'

'And why the pseudonym?'

'For discretion and propriety's sake,' she

answered. 'We thought that a widow would seem more respectable.'

'Miss Macclesfield did not seem to be travelling under one,' he observed.

'She was never asked for her name.'

There was a brief silence. 'Was there no one to whom you could turn?' he asked. Then because he could not hold the words back, he added, 'Lord Riseholm, for instance?'

'I would never have been guilty of such impropriety as applying to a gentleman for money,' she said indignantly.

'You accepted flowers from him,' Thurlby pointed out.

She blushed. 'Flowers are different,' she answered, carefully avoiding giving him a direct answer. 'You know very well that men send ladies flowers all the time.'

'Not usually as far away from London as Stamford,' the earl pointed out. 'But let that pass. I accept your assurances that you would never have asked Riseholm for money. Was there no one else to whom you might apply for help?'

She shook her head. 'I had few acquaintances in town. Mrs Stancross was never strong and we lived very retired, you see.' She paused for a moment before saying, 'Perhaps you should know that she was not strong even before I went to live with them.'

He coloured. 'I beg your pardon. I was angry, but what I said was unforgivable.'

'That's all right,' she answered. 'I should not have hit you; or implied that you had been drinking.'

He rubbed his cheek ruefully. 'It was certainly a surprise,' he admitted. 'As for your suggestion, I found it rather amusing. It's been some years since drink rendered me so out of control as to bruise myself on the furniture. But to return to your dilemma, why the deuce didn't you think of applying to me? A simple note would have sufficed. I would have come and fetched you myself, and saved you all this trouble.'

Lavinia thought of the week's anxiety that she had endured when she had thought that she might have to travel on the carrier's cart. She thought of her difficult interview with Mrs Wilbraham, her misgivings over Isobel's attachment to Riseholm, and the awkward situation created by Benjamin Twizzle. She imagined instead being transported in safety and comfort in the earl's chaise. Ill-mannered fellows would never come near, kept at bay by Thurlby's powerful presence.

She looked up into his face and suddenly realized that here was a man who would never let a woman down if it could be humanly prevented. 'Oh, how I wish I had,' she answered with a sigh.

For a moment, it was as if time stood still, and a shiver of feeling that was part excitement, part something else ran all the way down her back. Then his lordship cleared his throat, and said, 'I hope you will remember now that I would do so, if you were ever in similar circumstances.'

'Yes . . . yes, of course,' she murmured.

'We have known one another for some time, after all. I even remember when the news arrived of your birth.'

'Do you?' she asked curiously.

'Oh yes. My mother was beside herself with delight at the thought that she would be a godparent. 'Just think!' she exclaimed. 'A daughter at last!' I felt inferior for quite a half-hour after that.'

'No! So long?'

'Vixen!' He grinned. Then, after a brief pause, he said, 'There was a time when we were upon Christian name terms, you know.'

'You might have called me Lavinia, but I am sure that I never called you Victor — unless, of course, I was intending to vex you.'

'It would not vex me if you did so now; in fact, it would please me.'

'Then I will do so; and please call me Lavinia again.'

He inclined his head. 'Before we go into

the house, I must ask you one more thing: tell me that you are no longer in communication with Lord Riseholm.'

'Lord Thurlby . . . Victor . . . ' She turned away from him, but he caught hold of her arm, not roughly, but firmly, causing her to turn back and face him.

'I must insist upon knowing. Have you communicated with Riseholm since your arrival here?'

She coloured, but looked him straight in the eye. 'I have not,' she told him. 'Nor will I do so.'

He let go of her. 'Then I am satisfied,' he said. He smiled at her. Involuntarily, she smiled back. 'I think it must be time for breakfast. Shall we go in?' He offered her his arm and, after a little hesitation, she took it.

After they had had breakfast, Lavinia said to Isobel rather diffidently, 'I was wondering whether you would mind if I wandered into the village this morning? I was telling Miss Tasker at the table yesterday about a book in my possession which I believed she might find interesting, I thought that I might take it to her if you have no objection.'

'None whatsoever,' Isobel answered carelessly. 'In fact, I might join you. We could drop into the vicarage on our way back.' She patted her curls. 'I really thought that I made something of an impression on the vicar yesterday. I would like to fix my picture in his mind.'

As Lavinia went upstairs, she found herself hoping that Isobel would not come with her, although of course she could not say so. She felt a little disloyal for thinking this way, but she found the way that Isobel always regarded other women's men as possible prey a little tiresome. It was therefore with something akin to relief that she discovered Mr Hawkfield had called while she was putting on her bonnet, and that Isobel intended to stroll about the garden with him instead of walking to the village. Now, at least, she could enjoy a pleasant, uninterrupted conversation with Miss Tasker, whom she had judged to be a congenial acquaintance who could, with time, become a good friend.

'Pray give Caroline my love,' said Miss Wheatman, who was engaged upon the weekly inspection of the linen, which she had undertaken on the countess's behalf. 'And do tell her about the grasses that we found. She will be most interested.'

The little schoolhouse was joined to the village school by one wall, and comprised a kitchen and one other room downstairs, with a steep flight of stairs going straight up from the tiny hall.

Miss Tasker was delighted to see Lavinia, and her face beamed with pleasure. 'I was hoping that we might be able to continue our conversation,' she confessed. 'I thought you seemed to be a very interesting person.'

'That is quite strange, for I was thinking exactly the same thing about you,' Lavinia replied. They both laughed.

Miss Tasker was pleased that Lavinia had remembered to bring the book that they had been discussing, and for a time, the talk was all of books and poetry. 'It is so delightful to find someone who shares one's interests,' Caroline Tasker confessed eventually. 'Timothy enjoys a good novel, but he is not very fond of poetry.'

'Isobel isn't fond of any kind of reading,' said Lavinia frankly.

'How is it that you come to be acquainted with her?' Caroline asked.

Lavinia explained that they were school-friends, and that their fathers had both been attached to embassies overseas, thereby giving them something in common. 'Isobel is very good really; and very generous in lots of ways,' said Lavinia. There was a 'but' hanging in the air. Neither of them voiced it.

'Shall we have some tea?' said Caroline. 'Do you have time to stay a little longer?'

'Yes indeed,' replied Lavinia, following the

schoolmistress into the kitchen, where she began to gather together the things needed to make a pot of tea. 'Isobel had been intending to accompany me, but as she was about to go upstairs for her bonnet, Mr Hawkfield arrived.'

'He is a very handsome young man,' said Caroline in a matter-of-fact tone. 'Was Miss Macclesfield acquainted with him before you came here?'

Lavinia shook her head. She nearly said something about her friend's relationship with Hawkfield's uncle, but stopped herself in time. It was too early in their acquaintance for her to be expecting Miss Tasker to keep secrets for her. After a moment's hesitation she simply said, 'I'm afraid that Isobel is a terrible flirt. The fact that a gentleman may be already spoken for does not seem to matter to her. It is almost as if she constantly needs to prove her ability to attract.'

Caroline turned to look at her, the teapot in her hand. She smiled ruefully. 'I had already suspected it,' she said. 'And Timothy is very handsome, too.'

'Don't you mind?' asked Lavinia curiously.

'I feel sorry for her,' was the surprising response. 'I'm also anxious that she should not make a fool of herself; but I do not fear for my engagement, if that is what you mean. Timothy and I are in love, you see.' She paused and looked at Lavinia's startled expression. 'You are astonished. Many people are. They find it hard to believe that a handsome man like Timothy could have fallen in love with a plain little woman like me.'

'I assure you that that is not what I think,' Lavinia replied honestly. Her surprise had been at the other woman's frankness, rather than at what she had disclosed. 'I think you have a pleasing countenance. The person who judges on appearances only is superficial indeed, but many people do marry for reasons other than love.'

'You are very kind,' said Caroline, as she finished preparing the tea and arranged some biscuits on a plate. 'Some more of my own baking,' she added with a twinkle.

'Then I shall have one with pleasure, for the ones that we had the other day were delicious.'

'They are Timothy's favourites.'

When they were sitting down, Caroline said, 'Ours was not a love match to begin with; at least, it was on my part, but not on Timothy's. I had been attracted to him from the very first when he came to my father as his curate. When he proposed, I accepted, knowing that at that point he only saw me as a useful helpmeet. Half a loaf is better than no bread, you see.

'It was only when by chance he called upon me in a thunderstorm and found me in some distress that he realized his feelings were stronger than esteem. He has told me since that he had always thought me equal to anything. He found it quite endearing to discover that there was something that could confound me.'

'It seems to me that an attachment begun in the way that you have described must have a great chance of success,' said Lavinia, after a brief silence. 'Marriages based on passion alone may well turn cold when passion fades; but a marriage that was built first on esteem and mutual respect — these are qualities that will last a lifetime.'

Caroline smiled warmly. 'That has always been my opinion,' she said.

They talked for some time, touching on a variety of topics, and finding a degree of similarity in one another's views. Eventually, the talk got round to Miss Wheatman.

'I love her dearly,' said Caroline, 'but there is no denying that she is a little inclined to fuss.'

'She asked me to tell you about all the grasses that we managed to gather the other day,' said Lavinia. 'I am afraid that I cannot tell you about them in such detail as she would like.'

Caroline laughed. 'Pray do not even try,' she said. 'Grasses are not one of my interests. Her tendency to expatiate upon her current hobby horse can be a little tedious in ordinary conversation.'

'I had thought that searching for grasses would be very dull,' Lavinia responded, 'but by the time we had finished, I had discovered that there was a good deal more to the subject than I ever would have believed.'

'She really is very knowledgeable,' Caroline agreed. 'She sometimes comes to the school and gives the children a botany lesson for me.'

'I cannot hope to rival her in that area, but I would love to come and help you in some other way,' said Lavinia. 'Would you like me to come and sew with the children, perhaps?'

The schoolmistress readily accepted this suggestion, and they parted with mutual expressions of pleasure and esteem.

As she walked back to the Hall, the book safely delivered, and one that Caroline had lent her tucked under her arm, Lavinia decided to say nothing to Isobel about this conversation. She would be very unlikely to believe that the vicar and the schoolmistress were actually in love; and if she thought for a moment that it could be true, she might want to flex her muscles all the more to see if she could enslave him. That could only result in embarrassment at best, and heartache at worst. Far better for Lavinia to keep this knowledge to herself.

10

Whether because of the vicar's prayers, or for some other reason, the day of the outing to Folkingham Castle dawned bright and clear. *Now that dowdy spinster will see what I am made of,* Isobel said to herself as she put the finishing touches to her appearance. She had on a gown which she had hardly worn, and then only in London. It was made of muslin, low cut, and of a dazzling white that is seldom seen, sprigged with tiny silver flowers. When Isobel came to find her, Lavinia had to admit that it was undoubtedly becoming, if highly impractical for a day that was to be spent scrambling about ruins. If the vicar was ever to have his head turned, then it would be by that gown. The finishing touches to Isobel's outfit were added by a charming straw bonnet with silver ribbons and white and blue flowers, and a parasol of blue and white.

By way of contrast, Lavinia was in an older gown of pink and white striped cotton, with a bonnet of a similar age trimmed with pink flowers and tied with white ribbons. She had also taken care to put on stout boots, which were in marked contrast to Isobel's dainty kid slippers.

'You will not be able to do much scrambling about in those,' Lavinia pointed out.

'Perhaps not; but boots like yours would ruin the look of my outfit completely,' Isobel replied. 'Besides, if there are any obstacles, no doubt some gentleman will lift me over them.'

'One may not be on hand at the time,' Lavinia reminded her.

'I shall make sure that one is,' answered Isobel mysteriously. She had slipped down to the Horseshoe and collected a letter from Lord Riseholm the previous day. Just the sight of his firm, sloping handwriting did more to set her heart beating than an entire conversation with Timothy Ames, or an evening spent in Lord Thurlby's company. She had taken a letter of her own at the same time. After today's expedition, she would have more to write — perhaps even, a tantalizing account of a tryst with the handsome vicar! That would make his rakeship give a thought to what he was missing.

If only Benjamin Twizzle had not discovered her secret correspondence with Lord Riseholm! His appearance at the inn had been the most tiresome stroke of bad luck.

She had managed to scrape together twenty pounds, but very much resented the necessity of handing it over. Her meeting with Twizzle today was yet another reason for looking her best. She had not yet met a man whom she could not twist around her little finger. A little flirtation and perhaps even a kiss would no doubt be sufficient to appease him. Then she could keep the twenty pounds for something far more important. Giving up her correspondence with Riseholm was out of the question. She did not dare think too deeply about why this might be the case.

On descending to the hall, they found Miss Wheatman and Lord Thurlby waiting for them. Miss Wheatman had dressed practically; unlike Lavinia, however, for whatever reason she had not been able to combine practical considerations with stylishness. Her drab brown gown was at least twenty years out of date and did not go with her black boots or her straw bonnet with its blue ribbons. Whatever her appearance, she looked happy to be going, and had with her a number of books.

'We need not waste the journey, for I can make it very instructive,' she assured them.

'That is very good of you, ma'am,' answered the earl, 'but remember that the young ladies have not been on this journey before. They will want to concentrate on what they see about them.' He looked much as he always did, well dressed, but comfortable, in a dark-blue coat with tan breeches and top boots. In his hand, he carried a broad-brimmed hat.

'Very true,' Miss Wheatman agreed. 'I will save them for the return journey.'

'Allow me to hold them for you,' said the earl politely, as they waited for the carriage to be brought round. As they were all getting ready to climb into the barouche, he surreptitiously laid them down on a chair in the hall. Miss Wheatman was very well meaning, but he had no intention of spending either journey listening to her reading from some instructive book! He thought that nobody had seen him thus engaged, but when he looked around, he caught Lavinia's eyes upon him, and grinned ruefully. She was obliged to hide her answering expression of amusement.

The plan was that they should collect Mr Ames and Miss Tasker from the vicarage. Mr Hawkfield and Mr Laver would meet them at the Horseshoe, and travel alongside on horseback. The barouche was large enough to take six comfortably but certainly not eight. When they arrived outside the vicarage, the vicar and his betrothed were ready and waiting. Isobel had never supposed that Miss Tasker's appearance would rival her own, and she was pleased to note that she was correct in her supposition. The schoolmistress was dressed in a faded cotton gown, sprigged with golden flowers, and an old bonnet tied with yellow ribbon. Like Lavinia and Miss Wheatman, she was wearing sensible boots.

Lavinia and Isobel were sitting facing the horses, whilst Lord Thurlby and Miss Wheatman had their backs to them. When Miss Tasker and the vicar joined them, therefore, the former took her place next to the young ladies, leaving the vicar to join Thurlby and Miss Wheatman on the backward facing seat. This suited Isobel very well, for it meant that she was able to catch the eye of Mr Ames, and bat her lashes at him.

Once they had reached the Horseshoe, however, she gained more targets for her languorous glances, for both Mr Laver and Mr Hawkfield showed by appreciative looks how impressed they were with her appearance.

'All at once, the sun appears to have become more dazzling,' said Hawkfield, surveying all the ladies in turn, but allowing his gaze to linger finally on Isobel.

'Perhaps you should stay behind, then, if your eyes cannot cope,' Isobel suggested.

'Heaven forbid,' he replied, grinning

roguishly. 'Doubtless I shall soon become accustomed to the brightness.'

The journey was a pleasant one, as Lord Thurlby had predicted, taking them as it did through the bustling market town of Bourne, and then into some pleasant countryside. The weather remained good, the blue sky clear but for a few white fluffy clouds, and a light breeze saving the day from being sultry. Lavinia was interested to notice how frequently Lord Thurlby was obliged to acknowledge salutations from people walking, riding, or, like themselves, driving. Of course, as a prominent landowner who spent much of his time in this region, this was not altogether surprising. Nevertheless, Lavinia could not help contrasting this outing with one that she had made with friends of her aunt and uncle twelve months before.

On that visit, the three of them had gone out for a drive with Sir Antony Frew and his wife in the barouche belonging to the baronet. They had driven around their host's estate, but he had barely acknowledged the various greetings and reverences that had been paid to him by his tenants and others, limiting himself to a curt nod or a careless wave.

Lord Thurlby, on the other hand, really turned towards the person whom he was greeting, and returned every smile with another. It was a perfect display of cordiality, finely balanced with dignity.

'Who was that?' Miss Wheatman asked, as Thurlby raised a hand of greeting to a very broad, vigorous-looking man in his twenties on foot, who had saluted him in passing.

'A local farmer, Joe Habgood by name,' Thurlby answered. 'He recently inherited the property from his father.'

'He looks like a bit of a bruiser to me,' said Hawkfield, having eyed the young man measuringly. 'I'd like to see him in the ring.'

'I don't think you ever would,' Thurlby told him. 'There have been a number of attempts to persuade him, but he insists that he's too peaceable by nature.'

'Not enough money offered, no doubt,' Hawkfield surmised. Thurlby did not make any further comment, but contented himself with a wry smile.

Lavinia wondered whether Sir Antony would have been anything like as knowledge-able about any of his tenants or neighbours.

★ ★ ★

The village of Folkingham was very pretty, having a broad main street, with some very fine houses either side, as well as more humble dwellings, and an imposing coach house at the top of the street, called the Greyhound.

'We are on the main road from Bourne to Lincoln,' Lord Thurlby explained, 'so it is not surprising that this place should seek to provide well for travellers.'

As well as the Greyhound, there were one or two lesser establishments, including a chocolate shop, which the ladies all said that they would like to visit later. When they reached the top of the street, the Lincoln road veered off to the right, but the coachman steered them round to the left and through another part of the village. Ahead of them lay the church, a fine building with a spire, and Mr Ames expressed a desire to look around it if there was time. Lavinia was not surprised when Isobel endorsed this wish with enthusiasm.

It was as they descended a slight incline after passing the church that the castle came into sight. It was of grey stone, which could easily take on a gloomy look on a wet evening in November, but on this day, with the sun shining down and picking out the odd fragments of glass here and there, it fairly sparkled, seeming to share in the general merriment of the outing.

'I do hope that we did not have to ask

anyone's permission in order to visit here,' said Miss Wheatman. 'I should hate to be arrested for trespass.'

'As I am a magistrate, I should certainly find it embarrassing,' Lord Thurlby agreed. 'However, there is no need to be concerned. The ownership of the place has passed to a local landowner, who is happy for visitors to explore it, as long as they do no damage.'

The structure had looked to be quite a small one, but as they drew closer, they could see that it was much more extensive than they had thought at first. Surrounded by a moat which was now empty, it was more in the way of being a fortified house, rather than a castle of classic design. The barouche drew round to the front of the castle and set them down at the entrance, which could be approached by crossing a bridge which was set over the moat. From where they were standing, they could see through the open arch into a grassy courtyard.

'This is delightful,' said Isobel, looking about her as they strolled across the bridge. 'I declare that I could happily spend the rest of the day exploring.'

Lord Thurlby consulted his pocket watch. 'We have a little time before we need think about nuncheon,' he said. 'Shall we have a look around, and then reconvene inside the courtyard in, say, an hour?'

'That sounds eminently sensible,' answered Miss Wheatman. 'I have with me a written account of how and why buildings such as this came to be constructed. Would anyone care to sit down with me whilst I read the account out loud?'

More than one person of the party was wondering how to say that this idea did not appeal to them without being rude. To everyone's great relief, however, Lord Thurlby said, 'Were you referring to those books that you handed to me? I laid them down on a table in the hall, but I fear that in all the excitement of departure, I failed to pick them up again. I do apologize.'

Miss Wheatman looked anxious. 'Oh dear, oh dear,' she said. 'I am afraid that I have let you all down.' The rest of the company attempted to look downcast.

'No, indeed, the fault is Lord Thurlby's,' said Lavinia. 'For shame, my lord!' Nevertheless she was obliged to hide a smile. She was impressed with the way in which he had managed to sound regretful without telling an untruth.

Their eyes met briefly. The earl's lips twitched almost imperceptibly. 'I am justly reproved,' he said. 'What is to be done?'

'The day is too fine to spend in reading,

Aunt Daisy,' said Miss Tasker gently. 'We can enjoy such information on a day when it is raining. It will give us something to do, as well as providing a reminder of better days.'

'Very true, my dear,' answered Miss Wheatman. 'I think I can probably remember a good deal of what was written, in any case.'

'Then perhaps you will enlighten me,' said Thurlby with real heroism, as he gestured towards part of the gateway through which they had just walked. 'What is the purpose of those overhanging segments of brick, for example?'

Miss Wheatman proceeded to offer him a careful explanation, whilst the rest of the party split up. Lavinia would also have liked to learn more about the place, but Isobel tucked a hand in her arm, and began to chatter animatedly. Lavinia was a little surprised to see with what equanimity the other girl watched the vicar walk away with Miss Tasker on his arm. She could only assume that her friend was planning an assault upon the clergyman after nuncheon.

To the casual onlooker, Isobel, Lavinia, Mr Hawkfield and Mr Laver made a lively group, as Isobel and Hawkfield in particular discovered mutual acquaintances, and chattered about the London scene. It must be said that as Isobel dictated the pace, they did very little exploring of the ruins, owing to the dainty nature of her thin, kid slippers. By the time they all gathered together for nuncheon, the four young people had done little more than stroll around the grassy area in the centre of the keep.

No doubt her young companions of the morning would have thought that she was a trifle strange, but Lavinia had found it all a little dull so far. She had deliberately worn stout shoes, but she had hardly found them necessary. What was more, she would much rather have wandered around with Miss Wheatman and Lord Thurlby, and heard about the history of the place, than listened to gossip about a lot of people most of whom she had never met, and whom she was sure she would not have found particularly agreeable had she done so. However, it was much easier to allow Isobel to lead the conversation than to try to insert a new subject into their talk, particularly one that the other girl would not find congenial. Besides, she had a grave suspicion that any attempts to talk about the ruins would only result in her being condemned as a blue-stocking. She could but hope that she would have the chance to see more of the castle after nuncheon.

As she glanced around, she saw that preparations were being made for their meal.

The servants had brought blankets which Miss Wheatman was spreading out in a shady place on the grass next to the castle walls. Lavinia hurried to help her. She looked up from straightening one of the corners to see that one of the menservants was bringing a box which, from the rattling sound emerging from it probably contained cutlery. To her great surprise, however, a huge, two-handled wicker basket was being carried by a footman at one side and the earl at the other. The men were exchanging the odd comment as they walked. Obviously this was not the first time that Thurlby had lent assistance in such a way.

He had taken off his coat in order to perform this task, and Lavinia's eyes were particularly drawn to the way in which the light breeze moulded his shirt to his well-formed chest and biceps.

'Yes, very impressive,' Isobel whispered to Lavinia, causing her to blush bright red.

After everything was laid out on the grass, the earl put his coat back on with the footman's assistance, then said to him, 'Go and enjoy your own meal, now. I'll call if I need anything.'

Lavinia watched the man's retreating figure for a moment or two then said, 'The staff are picnicking too?'

'They have to eat,' he replied easily. 'As long

as they look after the horses, I see no reason why they shouldn't enjoy the day as well. We need no one to serve us here.' He wondered what had happened to embarrass her a short time before, but noted how a touch of colour became her. Some country air was doing her good after her stay in London, he decided.

The meal was a cheerful affair. After the basket had been unpacked and Thurlby had poured the wine, they all sat down to enjoy bread, pickles, cold chicken, cheese, and a fruit cake. It was warm and sheltered in the courtyard, and after a glass or two of wine, Miss Wheatman looked ready for a nap.

'I am happy to stay with you, Aunt,' said Miss Tasker cheerfully. 'Timothy has dragged me all over this castle already, and I would be glad to sit down for a while.'

'Perhaps if you have shown Miss Tasker the main points of interest, you would like to show them to me, now,' said Isobel prettily to Mr Ames. 'We did not get round to exploring properly this morning.'

The vicar eyed her slippers doubtfully. 'Will you be able to manage in those?' he asked her.

'If I cannot, then you will just have to help me,' she said, fluttering her eyelashes as she took his arm.

'What do you say to exploring the moat, and seeing if we can find a weakness in the defences?' said Hawkfield to Laver. The latter was quite amenable to this suggestion, and the two soon set off.

'You are now left with very little alternative by way of an escort, I fear,' Thurlby said to Lavinia. 'Shall we walk, ma'am?'

'With pleasure,' she replied truthfully. If she was honest with herself, she would have had to admit that she wanted to see whether she would again experience the strange sensation of attraction that she had felt in Lord Thurlby's company, or whether it had been something that she had imagined. Now, as she laid her hand upon his arm, she knew that it was real enough.

Determined not to betray some kind of interest that was almost certainly not returned, however, she said, 'I am hoping that you will have benefited from Miss Wheatman's instruction. What can you tell me about this place?'

★   ★   ★

In the meantime, Isobel was saying something very similar to Mr Ames. 'There must be a chapel,' she went on. 'You must show me the chapel.'

'Yes, there is indeed,' he agreed. 'It is this way.'

Perhaps because of reverence, or primitive

180

superstition, those who had plundered the castle had left the chapel alone and it was one of the parts of the building that remained more-or-less intact. It had a fine, high ceiling, decorated with stone bosses, and a balcony which looked down onto the high altar.

'This is splendid,' said Isobel looking around her. 'Now do not tell me that you would not like to be the vicar of a place like this. How romantic to live here!' She twirled around, holding her arms out, then stopped, and looked at him in a way that managed to seem both guilty and saucy at the same time. 'Oh dear! I fear that I have been disrespectful. Pray forgive me, sir!'

'Not at all,' the vicar responded. 'It is a lovely place, you are quite right.'

'What tales must have been told here! What joy! What sadness! What stories of romance must have been lived out over the years!'

'What coughs, colds and chilblains,' he replied with a twinkle. 'It is beautiful, I grant you; but I would not exchange the parson's living quarters here for my cosy vicarage.'

'Mr Ames, you are not romantic enough!' Isobel declared.

'It is a fault, I admit it.'

'I shall have to teach you,' she smiled. 'Show me something else.'

'I think I know what you would like to see,' said Lord Thurlby to Lavinia. He pointed to the highest tower. 'Would you like to ascend and take a look at the view? Miss Wheatman is not fond of heights, so we did not go up there this morning.'

'I would like to do so very much,' she replied. 'Is it safe?'

'Yes it is. The owner regularly checks the premises for structural soundness, as the castle attracts many visitors.'

They ascended the spiral staircase, Lavinia going first. It was a longer climb than was apparent at first, but when, as they reached the top breathless, they stepped out into the fresh air, they felt that all their efforts had been rewarded. The day was clear, and the view was splendid. Lord Thurlby knew the country-side well, and was able to point out what stood in each direction.

As he spoke with authority about the countryside which was spread out before them like a carpet, Lavinia made an interesting discovery. 'You have been here before, have you not?'

'Yes, I have,' he agreed.

'But you did not say so. Why ever not?'

'I was afraid you'd laugh at me if I told

you,' he said ruefully.

'I would never be so uncivil,' she replied.

'Would you not? Egad, I believe you. Very well, then. I came here with a party of friends some years ago. There was a young lady with whom I was besotted at the time. I was hoping to propose in this romantic setting.'

He fell silent. Eventually, Lavinia, who had been seized by a most unexpected stab of jealousy, said, 'I assume that she . . . refused you.'

'She didn't get the opportunity,' he replied. 'Discovering her entwined with a neighbour's son had the effect of banishing my ardour.'

She gasped. 'I'm not surprised. How very shocking. Did you knock him down?'

'I did not have the right. There was no understanding between us. Soon afterwards, they announced their engagement. He was several years older than me, you see. They are now living in a distant county. As I am sure you can imagine, this place did not hold very happy memories for me. I confess that I felt a certain reluctance at the prospect of coming here, but now I must be grateful for having had my hand forced. The ghosts seem to have gone.'

Lavinia smiled, and laid a hand on his arm. 'I am glad,' she said. 'I hope that you will now have happier memories to replace them.'

Suddenly realizing that he might think that she was attempting to flirt with him, she snatched her hand away quickly and said, 'But you have not told me about all the sights. What other landmarks can be seen from here?'

'Over there, you can just make out Lincoln Cathedral,' he replied, after a brief pause.

'Where? Where?' she asked, looking anywhere, but in the right direction.

'There,' he said, crouching a little, so that he could see from her point of view. He put one hand gently on her back, and leaned close to her, pointing again.

'I see it,' she said; but suddenly, the sight of Lincoln Cathedral was less significant than the way that he was making her feel. She looked at him, their eyes met, and her hand went to her throat.

Thurlby, too, was obviously affected in some way by their closeness, for he straightened, cleared his throat and put his hands behind his back. 'Shall we go and have a look at the rest of the castle? Would you like to see the dungeons?'

He is embarrassed at being up here alone with me, she thought to herself. He wants to go back down to the courtyard and join the rest of the party, so that a group of us may go to the dungeons together. 'Yes . . . yes, of course,' she said, anxious that he should not suspect the truth, which was that she had suddenly realized how very much she wanted to be alone with him. She turned away quickly, and, in her haste, caught her foot against a projecting stone, and stumbled. She was never in any real danger of falling from the tower; at the worst, she might have grazed her arm against the wall, but moving swiftly, Lord Thurlby prevented her from sustaining any injury by catching hold of her in his arms.

He drew her closer; he lowered his head; for a moment, she thought that he was going to kiss her and she held her breath. Some rooks flew overhead, cawing loudly and breaking the spell.

'Thank you,' she murmured, looking away from him.

He released her at once, flushing. 'You must take great care in these old buildings,' he said, sounding strained. 'The floors are often very uneven.'

'I will take more care in the future,' she answered, conscious of feeling disappointed as they descended the stairs.

Thurlby walked down ahead of her, so that he might break her fall should she trip. And while for her part, Lavinia was somewhat preoccupied by the pleasing sight of his broad shoulders, he found himself thinking about the young woman who was just behind him. If he paused, he might even feel her breath on his hair.

He had been sorely tempted to kiss her a few moments ago. The sound of the rooks overhead had brought him to his senses. He hardly knew whether to be glad or sorry. Now that the moment was past, he remembered how Lavinia had arrived in Lincolnshire having been the willing recipient of Riseholm's advances. She had never excused herself or given any explanation for her entanglement with his rakeship. Thurlby grinned humourlessly. Whatever his faults, the man had ever had good taste.

This visit to Folkingham may have laid some ghosts, but the memories remained. He could still recall how he had felt when he had encountered the girl he had set his heart upon in another man's arms. He had no desire to repeat the experience. Even so, he could not deny the attraction that he felt for Lavinia — an attraction which, despite any relationship she might have had with his rakeship would not go away.

She had assured him that that entanglement was over and done with, and he had no reason to doubt her word. Nevertheless, would a woman who had danced and flirted with men of the town during the London season be content with country life?

The direction of his thoughts almost caused him to miss his footing. Why should Lavinia live in the country? Her aunt and uncle would return to London eventually, and she would make her home with them again, surely? There were only two possible reasons that he could think of for her to live at Thurlby Hall. One would be for his mother to take the burden of her care off her uncle and aunt's shoulders. The other he hardly dared name; but the thought of it made his heart beat a little faster.

11

Isobel and Timothy Ames were already inspecting the dungeons. This had, inevitably, been at the lady's behest. Mr Ames had again suggested that her shoes might not be entirely suitable for such an expedition, but she had pouted, insisting that she did not want to miss something so interesting, simply because she did not possess the right sort of shoes. She managed to make it sound as though some unkind person had denied her the chance of having boots, and earned a thoroughly undeserved sympathetic look from the vicar.

'Of course we shall go down to the dungeons if you wish it,' he said kindly. 'I will assist you.'

'Thank you,' replied Isobel, laying her hand on his arm.

Lord Thurlby had taken the precaution of bringing some candles for the use of the party, and the vicar made sure that he had one with him when they went down to the dungeon. It was indeed very needful, for there were no windows at all in the lower chamber, and without a candle, it would have been impossible to see anything, except for the small area at the foot of the stairs. It was also damp and chilly — hardly the place to visit when wearing a thin muslin dress and very little else. Isobel, however, showed no signs of physical discomfort. She looked around the murky chamber, which was only faintly illuminated by the candle held high in Mr Ames's hand.

'What terror must have been felt by those who were escorted to this place,' she murmured, looking round and shuddering artistically. 'Just imagine how they might have despaired as the light disappeared and they were left in complete darkness! What horror!'

'Yes indeed, it is dreadful to contemplate,' Ames agreed.

His mind was not upon this present visit, but was busily recollecting what had occurred when he and Caroline Tasker had explored the dungeon before they had eaten their meal. Alone in the darkness, they had swayed together and he had dropped his candle to the floor where it had immediately gone out. Then he had pulled her into his arms and their lips had met in a long, passionate kiss. He had felt her capable hands stroke the curls at the back of his neck, and with a groan, he had pulled her closer, daringly allowing one hand to stray a little below her waist.

'Timothy,' she had whispered. 'This is very improper!'

'Not half as improper as some of the things that I would like to do with you,' he had admitted frankly. 'Dearest, I do not know how I am ever to wait until we are married.'

'You will have to do so, I'm afraid,' she had answered, softening her words by reaching up to kiss him again.

'Perhaps I shall be led into temptation,' he had suggested. 'Miss Macclesfield would be all too pleased to do so, I suspect.'

'Miss Macclesfield may do as she likes, just so long as you do not give her any encouragement.'

'Why should I ever want to encourage her when I have you?'

They had exchanged a few more passionate kisses before returning to the daylight to join the others. Nobody would have guessed from the composed appearance that they had presented, what had passed in the dungeon between the schoolmistress and the vicar.

Thus it was that he was quite unmoved by Isobel's preening and posturing. She would have been utterly astonished had she realized that the slightest turn of the head of plain little Miss Tasker inflamed him far more than her most calculatedly seductive gesture.

'Shall we return to the comforting

sunlight?' he asked Isobel. 'It is very cold down here.'

'Yes it is,' she agreed. 'Does it make you nervous, Mr Ames?'

'Not at all,' he replied, with more haste than truth as he scented danger.

'Suppose you were to drop the candle,' she suggested.

'I must take care not to do so. Come, Miss Macclesfield.'

'Oh, very well,' she pouted. She looked sideways at him as they ascended into the warm sunlight. Quite clearly he was interested in her. He could not fail to be when she had made herself look so stunning. He was obviously exercising considerable restraint. His evident agitation told her that. She would have to work out how to make him discard it and behave towards her as she was convinced he wished to do. A hint of a rival ought to provoke his interest. It had worked before with other men.

Upon reaching the sunlight, therefore, Isobel immediately waved to Mr Hawkfield and Mr Laver, who were returning from looking at the moat. Her intention had been to stroll about with them under Mr Ames's nose. At that very moment, however, she caught sight of Benjamin Twizzle signalling to her and her heart plummeted. In the excitement of the day, she had forgotten that he had said he would meet her here.

Unwelcome though the man was, however, it would do no harm to make use of him. 'Oh, good gracious!' she exclaimed, feigning surprise at seeing him. 'As if I did not have enough of men following me around in London, only to experience it here as well.'

'Would you like me to send the fellow about his business?' Ames asked, straightening his cuffs. He knew Twizzle by reputation, and what he knew he did not like.

'No, there is no need,' Isobel answered airily, misreading this chivalrous suggestion as a sign of personal interest in her. 'I shall go and speak to him myself.' Seeing him still looking doubtful, she added, 'I shall scream if I need rescuing and you can then come gallantly to my aid.'

Mr Ames might have protested further, but seeing his betrothed sitting with Miss Wheatman, he made no further objection.

'Well?' said Twizzle, as soon as they were alone together in one of the ruined chambers of the castle. 'Have you brought the money?'

'This is not very gallant, sir,' replied Isobel, dimpling at him, and twirling her parasol. 'You have not even asked me how I do, or commented on my gown.'

Although Benjamin Twizzle's very upright

father would have said that his weaknesses were manifold, the young man himself would have admitted to two: the need to cut a dash, and a liking for beautiful women. Isobel's undoubted beauty had attracted him from the first. Had he been challenged with being a blackmailer, he would vigorously have denied such an assertion. He was merely making the most of every opportunity. Life was to be enjoyed; and the purpose of those he met was to enable him to enjoy it, in every possible way. Flirtation was nothing if not enjoyable. This opportunity to extract money from the young lady with whom he was flirting merely added spice to the connection.

'It's dashed pretty,' he replied admiringly. 'Not nearly as pretty as the wearer, of course.'

'Oh Mr Twizzle,' answered Isobel, inwardly breathing a sigh of relief, for this was the kind of conversation that she understood. 'You flatter me, I fear.'

'Not at all,' he responded, lolling against one of the rugged walls, then spoiling the negligent effect by straightening and carefully brushing the dust off his sleeve. There was more than a hint of the dandy about him, dressed as he was in tight yellow pantaloons, jockey boots with tassels, and a blue coat with shiny metal buttons. None of these items had yet been paid for, a fact which made the acquisition of a sum of money all the more urgent.

'What a splendid place this is,' said Isobel, smiling at him, and half turning away. 'Full of secluded corners for . . . private conversations.'

'Exactly so,' he responded eagerly, taking two steps towards her and laying his hands on her shoulders.

Isobel was not unused to desperate flirtations in dark corners with flirtatious young men. Mr Twizzle, as Lavinia had observed on the coach, was exactly the kind of young man who often appealed to her. Since this was what she had been angling for from the first, it was rather strange, therefore, that she found herself thinking that she really did not want Benjamin to kiss her. 'Mr Twizzle! You are too hasty,' she exclaimed. She was surprised to hear a note in her own voice that sounded very like panic.

'Hasty?' he echoed.

'Why yes,' she responded, recovering herself. 'How many a good thing is spoiled through rushing.'

'True enough,' he agreed. 'You'll meet me again, then?'

'Why not?' she replied, smiling. 'I must return before I am missed.' She turned to go.

'Before you do so,' said Twizzle, who was

not quite as besotted as Isobel would have liked, 'Perhaps you could let me have my money.'

Quickly swallowing a cry of vexation, Isobel said, 'Mr Twizzle! Is not my company enough for you?'

'Your company is enchanting, but my purse is still empty,' he replied.

'Well . . . ten pounds, then,' she said, opening her reticule. 'Ten,' she repeated when he seemed about to protest, 'or not another meeting will I grant you.'

'Very well; ten,' he agreed. 'But meet me again in three days' time.'

'In a week,' she replied, pouting. 'Three days is too soon.'

'Three days in the wilderness garden at Thurlby Hall, or I shall come up to the house to see the earl.'

'Cruel,' answered Isobel, pouting. 'Three days, then.'

'And bring the rest of the money.'

She hurried off laughing, but in truth she was beginning to feel quite frightened.

★ ★ ★

Lord Thurlby and Lavinia never did manage to get down into the dungeons. After they had come back down from the tower, they saw

Miss Wheatman waving to them, and on drawing closer, they found Mr Ames crouching beside a distressed-looking Miss Tasker.

'The silliest thing,' she was saying, trying unsuccessfully to sound as if she was not in pain. 'I had gone all the way down into the dungeons without the slightest mishap. Then we were just sitting here quietly when a great bumble bee came and landed on my aunt's skirt.'

'And I cannot bear them, you know,' Miss Wheatman added. 'So foolish of me!'

'So I got up to chase it away, and before I had taken more than two or three steps, I caught my ankle in a hole.'

'Allow me to examine it,' said Lord Thurlby, bending down. 'I have a little experience in these matters.'

'It really isn't important,' said Miss Tasker weakly.

'Yes it is,' her fiancé retorted. 'You nearly fainted.'

'By your leave,' said the earl, speaking as much to Mr Ames as to Miss Tasker.

Lavinia watched as Lord Thurlby crouched down and gently examined the school-mistress's ankle. How strong and capable his hands were, she thought. They were not the kind of beautiful hands that would be chosen by a sculptor for him to model; they were perhaps too strong and square for that; but they were deft and assured in their movements. They were just the kind of hands that she would choose to help her in an emergency, Lavinia decided. Or to carry her if she were hurt, or even if she were not . . .

'I don't think it's broken,' he said, breaking into her reverie. 'A cold compress would help. Do we have any water?'

There was still some water left over from the picnic, and Lavinia damped a napkin with it, whilst Miss Wheatman gently held it to Miss Tasker's swollen ankle.

'We must get you home as soon as possible, I think,' said Miss Wheatman, in between making soothing noises.

'Home?' echoed the vicar. 'That will not do at all. She will be alone in the schoolhouse!'

'You are very right,' Thurlby agreed. 'She must come and stay at the Hall until she is better.'

'But I could not possibly impose,' Caroline protested.

'It would be no imposition,' the earl answered. 'Ames is right. You cannot go home to look after yourself when you are unable to put a foot to the ground. However would you manage to make yourself a cup of tea, for instance?'

'But — ' she began.

'No more buts,' interrupted the earl. 'You may go home as soon as your ankle is strong enough. Believe me; it will get strong more quickly if you have proper care. Neglect it and it could be a trouble to you for months.'

Miss Tasker sighed. 'Very well, my lord,' she said eventually. 'I agree, but only because I know that you are right.'

'Sensible woman,' smiled Thurlby. 'I will go and ask the servants to prepare to leave.' He turned to Ames. 'Will you find the rest of our party and apprise them of the situation? We shall have to think how best to convey Miss Tasker home without jolting her ankle.'

In the event, Lord Thurlby opted to ride on the box of the barouche, leaving extra space so that Miss Tasker could sit across the seat with her feet cradled by Miss Wheatman, after she had been carried tenderly to the vehicle by Mr Ames.

Isobel allowed herself a small secret smile. The presence of Caroline Tasker in the house would mean that Timothy Ames would be honour bound to come and visit. But after he had paid his obligatory visit to his dull, plain little fiancé, she, Isobel would entice him to walk in the garden with her. Then, if she did not manage to get a kiss or two out of him, she was not the woman that she took herself to be!

★　★　★

Lord Thurlby sent one of the servants on ahead in order for arrangements to be made for Miss Tasker's accommodation. As a consequence, when they arrived at Thurlby Hall, a room had been prepared by Mrs Bell, the housekeeper. Mr Ames lifted his fiancée down, and, following Mrs Bell, carried her upstairs. Caroline smiled bravely and made no complaint, but it was quite apparent to anyone who knew her that she was in some pain.

'I will send for the doctor,' said Thurlby to Miss Wheatman, 'if you will help her to get into bed.'

'I do not need the doctor,' the sufferer protested. 'You said yourself that it was only a bad sprain.'

'I am not an expert,' Thurlby replied. 'I would prefer the doctor to look at you.'

'I agree,' added Ames.

'Am I to have no say in the matter?' Caroline asked.

'No,' the two men responded in unison.

In the meantime, Isobel and Lavinia were entertaining Hawkfield and Laver in the drawing room. 'What a lot of fuss about nothing,'

Isobel was saying. 'The young woman only turned her ankle. I'm sure she could walk if she tried.'

'Tricky things, ankles,' remarked Laver, then paused.

The rest of the company waited for him to say something more. When nothing else was forthcoming, Lavinia said, 'How true. I am sure that it is better to be safe than sorry.' Then the conversation turned to something else.

12

Mr Hawkfield came to see them the following day, ostensibly with the purpose of enquiring after Miss Tasker, but actually with some very surprising news. 'I have received a letter from a schoolfriend who tells me something quite extraordinary,' he said. The day being fine and warm, Lavinia and Isobel were sitting outside on a wooden seat under a tree, when Lord Thurlby's butler conducted their visitor to pay his respects.

'Oh really,' said Isobel, fanning herself with deliberate casualness. 'Has he found his Latin primer?'

Hawkfield had taken the letter out of his pocket. Now he put it back again. 'Oh well, you obviously have no interest in it, so I will not trouble you. Did I tell you that Laver is planning to buy a new horse?'

'No, you did not,' replied Isobel. 'Pray, tell me, what is your extraordinary news?'

'Nothing worth troubling you with,' he replied, 'although I would never have thought such a thing of Riseholm. In fact, I would have said that he was the last man to . . . But there we are, it is of no interest to you. I always think that people who can do nothing but talk about their relations are intolerably tedious. Would you like to come and view Laver's prospective purchase?'

'Oh, who cares about Laver's stupid horse?' said Isobel angrily. 'Of course I want to hear your news. What about Riseholm?'

'Only that it seems as though he is about to become engaged.'

'Engaged? Engaged to be married?' said Lavinia hurriedly, seeing that Isobel had lost a little colour.

'Is there any other kind?' asked Hawkfield whimsically.

'But to whom?' put in Isobel. 'He said nothing of this in his — '

'Been writing to him, have you?' Hawkfield asked. She held his gaze with a defiant stare. He relented and looked down at his paper. 'To a Miss Egan, I think.' He scanned the page. 'Yes, Miss Hermione Egan. Now tell me that my news is not exciting.' He eyed Isobel a little maliciously.

'Hermione Egan,' Isobel repeated. 'But she will bore him silly in approximately five minutes. Has it been announced?'

'Not as yet,' he conceded. 'But he has been paying her very particular attention, apparently. All of London is waiting for the announcement. There has even been betting on it in the clubs.'

'It is amazing to me the things that gentlemen will bet on,' said Lavinia severely, seeing another means of drawing Hawkfield's attention away from Isobel, who had gone strangely still.

'Yes, isn't it?' Hawkfield agreed. 'Or so I'm told. Do you recall Miss Egan, Miss Muir?'

'There is precious little to recall,' Isobel put in bluntly, before Lavinia had time to say anything. 'Young, silly and stupid would sum her up, I think.'

'And exceedingly pretty,' put in Hawkfield.

'Oh yes, of course she's pretty,' said Isobel sarcastically. 'Riseholm would hardly look her way if she were not. Excuse me, will you? I have a hem that needs stitching, and this conversation has suddenly become very dull.'

She strolled back towards the house. Lavinia fully expected Hawkfield to make some remark about her reaction to the news, but instead, he went back to talking about Laver's plans for acquiring a new horse.

She nodded politely at everything that he was saying, but in reality, her mind was elsewhere. It was the first time that she had ever known Isobel excuse herself from a conversation with a young man in order to set a stitch in anything. In fact, if Isobel had so much as taken up her needle since their schooldays, she would be very much surprised. What was more, she had seen her friend's face at the very moment when Lord Riseholm's engagement had been mentioned. The girl had looked positively stricken.

If Hawkfield had hoped to see Isobel again, he was to be disappointed, for she did not come back downstairs and after the correct half an hour, he took his leave. 'Doubtless half the hem had come down,' he remarked with a little gentle malice. Lavinia could not think of a response to this, so simply bade him 'good day'.

★   ★   ★

Having drifted languidly away from her companions, Isobel went up to her bedchamber, forcing herself to walk in a leisurely fashion, even though every instinct was telling her to pick up her skirts and run. Eventually, she gained the sanctuary that she desired, and once in the room with the door shut, to her astonishment, found herself crying. What is the matter with me, she asked herself? Lord Riseholm is a rake, a flirt, an amusing dinner companion, but nothing more, surely?

Her mind went back over some of the occasions when they had met in London. Usually, this had been at some kind of society event, attended by members of the *ton*. At these functions, he had conducted himself towards her with his usual careless grace. When unobserved, however, there had been times when he had been more daring in his behaviour.

It had happened that she had visited Vauxhall for a masquerade one evening with Mrs Wilbraham and a party of her choosing. At such events, dancing became a much more exciting business, since disguise meant that it was possible to partner those with whom it might not, in other circumstances, have been permitted even to pass the time of day.

Isobel had been wearing a charming pink gown, with a domino of a darker shade, lined with white silk. She had just enjoyed a splendidly vigorous excursion with a slim, fair man whom she had not recognized, and who, she suspected, might have been a footman on his night off, when a familiar caressing voice had spoken from behind. 'Dance with me, fair Rosebud.'

Like everyone else, Lord Riseholm had been masked, and nearly everything he was wearing was of the darkest black. His linen was snowy white, trimmed with rich lace, and his domino was lined with purple shot silk. His teeth had gleamed in the lamplight.

'Thank you, kind sir,' Isobel had responded,

not giving away the fact that she had recognized him.

She had danced with him before, and had discovered their steps to be wonderfully well attuned. That evening had done nothing but confirm that impression, and when the dance had finished and he had slipped an arm about her waist, she had willingly gone with him off the dance floor and under the trees.

'Do you know me, sweet?' he had asked her, as he had pulled her into his arms.

'I believe so,' she had responded demurely.

'Then prepare to have your education extended, for you are about to know me a good deal better,' he had said, before kissing her. At first his kisses had been languid, seductive and assured. Then as she had gained in confidence and begun to return his caresses, his languor had appeared to diminish and his passion increase. They had remained in seclusion, kissing and murmuring endearments for quite some time; and when at last he had led her back to the dance floor, she had felt breathless and not quite steady.

From that moment on, Riseholm had been the man she had looked for at every gathering. Anyone could have told her that the wisest course would have been to avoid him completely; she knew it herself. She had quite deliberately set up other flirtations so that her interest in him would not look so particular. It was only Riseholm who made her heart beat faster, however, and she had been foolish enough to allow her preference to lead her into indiscretion. The occasion when Lavinia had seen them together in the street had not been the first time that they had met thus. Eventually the scandal had forced Mrs Wilbraham to take the step of threatening to send her away from London, but this had been the last thing that she had wanted. She had managed to manipulate things so that she could come to Thurlby, rather than be sent to Harrogate. Truth to tell, wherever she had gone, she would have found a way of keeping in touch with Riseholm. She did not by any means wish to be parted from the earl.

Circumstances had fortuitously combined to enable her to find a way of writing to Riseholm. This did not mean that she was unaware how wrong it was to engage in a secret correspondence with a libertine in the way that she had. Why else would she keep this secret from Lavinia? Nevertheless, she found herself wanting to know everything about him. She had asked him questions which he had answered, before asking some of his own in his response. Why had he said nothing about an engagement? Had he said anything about Miss Egan at all? Could Hawkfield's friend have been mistaken?

She hunted at the back of the cupboard where her clothes were kept, and got out the box in which she kept all his letters. Carefully she re-read each one, but there was nothing about the wretched girl. With a man like Riseholm, she knew that there was a great danger of out of sight, out of mind. She now realized with added force that the notion of his forgetting about her was very disturbing, to say the least.

She sat nibbling the end of her finger before making a decision. She decided to write to Riseholm playfully, teasing him a little about his conquest of Miss Egan. Then in the same letter she would boast discreetly about her success in enslaving the vicar. He was, after all, the nephew of Lord and Lady Smilie, a wealthy childless couple. Yes, a hint that she was on the point of contracting an alliance with Timothy Ames would make his rakeship think!

She was also aware that she needed to do something to get rid of Benjamin Twizzle. Short of a torrential downpour, she could not see a way out of meeting him in the wilderness the day after tomorrow. Thanks to her craftiness, she had some money to give him, but her allowance was not a bottomless pit, and what would he do when her money was gone? If he told Thurlby, as he had threatened, then Thurlby would send her back to London, and Mrs Wilbraham would send her to Harrogate to her grandmother's house. She could not think of her grandmother without a shudder. She remembered a cold voice, the grip of bony fingers, and a thin switch, vigorously applied. Her grandmother was the only person of whom Isobel had ever really been afraid. Getting rid of Benjamin Twizzle was becoming a matter of urgency.

The only certain way out of the situation, as far as she could see, would be to become engaged. Then any tiny scandal of the past would be covered by a cloak of respectability. There were four men in her immediate orbit who might fit the bill. Lord Thurlby she discounted immediately. In a private conversation before she had left London, she had suggested to Mrs Wilbraham that she could exert herself to attach him. She might have done, too, had it not become perfectly plain to her that he was in love with Lavinia, and she with him if only they would pull themselves together and realize it. Isobel had very few scruples, especially with regard to attracting men, but not spoiling her friend's romance was one of them.

Mr Laver would never do. He had an irritating laugh, and was so self-effacing that she could imagine him agreeing to pay Twizzle twice as much rather than getting rid of him. Hawkfield would not do either. He looked too much like Riseholm for comfort, and Isobel had a suspicion that he would not take any of her overtures seriously. It would have to be Timothy Ames. She had no scruples about breaking *that* engagement. Caroline Tasker was not a friend of hers after all and she was as she, Isobel, had already observed, a dyed-in-the-wool spinster. Her own engagement to the vicar would be announced; Twizzle would retire in discomfort, and Riseholm would be made to think twice about engaging himself to that insipid creature. She was not sure which eventuality would give her the more satisfaction.

★ ★ ★

'Really, Timothy, I am not an invalid,' Caroline protested the following morning. 'There is no need for me to stay in bed. The doctor said so.'

'The doctor said that you must keep the ankle still,' the vicar retorted. 'If you remain in bed, then that is the best way of ensuring that you do not move it. The doctor said that as well.' He had just come from making a formal call, and was dressed all in black, with a high stock and bands. Caroline thought that he looked exceedingly attractive, but did not say so.

'Well when *can* I get up? Did you ask him that?'

The vicar smiled down at her. She was wearing a nightgown which had been lent to her by Lavinia, and had a frilly cap on her head. Her hair, which waved gently, was gathered loosely under the cap, allowing a few tendrils to escape. This more casual arrangement was much more becoming than her usual severe style and Ames thought how desirable she looked. He smiled. 'How very dear to me you are, my darling,' he said, sitting down next to her and tilting her chin with his long fingers so that he could press a kiss upon her lips.

'Timothy!' she exclaimed, intending to reprove him, but sounding half-hearted about the business.

'Now now,' he said in minatory accents, wagging a finger at her. 'You are not to move. The doctor said so.'

The interval that followed was very satisfactory to both parties, and when the vicar got up to leave, not forgetting to say a brief prayer for the speedy recovery of his future wife, Miss Tasker lay in a happy daze until eventually she dropped off to sleep.

Perhaps because his mind was still more than half upon his betrothed, Ames was not as alert to danger as he might have been. When Isobel, catching him at the bottom of the stairs as if by chance (for she had been waiting for him ever since he had gone up them) said that she would be grateful for his advice, and would he please stroll in the garden with her so that they could have some private conversation, he therefore agreed at once.

Isobel was determined to make the most of this opportunity. She had not slept well the previous night, for she had lain awake for some time, thinking about Lord Riseholm and Miss Egan. When Hawkfield had raised the subject of the earl's prospective engagement, she had followed her instincts and fled the scene as quickly as possible. Now, she could have kicked herself for not lingering. Had she not been so anxious to show no undue interest in Riseholm, she could perhaps have discovered more by judicious questioning. She had tried to extract further information from Lavinia, but it appeared that the subject had been dropped soon after her withdrawal.

The more she thought about the matter, however, the more she decided that Mr Hawkfield's friend must be correct in his opinion. Miss Egan was not just pretty; she was very well behaved and virtuous, the kind of debutante who never put a foot wrong; quite unlike herself, in fact. To put it bluntly, Miss Egan was the kind of biddable young woman whom men like Riseholm ended up marrying. By way of contrast, she, Isobel, was the sort of girl with whom such men flirted and misbehaved as much as they could, but whom they never took seriously.

It was essential, therefore, that Riseholm should be brought to realize that someone *did* take her seriously, even if *he* did not. Having written to Riseholm indicating that Ames was almost on the point of proposing, it followed that she would need to make some solid progress that would warrant such boasting. Little Miss Tasker was up in her room after her handsome fiancé's duty visit. Thurlby was in his study, and Lavinia was helping Miss Wheatman to identify her grasses. There would be no one to interrupt.

She had thought long and hard over what private affair she might consult the vicar about. It ought to be some romantic entanglement in which she would feature as an innocent victim, then she could make play with wet eyelashes. After a little heart-searching, she had decided to give a carefully doctored version of her connection with Riseholm. There was always the possibility that Benjamin Twizzle might not keep quiet about his rakeship, so telling the vicar about his lordship's 'unwanted' attentions would at one and the same time arouse the clergyman's chivalry and spike Mr Twizzle's guns. She was aware that she would be taking a bit of a risk, since it was essential that Lord Thurlby should not hear of her connection to Riseholm. If she bound Ames by the seal of the confessional though, he would have to keep quiet. Once she was engaged to him, it would not matter who knew.

'Now, Miss Macclesfield, how may I be of assistance?' Mr Ames asked, as they descended the terrace.

Isobel looked about her intently. 'Not just yet,' she said. 'I fear being overheard. Let us get a little further from the house.' They crossed the grass and walked down to a little bridge over an artificial stream which fed into an ornamental lake. Once across the bridge, they began to walk along a slightly rougher path, which took them through a pretty wood which in spring was carpeted with primroses, celandines and bluebells. 'Oh,' exclaimed Isobel. 'It is a little uneven underfoot along here. Do you mind if I take your arm?'

The vicar politely disclaimed and extended his arm to her. She took it and smiled up at him; suddenly at that moment, he scented danger. 'What a comfort it is to be able to walk along with you like this,' Isobel said. 'With any other gentleman of course it would not be proper, but with a clergyman, I know that all will be well.'

At this, Ames experienced a feeling of relief. It was as a clergyman that she had sought him out. His instinct for danger had been wrong. 'Tell me how I may advise you,' he said kindly.

'Before I do so, I must have your assurance of secrecy — your word as a clergyman.'

Mr Ames hesitated. He had been asked to keep secrets before and on one or two occasions, he had wished that he had not made any such promises. 'I do not know . . . ' he began hesitantly.

'The matter affects no other person,' she insisted. 'If I cannot unburden myself to you, I do not know where else I can turn.' She dabbed her dry eyes with a handkerchief.

'Then of course you must confide in me,' he replied. 'I will pass nothing on, I promise.'

'Well you see, I have just come from London,' Isobel began. 'I am sure you know, Mr Ames, that London is a dangerous place, especially for a young girl like myself. It is difficult to tell the true from the false, and the virtuous from the wicked.' She glanced sideways at him under her lashes. He seemed to be paying close attention. 'It was when I first arrived in town that I met Lord Riseholm,' she went on. 'He was very kind and friendly to me when I was feeling awkward and shy.' Lord Riseholm would have spluttered with laughter at this point. Timothy Ames did not know Miss Macclesfield so well, and although this sounded unlikely, he accepted that such could indeed be the case.

'I was grateful for his kindness,' Isobel continued, 'and for that reason, perhaps, he began to think that I would welcome rather warmer advances. Lavinia's invitation came at just the right time, as it meant that I could escape his attentions. Now, however, he has threatened to pursue me even to Lincolnshire. What should I do?'

By now, they had walked through the little wood, and were strolling along a path which continued on around the edge of the lake. They reached a fork in the way, one side of which would take them deeper into the wood, whereas the other would lead them back along the edge of the lake and eventually back to the lawn again. Determinedly, the vicar led

Isobel along the second of the two paths. 'There is no doubt about your course of action,' Ames replied. 'I take it that your father is not aware of this situation? He must be informed so that he may take steps to make this man keep his distance. Your first duty must be to obey him.'

'Yes of course,' Isobel replied demurely. This time it would have been Isobel's own father who would have been doing the sniggering. 'However, he is abroad and my guardian in London is not a very motherly person. I can expect no help from her.'

'Then in that case, Lord Thurlby would be your natural protector. You must unburden yourself to him and ask for his help.'

'Oh I would, believe me; I have thought about it many times. But I do not find him truly sympathetic.' She looked meltingly up into his eyes. 'What must I do?' she whispered. 'You, of all people, must be able to tell me. I felt a strong pull of sympathy between us from the very first. Did not you?'

Ames looked down at her, horrified. Now, the letters of the word 'danger' flashed before his eyes, huge and flame coloured. 'Why, I . . . I . . . ' he began.

Isobel knew better than to push things at this stage. She would only frighten him off. 'Pray give my situation some thought,' she said. 'I know that your wise counsel will enable me to deal with Lord Riseholm should he dare to come near this place.' Briefly, she squeezed his arm, then slipped her hand away, and strolled elegantly back towards the house, a smile on her lips. Of course he had been startled. Doubtless in this restricted society he would be unaccustomed to the admiration of someone as glamorous as herself; but he would soon come round.

13

Lavinia had gone out into the garden to pick some flowers. She had made a good selection of the summer blooms, but needed some greenery. She was just walking past one of the tall hedges near to the kitchen gardens, when she heard hasty footsteps, and around the side of the hedge came Mr Ames. When he saw her, he gasped with shock, then let out a sigh of relief. 'Thank God! I thought it must be her!' he exclaimed with real fervour, briefly losing control of his grammar.

'Her? Whom can you mean, sir?' Lavinia asked in puzzlement.

He turned brick red. 'I beg your pardon,' he said. 'My . . . my wits have gone wandering, I think. You . . . you must excuse me.'

He would have turned away, but Lavinia touched his arm. 'Forgive me, sir, but you are distressed. Can it be that you have encountered my friend, Miss Macclesfield?'

He did not speak at once, but glanced at Lavinia hesitantly. 'It's all right,' she said reassuringly. 'Isobel is an old friend, but I suffer no delusions about her.'

He closed his eyes briefly. 'I do not know what to say,' he said. 'I hesitate to criticize one who is close to you but I . . . '

Lavinia put her basket down and invited the vicar to join her on a seat in the shade. When he hesitated, she added, 'I promise not to flirt with you.'

He sighed and smiled ruefully. 'That would indeed be a relief,' he said, taking his place next to her. He told Lavinia in general terms about what had transpired, needless to say without disclosing matters that Isobel had asked him to keep confidential. 'What do I do, Miss Muir?' Ames asked eventually. 'I do not want to be unkind, but really, I have to consider Caroline above anyone else. I will not have her distressed.' He glanced at Lavinia then looked away, almost shyly. 'I love her so much, you see.'

'Yes, I know that you do,' Lavinia replied warmly. 'If it is any consolation to you, Isobel's flirtations do not generally last very long.'

'So what would you advise me to do?' he asked earnestly.

'Whatever you do, avoid being alone with her. And perhaps try to talk about something in a very dull, sanctimonious way. She cannot bear to be dull.'

'I could explain the Greek origins of some

of the words in the New Testament at considerable length,' he said after some thought.

'That should do the trick,' she answered with a smile.

* * *

On the following day, which was Sunday, Lavinia visited Miss Tasker before the morning service and found her feeling very disgruntled.

'As if it were not bad enough having to miss church, I am also very unlikely to see Timothy later in the day,' she explained.

'Oh dear,' said Lavinia sympathetically. 'Does he have to go elsewhere?'

'The curate at St Philip's in the next village is unwell, so Timothy has promised to ride over and take the service after he has led worship here,' she said.

'Why can he not come straight back here after the service?'

'Because poor Mr Blenkinsop lives alone,' Caroline answered. 'Timothy told me so with the utmost patience. He would not come home with a clear conscience if he did not make sure that the curate had good fires lit and something hot to eat.'

Lavinia sat in sympathetic silence before

saying, 'I was just wondering if you had any messages for Mr Ames?'

'Bother Mr Blenkinsop,' Caroline said crossly.

'Shall I tell him that?' Lavinia asked playfully.

Caroline grinned reluctantly. 'Give him my best love, if you please, and tell him that I am looking forward to seeing him tomorrow.'

'Would you like to come with me to Caroline's room to entertain her this afternoon?' Lavinia asked Isobel as they walked to church with Lord Thurlby and Miss Wheatman walking behind.

'Good gracious, no,' Isobel responded. 'I have something else I need to do.' A note had arrived from Benjamin Twizzle, asking for another interview. She had no desire to meet him, but she did not want to antagonize him by putting him off.

They arrived at church at the same time as an acquaintance of Miss Tasker who had met Lavinia in Caroline's company. As this lady wanted to enquire about the health of the schoolmistress, Lavinia was delayed for a few moments, so she was the last of the party to enter the church.

Miss Wheatman and Isobel had already entered the earl's pew, and Lord Thurlby was waiting politely for her to go in before him. It happened, therefore, that Lavinia found herself with Lord Thurlby on one side and

Miss Wheatman on the other.

The splitting up of Lavinia and Isobel was a very desirable situation, as far as Miss Wheatman was concerned. The older lady disapproved of any kind of acknowledgement of others in the service, and Isobel was a little inclined to whisper and giggle. The girl would not do so if she, Daisy Wheatman, was her neighbour!

Miss Wheatman was so determined not to be distracted from the service that she only raised her eyes from her prayer book in order to look at Mr Ames. Lord Thurlby, on the other hand, whilst properly attentive, was also aware of his neighbour in the pew, and when the vicar referred to meadow grasses by way of an illustration to his sermon, his lordship looked down at Lavinia and smiled. I like the way his eyes crinkle up, she thought to herself as she smiled back.

They were about to stand for the final hymn when Lavinia accidentally caught the corner of her book with her hand and knocked it onto the floor. She bent to pick it up, but Thurlby was too quick for her. As he gave it to her and their hands touched, that familiar dart of feeling shot through her and she almost dropped it again. Their eyes met, and this time, his expression told her that he had had exactly the same experience.

The earl's rank meant that their party was the first to leave the church and shake hands with Timothy Ames. Isobel lingered for a moment to tell him how very moving she had found the service. If she had listened to a single word, it would have been for the very first time, Lavinia reflected. She smiled as she overheard the clergyman telling Isobel about some of the Greek words that he had been obliged to look up in order to write his sermon.

Whilst Miss Wheatman exchanged remarks with a friend who was just coming out of church, Lord Thurlby said to Lavinia, 'Forgive me, I did not mean to eavesdrop, but I overheard you asking Miss Macclesfield if she would like to help you entertain Miss Tasker this afternoon.'

Lavinia smiled. 'Poor Caroline! She will be so glad to be up and about again. Mr Ames's daily visits help to make her situation tolerable. She will miss him today.'

'If I may make a suggestion, perhaps we might entertain her together, if you have no objection,' said the earl. 'I could have a look in the nursery and see if I could find some of our old games.'

'I think that she would really like that,' Lavinia replied.

'But would you?' he asked in a lower tone.

At that point, Miss Wheatman approached them, so Lavinia was not able to ask him to repeat his remark. She was convinced that she must have misheard.

After dinner was over — that meal being eaten in the middle of the day on a Sunday — Lavinia went up to Caroline's room, where Thurlby joined them after hunting in the schoolroom as he had promised, but with limited success.

'I've found some packs of cards,' he said, 'and a set of spillikins. I'm sure there were some other things, but I don't know where they've got to.'

Miss Tasker was now allowed to lie on a day bed, so they set up a table next to her elbow and she took up one of the packs of cards. 'These appear to be marked,' she said after shuffling them.

'Oh dear,' murmured the earl, flushing a little. 'My sins have found me out.'

'You played with *marked cards?*' Lavinia exclaimed in shocked tones.

'I wanted to win,' he said defiantly. There was a short silence during which both ladies looked at him reproachfully.

'Lord Thurlby, how old were you?' Caroline asked.

'Seven,' he answered. 'Don't look at me like that! My brother was seventeen! I *never* won.'

'That is no excuse,' said Lavinia severely. 'I trust you paid a severe penalty.'

'My father was very shocked, and quite ready to tan my backside for it,' he admitted. 'Luckily for me, my brother took the responsibility. He told my father that he was showing me what some unscrupulous people might do so that I would be wary.'

'What an excellent brother,' remarked Caroline.

'He was the best,' the earl agreed.

After they had played a game or two of cards, they turned to the spillikins for further amusement. Although Lord Thurlby's hands were large, he proved to be surprisingly deft, and far more successful than Caroline, who, in her efforts to remove one of the pile of thin wooden sticks without dislodging any of the rest, managed to destroy the whole structure when she leaned over too far, knocked the table over and nearly fell off her day bed, to the great amusement of all concerned.

Lavinia, whose life in London had always been rather subdued, even before Mrs Stancross's illness, found herself laughing more than she remembered doing for a very long time. Lord Thurlby's laughter, too, rang out over and over again, making him look a good deal younger and exceedingly handsome, or so it seemed to Lavinia. When they had had enough and the tea tray had been called for, Caroline declared herself to be amazed at how much time had passed. 'I had quite thought that today would seem endless, but thanks to you both, the afternoon has flown by. What a happy time we have had.' Both Lavinia and Lord Thurlby agreed wholeheartedly with this opinion.

Just two days later, the doctor pronounced that Miss Tasker could go home, if she promised to be very careful. 'Make sure that you rest the ankle for some time each day for a week. Every afternoon with your foot up would do you no harm,' he said.

'Oh yes, and how would the children learn anything if I did that?' Caroline asked. The doctor had come to see her at Thurlby Hall. She was up and dressed, but sitting on a day bed in one of the downstairs parlours, whence Lord Thurlby had carried her that morning.

'That's perfectly simple,' put in Thurlby. 'They will have an extra holiday, that's all. The school can be closed until you are better.' His lordship, together with Mr Ames and Lavinia, had gathered together to hear the doctor's pronouncement after he had finished his examination. Isobel was upstairs writing a letter.

'But that will never do,' Caroline insisted.

'The children will get out of the way of learning. They need to keep the good habits that they have acquired.'

'I could help you,' said Lavinia after a moment's thought. 'You know that I have been into the school now on a number of occasions to sew with the children, and they know me quite well.'

'Forgive my saying so, but you are not the teacher,' said Caroline diffidently. 'It hardly seems fair.'

'You would be there to refer to, my dear,' the vicar pointed out. 'And, of course, I could pop in as well from time to time.'

'You could even borrow this day bed,' suggested the earl. 'It could be set up at the front of the school. You would still be in charge, but Lavinia could do the tasks that required moving about. Would you have any objection to that, Doctor?'

'None at all,' the doctor replied. 'As long as the patient keeps off her feet as much as possible, then that is all that concerns me.'

'I shall look like the Queen of Sheba,' Caroline grumbled; but as it seemed that she was to be allowed to teach after all, she made no further objection.

14

Although it was midday, the corridors of Riseholm House were still hushed. The earl's staff knew better than to disturb him, particularly when he had been from home until the early hours. His valet, Stimpson, had not put his noble master to bed very much before five that morning, and had had strict instructions not to rouse him until noon. He knew better than anyone that when his lordship stipulated noon, he did not mean one minute before. He had been the earl's valet for twenty years, ever since Riseholm had first gone on the town aged just nineteen. Stimpson himself was only two or three years older.

The earl's habits had never varied greatly. He rose late, frequently dined out, waited upon whichever obliging female currently enjoyed his favours and attended various entertainments until the early hours, and expected his valet to wait up for him. In return, however, Stimpson was permitted to keep roughly the same hours. As long as he was available when his master needed him, then that was all that mattered to his lordship.

Today, for example, he had risen just one hour before, at eleven o'clock.

He was grateful for the earl's consideration. He had a colleague whose master kept the same hours as Riseholm, but who slept erratically and often needed his valet to dress him for an early morning ride, when he might only have retired to bed three or four hours earlier. His manservant, therefore, was obliged to catnap when he might. Stimpson, on the other hand, seldom missed a good night's sleep.

As instructed, he entered the earl's chamber with his master's chocolate, set the tray down, drew the curtains and turned towards the bed. 'A fine morning, my lord; or rather day, as I should say.'

The earl sat up and stretched. 'Is it? You know, Stimpson, sometimes I wonder whether it is a mistake to miss the mornings.' Not many people saw his lordship as did Stimpson. He was considerably more dishevelled than the world was accustomed to see him, clad in a nightshirt with the neck open to reveal a few curls of chest hair, his chin shadowed with a night's growth of beard, his hair tousled from sleep. Even those ladies who enjoyed his favours only benefited from an hour or two of his company before he retired to his own quarters.

'That rather depends on the mornings, my lord,' his valet replied, adjusting the pillows at his lordship's back so that he could sit more comfortably. 'The letters have arrived. Would you like to look at them now, or would you prefer to dress first?'

'Is there anything of interest?'

'That is not for me to say, my lord.'

'Don't talk rot, Stimpson. Who's written to me?'

After twenty years in the earl's service, the valet knew the handwriting of his lordship's correspondents as well as did the earl himself. 'There is something from Riseholm Halt, my lord. There are some invitations, a trades-man's bill, and I believe that . . . '

'Well?'

'I think that there is one from Miss Macclesfield.'

'Is there, by God? Hand it over then, and come back in half an hour.'

'Very good, my lord.'

Riseholm's eyes gleamed as he opened the letter. The little Macclesfield intrigued him. She had indulged him with an agreeable flirtation, and in general, with young women of good family, that would have been enough for him, for them, and certainly more than enough for their chaperons!

There were always a few young ladies of a

faster persuasion who were inclined to pursue him, and these he avoided for the most part. He much preferred to do his own chasing. In Miss Macclesfield, however, he had sensed a charmingly subtle blend of boldness and innocence. This, coupled with her undoubted beauty, had been enough to tempt him to allow her to think that she had succeeded in her pursuit.

Their little game had come to a head at Vauxhall, where he had turned the tables on her, and obliged her to understand that she was in fact the quarry. Much to his surprise, however, when they had kissed, he had felt his senses reel in a way that they had not done since his first love. It had unsettled him to feel that a woman should have power over him in that way. He was always the one who dictated the pace; with Isobel, he had felt perilously close to being swept off his feet. He had backed off, and soon afterwards, she had gone to the country.

To his surprise, he had viewed her departure with some regret. He could never find it in him to feel very much sympathy for those who managed to embroil themselves in scandal and then grumbled about the consequences. He had been shocking the ton for a number of years now. He knew that respectable people avoided him and that consequently there were places where he was not welcome. He had decided long ago how he wanted to live his life, was prepared to pay the price, and felt that anyone else who deliberately flouted society's rules should be ready to do the same. Surprising, then, that when he thought of Isobel, he should feel a twinge of guilt. This feeling had been increased if anything by an encounter that he had had shortly after Isobel's departure with a man whom he knew slightly, but whose wife was a close friend of Isobel's chaperon.

Maurice Craig had been taking a short break after an energetic fencing bout when Riseholm had wandered in through the doors of the fencing school in Piccadilly, looking for someone with whom to exchange a parry or two. The two men were evenly matched, so when Riseholm had been helped out of his coat, waistcoat and boots, he had not been displeased to discover that Craig was ready to resume his exercise.

After a bout during which Riseholm had emerged the winner by a narrow margin, having achieved two hits to Craig's one, the two men had paused for a while, watching the others.

'You've lost none of your skill,' Craig had remarked.

'Nor you,' Riseholm had answered. 'Are you staying in London for the summer?'

'You'd better ask my wife,' had been the rueful response. 'I'll tell you, Riseholm, you're a lucky man. Cling to your bachelor state — that's my advice.'

Riseholm grinning, had not corrected him, judging that the other man had not recalled that he was a widower. 'I intend to,' he had said.

'Hope you don't mind my saying so, but I quite thought the little Macclesfield might have snared you. Still, danger over now, eh?'

'As you say,' Riseholm had answered, his tone even.

'Time for a fresh pursuit? Apparently, Wilbraham has washed her hands of the chit, and sent her out of town to rusticate. If she doesn't snag a husband, she'll be packed off to her grandmother in Harrogate.'

Riseholm had not responded to this comment, and had merely suggested another bout. This time, however, Craig had emerged the winner.

Now, as then, Riseholm thought about what he knew of Isobel Macclesfield's grandmother. Known as the Wimbledon Witch before her retirement from London, she was universally loathed, and no one had been sorry to see her go. Unsurprising if Isobel would do anything rather than be banished to live with that loathsome female.

When she had, rather naively, informed him of the route of her journey into Lincolnshire, where she was to stay with her friend's godmother, instead of dismissing this information from his mind, he had arranged for flowers to be delivered to her *en route*. Part of his motive had been to pander to her vanity. Ruefully he was bound to acknowledge that he also wanted to impress himself upon her memory.

Not long after her departure, she had begun to write to him, and her correspondence had intrigued him. Unlike other ladies, she did not write on sickly scented paper. She wrote fluently and amusingly, too, her letters pleasingly free of cloying sentiment, and he often found himself laughing out loud at what she had to say. Rather to his own surprise — for he was not usually much of a letter-writer — he had begun to reply to her missives, carefully not committing himself in intention or sentiment, and sending them to a Mrs Hedges, care of the inn in the village, as she had requested.

He would have a very entertaining story to tell her in his next letter. It involved the machinations of a certain little Miss Egan who had clearly thought that she was destined to be the next Lady Riseholm, and had tried to manipulate him into offering for her. He had had to be quite cunning there. Not even his boon companions had known what he was about. Still, now the danger was past, and he could tell Isobel about it and imagine her laughing at his lucky escape.

He had read little more than the opening greeting when the whole letter began to unfold in ways that he had not expected.

And so, it appears that your days of singleness are numbered, as I have been reliably informed that you and the exquisite Miss Egan are engaged to be married. I'm sure that congratulations must be due to someone. Just now, I am hedging my bets as to whom!

When is the wedding to be? I am sure you will make a charming groom as you take on the shackles of married life. Oh, did I say shackles? I meant delights, of course. It may not be too long before I follow you to the altar, my friend. I believe that I may have mentioned before that there is a most charming vicar here, of noble blood, related to Lord and Lady Smilie. His attentions have become more marked by the day, and I am in hourly expectation of a declaration from him. He is so handsome, that I really do not think that I shall be able to say no. You will have observed that I like extremes in my suitors, and if I can't have one, then I might as well embrace t'other . . .

He began by laughing at her error, but once he had grasped what she intended to do by way of retaliation, he soon lost all desire to laugh. What was the foolish girl about with this vicar? What was more, how had she come by such a misunderstanding over Miss Egan in the first place?

Where exactly was Isobel now? He had kept all her letters. They were in his desk downstairs. Once dressed and ready for the day, he would go down and remind himself of where she was staying. Then perhaps he might go and see what she was up to. If nothing else, it certainly behoved him to rescue this poor vicar. A worse parson's wife he could not imagine!

When eventually Lord Riseholm opened his desk, his appearance had undergone a transformation. He was now dressed in dove grey pantaloons with a white waistcoat and a black coat with silver buttons, and his hair, neatly brushed, hung loose over his shoulders.

He took out Isobel's letters, wandered over to the window, and sat down so that he could examine them properly. Ah yes, he remembered now. She was staying with Thurlby.

This parson fellow must be Thurlby's chaplain, he supposed. No doubt he had become dazzled by the chit's remarkable beauty, but propose? Never! And even if he had, Isobel would no more wed a parson than she would take the veil. She had obviously decided that what was sauce for the gander was sauce for the goose.

He got up and walked back to his desk, where he sat down, took out a fresh sheet of paper, and mended his pen.

My dear, foolish, Innocentia
How very naïve of you to believe every rumour you hear. But then, your naïveté has always been one of your charms.

He stared at the sentences that he had written, gently tapping his lips with the feather of the quill before screwing up the paper and throwing it into the fireplace. No, that would never do. It would be much more delicious to tantalize her with the notion that he really was engaged. Smiling, he took up his pen again.

My dear, perceptive Innocentia
How very kind of you to offer your con-gratulations. Miss Egan, you will be pleased to hear, is in great beauty. (That, at least

238

was true; he had caught sight of her at a ball before her wary chaperon had hustled her away.) *Would you like me to bring her so that we can dance at your wedding? Tell me, I have always wondered who officiates at a parson's wedding? Will the bishop honour you, or does your parson have to ask the questions, then leap the altar rail in order to make the responses?*

He leaned back in his chair and chuckled to himself. That was much better! He would tell her the truth eventually, of course. For now, let her think that she had hit the nail on the head. He would let her stew for a little while, but he would not leave it very long before following his letter into Lincolnshire. He would like to see for himself what she was getting up to. Did she really mean to marry this parson? It would be worth discovering whether the fellow was actually worthy of her.

Now that was a novel thought. Where had it come from? He pondered for a moment or two, then gave himself a mental shake, took up his pen once more and got on with his letter.

His correspondence completed, franked, and taken for delivery by a footman, he decided to walk to his club and, by the strangest fortune, he found himself reaching out for a newspaper at the same time as Lord Smilie. He barely knew the man, but on impulse mentioned his nephew who had a hunting box in Lincolnshire. 'I understand you also have a nephew who lives in that county,' he said.

'Indeed I do,' Smilie answered, a little puzzled at being addressed by a man who would not normally pay him any attention at all. 'He is a clergyman.'

'Really?' replied Riseholm. 'Is he your only nephew?'

'And my only heir,' Smilie agreed. 'However, he's now engaged.'

'My congratulations.'

'Mind you, I think he could have done better, but there's no reasoning with a man in love.'

'The devil he could,' said Riseholm, before walking away, leaving the other man completely nonplussed.

The vicar might be in love, but Isobel certainly wasn't, Riseholm decided, as he walked home. Damn the wench! She was creating havoc with his social life, and with his mental state. There was nothing for it but for him to go to Lincolnshire to put a halt to whatever folly she had stirred up. Then perhaps he might have some peace.

15

Although Caroline had grumbled at having to preside over her class sitting down, there was no doubt that it had helped her foot to heal, and within a few days, she was walking quite well, provided that she did not overdo things.

For her part, Lavinia found that she was very much enjoying the chance to teach in the school. The children were generally polite and responsive, and she discovered in herself a gift for teaching reading, as well as an enjoyment in the task, which encouraged and surprised her.

Mr Ames had his own church duties to perform, but he had always made a point of coming into the school once a week to help the children learn their catechism. Now, he came more frequently and took the children for scripture classes as well. Lavinia was fascinated by the way that he often told the Bible stories in his own words rather than always reading them, and made them lively and interesting for the children. She was also impressed by the way that neither the vicar nor the schoolmistress was betrayed into any unbecoming familiarity in front of the children. They might be in love and engaged to be married, but they kept all demonstrations of affection for their private moments together.

On one occasion, Isobel, who had wandered into the village in search of pink ribbon at the shop, had come into the school at the end of the session. She was there ostensibly in order to walk home with Lavinia, but in fact to show the vicar what he had been missing. She had been keeping away from him for the past few days, much to his secret relief.

'Thank you very much, Mr Ames,' Caroline had said, very correctly, for a child was still putting the slates away. 'Your help has, as always, been invaluable.'

'I am glad to have been of service, Miss Tasker,' the vicar had replied. He bowed, and picked up his hat. 'I shall see you in church on Sunday, no doubt.'

'Not a wildly passionate romance,' Isobel had remarked to Lavinia, as they had walked back to the Hall. 'On the other hand, did you see how he couldn't keep his eyes off me?'

'I did see him looking at you,' Lavinia had replied, remembering that she had noted a distinctly hunted expression on the vicar's face. 'But Isobel — '

'Really, if one thinks about it, I should be

doing her a service to take him away,' Isobel had continued, interrupting without even noticing that the other girl had something else to say. 'He would be bound to turn to someone else in the end.'

Lavinia said nothing in response. Part of her felt guilty about not informing her friend about the true nature of the vicar's relationship with his fiancée. Every time she thought she might say something, however, she remembered that Isobel might well see this as a challenge. She no longer feared that Isobel's beauty might prevail; rather, her concern was that the other girl might make a fool of herself, and she did not want this to happen to her friend, however vain she might be.

★   ★   ★

'This is very good news,' said Lord Thurlby, as he opened a letter at the breakfast table. 'You will recall that I escorted my mother to pay a dying friend a final visit. Contrary to every expectation, Mrs Jacklyn is making a good recovery, and consequently, my mother has asked me to fetch her home.'

'That is good news indeed, my lord,' said Miss Wheatman, beaming. 'When will you leave?'

'As soon as I have finished my breakfast,' he replied.

'It will be good to see Aunt Phyllis again, especially under such happy circumstances,' said Lavinia warmly.

Isobel agreed, but inside she was feeling far less sanguine. Instinct told her that it would be much harder to keep her correspondence with Lord Riseholm a secret once Lady Thurlby was in residence again.

After breakfast was over, they all got up from the table, and left the room to go about the business of the day. Lavinia made as if to go upstairs with Isobel, but to her surprise, Lord Thurlby asked for the favour of a few words with her in his study.

The last time that she had been in this room alone with him, he had reprimanded her and she had responded by slapping his face. As she crossed the threshold, therefore, she found herself examining her conscience to try to think what she might have done that would merit his anger.

'Don't look so anxious,' he reassured her. 'You must think me a dreadful fellow. You look as though you expected a reproof.'

'Yes,' she said. 'I mean, no.' She took a deep breath. 'I do beg your pardon. I did not expect anything of the kind. It is just that last time I was in here . . . ' Her voice faded away.

'Indeed,' he said into the silence left by her uncompleted sentence. 'Shall we agree to draw a line under an episode which does not really reflect creditably on either of us?'

She laughed. 'I think that it would be as well,' she answered.

He was silent for a time. 'I cannot let this opportunity pass without telling you how regretful I am for misjudging you so seriously,' he said eventually. 'I remembered the child that you were — '

'The *foolish* child that I was,' she interrupted.

'Just so,' he agreed with a faint smile. 'I remembered the child, and when I detected you doing something I thought unwise, I treated you like a child, and forgot that you are a woman.'

Something in his voice brought forcefully to her mind the fact that if she was now a woman, he was very much a man. 'I was foolish,' she agreed, flushing. 'But I shall not behave in such a way again.' She was thinking of the journey that she had made without applying to him for help.

'I know that you will not,' he answered, looking steadily at her. Somehow, she was aware that he was speaking of Lord Riseholm.

He walked towards her and took her hand, looking down at it, then straight into her eyes.

'When we were at Folkingham, on top of the tower . . . ' He paused. 'Lavinia, you know what almost happened between us at that moment, don't you?'

'Yes . . . yes, I do,' she agreed. She wanted to look away for very embarrassment, but was unable to tear her gaze from his.

'I must not take advantage of you whilst my mother is not here,' he said. 'I may spend a few days with the Jacklyns for courtesy's sake, now that the emergency is over; but after I have brought her home and spoken to her as your guardian at this time, it is my most ardent desire to bring that moment to its proper conclusion.'

'I . . . I . . . ' she said, in a tone almost too low for him to hear.

'I do not ask you to say anything,' he assured her. 'The fact that your hand still rests in mine allows me to hope. May I speak to her?'

'Yes . . . yes, you may,' she said in the same low tone. For answer, he raised her hand to his lips.

* * *

A few days after Lord Thurlby had gone to fetch his mother home, the vicar came into the school after lessons had finished, just as the last child had left. 'Would you like to come back to the vicarage for a cup of tea?' he asked.

'I thought that you were due to visit Mr Heggarty,' said Caroline.

'So did I,' the vicar answered. 'However, apparently he forgot all about it and has gone into town for another appointment. So I am free to entertain you. I thought we might celebrate the banishment of the day bed.'

'With pleasure,' replied Caroline devoutly. 'It is not that I was ungrateful to Lord Thurlby, but I do hate looking like an invalid.' To her great relief the doctor had decided that very morning that she need not use the day bed any more, provided that she remembered to sit down from time to time during the day.

The rest of the tidying up was done, and in no time they were making the short journey to the vicarage. 'How are the wedding plans going?' Lavinia asked, as they were walking.

'Is this where I stroll half-a-dozen steps ahead and sing very loudly?' Timothy asked.

Caroline laughed. 'I shall not give any details away,' she said. 'There is not a great deal to plan. Timothy and I both want a very simple wedding, but . . . ' She paused.

'But?' prompted the vicar and Lavinia in chorus.

'Timothy, I hope you will not mind that I have not consulted you first, but I would very much like Lavinia to be my attendant. I know we said that we would not have any, and I agreed because there was no one that I wanted to ask, but . . . '

Lavinia very much wanted to express her delight straight away, for no one had ever made such a request of her before. She did not want to do so unless the vicar also agreed, however, so she held her peace and, it must be admitted, her breath. She need not have worried.

'What a splendid idea,' he said, beaming. 'She has been a good friend to you, my dear. It would be a lovely way to acknowledge that friendship.'

'Then we have even more to celebrate than the passing of the day bed,' smiled Caroline, as they walked up the garden path to the vicarage.

The weather was so fine that they decided to have tea in the garden. There was an ideal spot just next to the hedge, where a small tree provided a little much needed dappled shade, for the day was quite warm.

Once the tea had been served, there was no need for concealment, and the vicar and his lady sat quite close together, so that if neither was eating or drinking, they could hold hands.

'I have very much enjoyed working in the school,' Lavinia confessed. 'I shall really miss it.'

'But you will be welcome to come and help at any time,' Caroline assured her.

'You are very good, but I must give some time to Isobel,' Lavinia replied. 'I have rather neglected her recently.' There was a brief silence, during which all of them thought of things that they might have said about the absent Miss Macclesfield. Since they were very well-brought-up people, they did not give voice to these thoughts, however, and began to speak of other matters.

★ ★ ★

It had recently occurred to Isobel that she might easily take the opportunity of going to the vicarage whilst Lavinia and Miss Tasker were at the school, and thus catch the vicar on his own. After having made her first approach, she had deliberately whetted his appetite by keeping tantalizingly out of his way. Now was the time to remind him of what he had been missing and, if she knew anything about men — which she flattered herself that she did — she would now find him eager to see her again. When she had encountered him in the school, his eyes had followed her everywhere. Today would be the day. She had indicated to Riseholm that she was to be engaged to the vicar. It was time to make good her boast.

When she had made her calculations, she had not realized that each week on a Wednesday, the school finished early, and that the vicar might therefore be entertaining his fiancée and her friend. She approached the vicarage from the garden, thinking that on such a lovely day, Ames might be reading outside. That would be a delightful setting in which to surprise him. She imagined herself approaching silently across the grass, her parasol in her hand. It was a charming creation in a rich gold colour, trimmed with gold ribbons, and its colour matched the trimming of her bonnet and brought out the gold of the flowers on her gown. As she drew nearer, he would look up from his book, frowning at first at the distraction, but then smiling at the charming picture before him. He would lay his book aside and rise. She would hold out her hand . . . She came back to the present all at once. No, he certainly would not laugh; and yet, it was the unmistakable sound of laughter that she had just heard.

'It is no use, Timothy, you will not manage to surprise me into disclosing a single detail of my wedding gown, so you might as well abandon the attempt,' Miss Tasker was saying.

'Admit that there is nothing to disclose, my darling, for I am willing to wager that you have not ordered it yet,' was his reply.

'No, I have not,' Caroline answered, 'and I am glad of it, for I would very much like to consult Lavinia on the subject.'

'I should be delighted,' said Lavinia.

'I am sure that she will advise you well, for she has excellent taste,' said Ames. 'But you know, my love, that I am quite indifferent as to what you wear. All that matters to me is that you will be mine in the sight of God.'

'That is what I want as well,' responded Caroline softly.

Through the gap in the hedge, Isobel witnessed the vicar raising Caroline Tasker's hand to his lips. The look of adoration in his eyes was quite unmistakable. She stepped away from the hedge and hurried away, before any of them could so much as detect her presence.

16

There could have been no one more delighted than Lady Thurlby when her son disclosed to her the nature of his hopes. She had had a very testing time at her friend's house. During the visit, her emotions had veered wildly between distress at Mrs Jacklyn's illness — from which she had really not been expected to recover — to thankfulness as the lady's condition had most unexpectedly improved, to irritation, as she had remembered what a tiresome man her friend's son had always been. Consequently, Thurlby's arrival to fetch her home had come as a very welcome relief.

Clarice Jacklyn had still been confined to her room, but was looking so much better that the countess had ventured to suggest that she might like to pay a visit in the not too distant future. 'As long as she comes without tedious Thomas,' Lady Thurlby told her son as they began their journey straight after an early breakfast. 'As soon as his mother was on the mend, he began telling interminable stories of people that I had never met, and interspersing them all with phrases like 'as one does' and 'strangely enough' until I thought I would scream.'

Her son agreed. He had been obliged to endure more than one tiresome half-hour with Jacklyn whilst his mother had sat with her friend upstairs. The other man had pronounced upon farming methods in a very self-important manner. His opinions had been so misguided and his ponderous advice as to what Thurlby should do with his acres so ill-judged that it had taken every ounce of the earl's self-control not to speak in a most unbecoming way to one who had been his mother's host.

'I hope you will not feel obliged to invite him to the wedding,' he said.

'The wedding?' said his mother, wrinkling her brow. 'But that will be up to Miss Tasker and Mr Ames, surely.'

'Not that wedding; mine,' he said.

His mother's surprise and excitement were all that he could have hoped for. 'Yours! Victor! My dear! But who?' A look of horror crept across her face. 'Not Isobel Macclesfield?' she ventured. He shook his head. Her expression turned to one of delight. 'It's Lavinia!'

'You've guessed it,' he answered with a smile. 'You're pleased, then.'

'My dear boy, I couldn't be happier,' the countess answered, leaning forward to grasp his hand. 'I always thought that you were very well suited, but . . . ' She paused.

'But?'

'Forgive me, but when I left for Clarice's house, it seemed to me that things were decidedly chilly between you.'

'Yes, they were,' he replied. It was his turn to pause. 'I did not tell you before, as I did not want to add to your anxieties, but she and Isobel Macclesfield travelled up from London on the stage,' he said at last. 'Stancross and his wife left London without providing Lavinia with the means to travel here. The two girls put their resources together and bought tickets. They gave themselves false names for discretion's sake.'

'How resourceful,' commented his mother.

He grinned reluctantly. 'Yes, it was, wasn't it? Unfortunately, I assumed that they had done it for a prank, and raked them down — Lavinia in particular — without giving them a chance to explain.'

'That was not very fair — and not like you, if you will forgive my saying so,' said the countess. 'How did Lavinia react to that?'

'She smacked my face,' he admitted. 'But in all fairness, I must tell you that that was not all. I discovered that while in London, Lavinia had somehow got herself involved with Riseholm.'

'Riseholm!' The countess's shocked tone told him that she was as familiar with the earl's reputation as was he.

'I blame her aunt and uncle,' said Thurlby, flushing. 'I know that Mrs Stancross was unwell, but they should have made better provision for Lavinia. No doubt they thrust her upon any willing woman who was prepared to chaperon her. How could she then be anything but easy prey to someone like Riseholm?'

'She has told you this?' His mother asked, frowning.

He shook his head. 'Not in so many words; but she has assured me that all is at an end between her and Riseholm, and I believe her.'

'I am sure that you are right to do so,' she replied. 'Indeed, I wonder . . . ' Her voice tailed off. 'But enough of that for now. Tell me — for a woman likes to know these things — where did you propose, and what did she say?'

He looked a little sheepish. 'I have not proposed as yet,' he said.

'Not yet? Then forgive me, but how — ?'

'How do I know that there will be a wedding? I told her of my hopes before I came to fetch you, but said that I would not ask her for an answer until you had returned.'

She eyed him, a little mystified. 'Victor, are

you in love with the girl, or not?'

'Yes, I am,' he acknowledged.

'Then surely you could have been a little bolder.'

'As bold as Riseholm?' he suggested, an eyebrow raised. 'No, Mama, I am no rake. I will treat the woman, whom I hope is to be my countess, with respect, right from the beginning.'

★ ★ ★

Isobel hurried away from the vicarage, and back towards Thurlby Hall, without even dropping in on the Horseshoe as she had intended. At first, all she could think of was how thoroughly she had been deceived. 'How dared they?' she muttered to herself. 'How dared they?' They had all conspired against her, and Lavinia was the worst of all. She knew all about this romance and she had said nothing. No doubt her so-called friend had been sniggering behind her hand when she had been talking about attracting Mr Ames. She had probably told the whole story to the vicar and Miss Tasker so that they could all have a good laugh at her expense.

She, Isobel, was always the one who was talking secrets. It was a strange sensation for her to feel left out. Worse still, the look of love that she had wanted directed towards herself was being turned upon the plain schoolmistress whilst she, the belle of every ball, had become a wallflower.

Why had Lavinia not warned her? Surely she owed her some loyalty, especially after she had provided the wherewithal for them both to travel to Stamford! No doubt Lavinia had been too wrapped up in falling in love herself to think about her friend's needs. She was not even aware that her friend was being blackmailed by Mr Twizzle — Twizzle who this very afternoon was coming for more.

Her plan for getting a respectable fiancé was in ruins. What could she do now? Ames was beyond her reach, whilst Lavinia had snapped up Thurlby. Hawkfield and Laver had both gone to London. They had called upon her a few days ago to make their farewells, and Hawkfield had asked her, with a look full of mischief, if she had any messages for anybody.

She had not made the mistake of sending a message direct to Riseholm; but she had told him with a flirtatious toss of her head that those with whom she was acquainted would no doubt be invited to dance at her wedding, which might be sooner than any of them expected. Now there would be no wedding, and she would be made to look a fool in front of everyone.

Once back at Thurlby Hall, she went to sit in the garden. She thought about the earl, remembering how angry he had been when he had seen them getting down from the stage. Why, even Benjamin Twizzle had slunk away from him! She sat up straight, a thoughtful expression on her face. If Thurlby could somehow be persuaded to help her, then Twizzle would not dare menace her any more.

Lavinia ought to be the one to persuade him; but she did not want to ask Lavinia for anything. Lavinia had conspired against her with the vicar and his fiancée. Her friendship could not be trusted. The idea of begging for her kindness made Isobel's mouth set in a mutinous line. This would need careful thought. Perhaps she could dare to address Lord Thurlby herself? She could give him the same story that she had told Timothy Ames. His very disapproval of Lord Riseholm might work in her favour.

★ ★ ★

Lavinia left the vicarage a short time after Isobel had hurried off. She had a good deal to think about, much of it very agreeable indeed. She had no sisters or cousins, and had never supposed that she would ever be asked to be someone's bridesmaid. That was something to look forward to. Then there was the prospect of the return of Lord Thurlby. She had been offered nuncheon at the vicarage but she had refused, not wanting to miss Lord Thurlby's arrival.

His meaning could hardly have been plainer when he had spoken to her before his departure. He meant to propose, and she had no doubt as to what her answer would be. She had always liked and admired him; hero-worshipped him, even. Over the days since their arrival, after an unfortunate start, she had found herself thinking about him more and more. They had enjoyed outings, conversations and jokes, and she had seen how much he was liked and admired by those who depended upon him. Yes, his temper could be quick, but he was man enough to acknowledge his mistake. The strange bolt of feeling that shot through her every time they touched hands could not be ignored. Nor could that moment when they had almost kissed, and she had felt vaguely disappointed for the rest of the day because he had not done so. At last, she had had to acknowledge that she had fallen in love with him.

Upon his return, she would tell him about

259

who had been the real recipient of Riseholm's advances. By that time, she hoped, they would be engaged, and he would be too happy to send Isobel away in disgrace.

She popped into the Horseshoe with a note to the landlady from Miss Tasker. Having handed it over, she was about to leave, when the landlord called out to her, asking whether she would be seeing Mrs Hedges.

Lavinia turned, completely taken by surprise by this reference to a pseudonym that he should not have known. 'I beg your pardon?' she said.

The landlord repeated his question. 'Only there is a letter for her here, miss. This is a busy place and I like to get these off my hands as soon as possible, so as not to lose them.'

'Yes, I shall be seeing her,' Lavinia answered, taking the letter and looking down at the sloping handwriting that she had seen before, generally on notes attached to bouquets of flowers. 'Does Mrs Hedges send and receive many letters?'

'Quite a few,' the landlord answered.

Thanking the man, Lavinia left the inn and set off back to Thurlby Hall. 'Isobel!' she declared out loud in an exasperated tone. 'I'll wring her neck!'

As Lord Thurlby's carriage entered the village at about midday, the earl knocked on the roof with his cane. 'The landlord of the Horseshoe promised to set aside a barrel of beer for me, but I think he may have forgotten. I'll just go and remind him.'

Lady Thurlby smiled as he got down from the carriage. She could not remember ever having seen him look happier.

'John,' the earl called. 'Hey there, John!'

'Coming, my lord,' the landlord replied, entering the tap room and bowing.

'Have you forgotten that beer of mine?' Thurlby asked.

'I'll admit it slipped my mind,' the man acknowledged. 'But I did remember earlier. In fact, I meant to send a message back to the Hall with the young lady.'

'Which young lady?'

'Why, the fair-haired young lady that collected the letter for Mrs Hedges,' the landlord answered.

Just as surprised as Lavinia had been earlier, Thurlby responded with exactly the same words. 'I beg your pardon?'

'The letter for Mrs Hedges, my lord,' the landlord repeated. 'She's a powerful diligent correspondent is Mrs Hedges. The lady that made the arrangements did say that the letters weren't to go to the Hall.' He looked self-conscious. 'I hope I haven't been indiscreet, my lord.'

'You have done quite right,' said the earl in neutral tones. He put his hand in the pocket of his breeches and drew out some coins. 'With whom does Mrs Hedges correspond?'

The landlord's loyalty to the inhabitants of Thurlby Hall had developed over a lifetime, and he might well have told the earl what he wanted to know without any pecuniary incentive; but the money was nonetheless welcome.

'The letters are for a gentleman named Lord Riseholm, and the replies are always franked by him,' the landlord answered.

'I see,' said the earl, this time stony-faced.

'May I serve you in any other way, my lord?' the man asked, a little concerned.

'I don't think so. Good day to you.'

'Victor, what upon earth has happened?' his mother asked when he got into the carriage.

'Nothing that cannot be mended, thank God,' he replied.

'But what — '

'Not now, Mama,' he said, in the voice of one reining in his temper with difficulty. 'For pity's sake, not now.'

★ ★ ★

As Lavinia walked up the drive, she caught sight of Isobel sitting in the garden, so she walked straight over to her. 'Isobel, what is the meaning of this?' she asked, holding the letter out in her hand.

'It looks like my letter,' Isobel replied, standing. 'May I have it, if you please?'

'But it cannot be,' answered Lavinia. 'This is addressed to Mrs Hedges, and we both know that there is no such person, don't we?'

'What was I supposed to do?' Isobel asked, turning away impatiently. 'I knew that I could not send letters and receive them here under my own name.'

'Yes you could,' Lavinia retorted. 'Just not those letters. They're from Riseholm, aren't they?'

'If they are, what of it? Anyway, I'm not the only one keeping secrets. What about you concealing from me the true nature of the romance between Timothy Ames and Caroline Tasker?'

'A man is entitled to be in love with his own fiancée,' Lavinia answered reasonably.

'Yes, I dare say he may be; but why did you not tell me? I suppose I have you to thank for the fact that I have been made to look a fool.'

Resisting the urge to say that if anyone had made a fool of her, it had been Isobel herself, Lavinia simply added, 'The signs were there for all to see. But never mind that. For how long have you been corresponding with Riseholm?'

Isobel stared at her defiantly for a moment or two before turning away. She picked a nearby bloom, a large ornamental daisy, and began to pull off the petals. 'Ever since we arrived,' she answered. She paused in her work and looked up. 'And now I am in the most awful situation.'

Lavinia was very strongly tempted to tell Isobel that clearly the mess was of her own making so she could not expect any help to get her out of it. That kind of callous approach was not in her nature, however. She sighed, tugged at her friend's arm so that they could both sit down together, and said, 'What is it, then?'

Isobel explained all that had happened with Benjamin Twizzle. 'I thought that once I had paid him, he would go away,' she sighed. 'He did seem to be very taken with me, and I hoped that a flirtation would be sufficient for him, but he wants money, and I have no more to give him.' She glanced at Lavinia then looked down again.

'Don't look at me,' Lavinia said frankly. 'I don't have any money; you know I don't.'

'No, but . . . ' She paused. 'Lavvy, anyone can see that you and Lord Thurlby are meant for each other. Do you think that he might prevail upon Mr Twizzle to go away? Oh, Lavvy, would you ask him?'

Lavinia had blushed at the first part of Isobel's speech. Now she said, 'There is no understanding between us, you know.'

'Not yet, but . . . Would you? Please?'

'I'll see what I can do,' Lavinia answered. They both turned their heads at the sound of an approaching carriage. 'He's here,' said Lavinia, the tone of her voice betraying her feelings.

'Then go and see him,' said Isobel. 'But give me my letter first.'

Lavinia hurried across the lawn, a smile on her lips. She did not see Isobel read the first line of her letter, then lift her hand to her mouth, her eyes stricken.

A tiny part of Isobel had wondered whether this letter might be full of words of love and reassurance; words which might encourage her to think that there might be a chance for her with Riseholm. Instead, he wrote of his forthcoming marriage. It was over, then. Lord Thurlby was her only hope. She put her letter away and walked slowly across the grass.

17

Lavinia could feel her heart beating faster as she approached Thurlby Hall, a smile on her face. He had as good as promised that he would ask for her hand once his mother was in residence. Now, he had come back, and presumably Lady Thurlby was with him.

She had gone over the scene in Lord Thurlby's library countless times since he had left. The memory of his lips against her hand had been her last waking thought each night, as she had cradled her hand against her cheek before settling down to sleep.

She wondered whether to go and greet them at once, or to go to her room and put on a prettier gown. Before she could make that decision, Lord Thurlby himself emerged onto the terrace, glanced around, saw her, then came towards her with hasty strides. At first smiling, Lavinia's smile faded as she saw the thunderous expression on his face.

'Victor,' she exclaimed, 'what has occurred?'

As he reached her side, he caught hold of her arm, constraining her to walk with him, almost at a run. 'You might well ask,' he responded.

'Pray, what is the meaning of this?' she asked, astonished, and now becoming angry. 'Let go of me at once.'

'Be silent,' he demanded, still holding tightly to her arm, and leading her towards a sheltered area, where small clearings were surrounded by high hedges. 'Now, *Mrs Hedges*, you can explain yourself.'

'Mrs Hedges?' she echoed.

'You remember, surely,' he answered sarcastically. 'It is the assumed identity under which you travelled to Stamford.'

'Yes, I know,' she responded. 'And so did you. We spoke of this before.'

'We did indeed,' the earl agreed. 'You may also recall that during that same conversation, you assured me that your correspondence with Lord Riseholm had ceased.'

'I have not corresponded with Lord Riseholm,' she told him. She was so shaken by his ungentlemanly handling of her that she could not grasp what he was talking about.

'Then kindly explain to me why the landlord of the Horseshoe is able to describe Mrs Hedges as a 'diligent correspondent',' he demanded.

Now, she understood. She blushed, and to his eyes, she looked guilty. It was the time for her to tell him that it was Isobel who was corresponding with Lord Riseholm, but she could not think how to say it. After all, she had only just learned about it herself.

'Your silence tells its own tale,' he said, before she could frame a reply. 'To think that I believed you! You told me . . . assured me that your relationship with him was over and I believed you. I even . . . gullible fool that I am, I even fell in love with you. But the woman I fell in love with does not exist.'

'Victor, please!' exclaimed Lavinia, anxiously.

'To think that I held back from making an offer for your hand out of respect!' He laughed derisively. 'Respect! That's rich! You don't know the meaning of the word.'

'Indeed, you are mistaken! I — '

'Were you laughing at me when I professed my devotion to you?' he asked, hurt as well as anger in his voice. 'Was it a choice titbit with which to regale his rakeship in your next letter? How you must both have laughed at my folly! Well no more, madam, no more. Since a rake is what you want, a rake is what you had better have.'

Before she could discern his intention, he had seized her and pulled her into his arms. Then with insolent fingers, he forced up her chin, and pressed his mouth down onto hers in a cruel travesty of a kiss.

She had shyly anticipated the first time

when he would kiss her properly. Never had she imagined something so savage, so brutal, without a vestige of the love that he professed to feel for her. At last he released her and they stood staring at one another, both a little out of breath, he still with rage in his eyes, she with unshed tears in hers. 'Get out of my sight,' he said in a low tone that was not quite steady. 'Just get out of my sight.'

She stared at him for a long moment, before whirling around and running into the wilderness.

Isobel, who had approached unseen, and heard the last little bit of this exchange, also turned away. There would be no help from this direction, for if the earl had been so angry with the woman whom he was supposed to love, how great would be his anger towards one for whom he did not care two straws? Now she would have to face Bernard Twizzle, not only without any money to offer him, but without any prospect of getting any and with no possibility of rescue from any other quarter. Her lips set in a tight line. Mr Twizzle had had it his own way for too long. It was high time that *he* was of use to *her*.

★　★　★

It was some time before Lavinia returned to the house, and when she did, it was with the resolve that she must find somewhere else to stay. She refused to spend so much as one more night underneath the roof of a man who was so unreasonable that he would not listen to an explanation, even when he had asked for one. As he had hurled accusations at her, she had been too confused to speak. Later, distress mingled with indignation that he should believe this of her when he was supposed to be in love with her had ensured her continued silence. She had greeted his return, full of hope for a happy future. Now, all that was gone; and although she knew that she bore some responsibility for not being open with him, he had shown a deplorable lack of trust that would be hard to forgive. Furthermore, the notion of facing him when he had kissed her so brutally was utterly mortifying.

She would go to Caroline Tasker, she decided. Her cottage was tiny, but at least she was a true friend. From there, she would write to Mr and Mrs Stancross. She would be able to make herself useful to them at Lyme Regis, she was sure. All her dreams were shattered now. It was time to face reality.

She went into the house by a side door hoping to escape notice. She was successful until she got to her own room, and found Lady Thurlby waiting inside, in a chair by the window. 'Aunt Phyllis!' she exclaimed.

Lady Thurlby got gracefully to her feet. 'My dear,' she said, opening her arms. Lavinia, who had thought that she had regained control over her composure, ran into them and burst into tears.

★ ★ ★

'I *knew* that it was a mistake for me to go away,' said Lady Thurlby when Lavinia had spilled out the whole story. 'Miss Wheatman, excellent though she is, does not know you as I do and would, perhaps, be more diffident than I about making enquiries when she is not living in her own house. And of course, my pig-headed son has leaped to his own conclusions in a way that only a man of this family can. Would you like to remain here with me whilst I send *him* to live in a cottage in the village?'

Lavinia gave a watery chuckle. 'This is his home,' she said. She remembered that she had thought that it would be hers too, and she gave another little sob.

Instinctively understanding the direction of her thoughts, Lady Thurlby said, 'My dear, it will all come right in the end, I am sure.

271

Victor has a temper, I know, but it is an honest and open one. He has gone out riding now but when he comes back I am convinced he will see reason.'

'I hope he falls off into a ditch and has to come home covered in mud,' said Lavinia savagely.

Lady Thurlby laughed. 'If it brings him to his senses, then I hope indeed that he may,' she said. 'I do think that there can be no harm in your going to Caroline Tasker. I have only one concern, and that is your friend, Miss Macclesfield. I doubt very much if Victor will want to give her house-room when he hears that she is Lord Riseholm's real correspondent.'

'He must not be told,' said Lavinia quickly. 'He has made some stupid assumptions and I do not see why anyone should put him right.'

'I thought that you would say that, and although I am not in complete agreement with you, I can understand your feelings,' replied her ladyship. 'But you must understand mine. Even if he does not know, *I* will do so. I do not scruple to say that I should find it hard to be civil to her under such circumstances.'

'I suppose I had better go and speak to her,' said Lavinia with a sigh. 'I just have no idea what I am going to say.'

'I think your determination to speak to her at all is quite admirable,' said Lady Thurlby. 'In your place, I should be wanting to wring her neck. Shall I wait here?'

'Please.'

As she left her room and walked down the passage to Isobel's, it occurred to Lavinia that whilst her feelings towards her friend amounted to little more than irritation, her anger was reserved for the man who had asked her to explain herself, and had then refused to listen. She hoped that he would not just be covered with mud from head to toe, but that his horse would bolt and he would have to walk all the way home. 'In leaky boots,' she added savagely to herself, as she scratched on Isobel's door.

There was no reply, so after calling her friend's name softly, Lavinia opened the door and walked in. Isobel was never a very tidy person, but her belongings seemed to be in more of a mess than usual. Gowns had been taken from the cupboard and thrown across the bed. One bonnet was also on the bed and another was on the floor. Drawers had been left open, and things were spilling out of them. One or two papers were lying on the floor. The impression was of someone having made a hasty departure. It was impossible to discern whether anything was missing.

Lavinia looked around her, quite unable to decide what to do next. Eventually, she went back to her own room, thinking to fetch the countess. 'She is not there,' she began. Then because she had walked into the room thinking about Isobel and not, as on the previous occasion, about her own troubles, she suddenly noticed the note on the mantelpiece. With an exclamation, she hurried across the room and opened it.

Dear Lavvy

I have gone with Benjamin Twizzle, so pray do not try to come after me. I can't go back to London, since Willie will be as mad as fire and send me to Harrogate to my grandmother, and I can't face that. Riseholm is spoken for. Timothy Ames can't help me and I daren't face Thurlby after seeing how angry he was with you today, so Twizzle it must be! I dare say he may make an amusing enough husband in the end, and since I can't have Riseholm, anyone will do.

Once I've gone, you can tell Thurlby about who was really writing to his rakeship. He'll come round then, I'm sure. Be happy. At least one of us will marry the man she loves.

Isobel

'What does it say?' her ladyship asked. She had got up from her place and was standing next to Lavinia, although very politely refraining from looking over her shoulder at her correspondence.

'She has gone with Benjamin Twizzle,' said Lavinia looking up incredulously.

'With Twizzle!' exclaimed Lady Thurlby. 'Good heavens, why?'

'She has heard from Lord Riseholm. Apparently he has got engaged to Miss Egan. Isobel had other hopes, but they are not to be.'

'What might those have been?' asked her ladyship, wrinkling her brow.

'I'm not at all sure,' Lavinia answered, reluctant to reveal how her friend would have destroyed Mr Ames's engagement without a qualm.

'But how has she come to know Twizzle well enough to take such a step?'

'We met him on the stage as we were travelling to Stamford, and I'm told he was at Folkingham when we went there on an outing. At the time, I thought that he was there by chance, but today she told me that he has been taking money from her as payment to say nothing about her involvement with Lord Riseholm. She had decided to tell Lord ... Lord Thurlby' — she hesitated on the name — 'about her difficulties, but then — ' She stopped abruptly.

'I can guess,' said the countess. 'She heard Victor upbraiding you about Riseholm and concluded that no help was to be had from that direction. Poor girl! She had nowhere to turn.'

Lavinia had to smile at that. 'Isobel is not usually the kind of girl whom one would describe as 'poor',' she said. 'Although I suspect that her chaperon in London was not very kind, so no doubt she could not bear to go back there either. What's more, Mrs Wilbraham has threatened to send her to her grandmother in Harrogate if she returns to London unattached.'

'And who is her grandmother?'

'She is called Mrs Scales,' Lavinia answered.

Lady Thurlby blenched. 'The Wimbledon Witch,' she breathed. 'Married three times and all of her husbands dead; from what cause one dare not guess! No wonder Miss Macclesfield is desperate not to go there.'

'Izzy has been very foolish, but I cannot bear to think of her being at the mercy of such as Benjamin Twizzle. I shall have to go after her, I suppose.'

'Our horses are at your disposal, of course,' said the countess. 'I wonder whether Mr

Ames and Miss Tasker would go with you?'

'You forget that Miss Wheatman and Miss Tasker have gone to visit Miss Tasker's father today,' Lavinia reminded her.

'Oh dear,' said the countess. 'Then, of course, I will go with you myself.'

'But you have only been home for five minutes,' Lavinia responded. 'It hardly seems fair.' At that moment, they heard the sound of the front doorbell.

'Perhaps Miss Wheatman has come back early,' said the countess hopefully. They left Lavinia's chamber and walked along the passage, descending the stairs just as the butler was admitting a caller. As they stood at the top of the flight, they looked down, just as the visitor looked up. He was dressed for travelling in the finest London fashion.

'Lord Riseholm!' Lavinia gasped.

Riseholm executed an elegant bow. 'Your servant, Lady Thurlby. And Miss . . . Muir, is it not? Your pardon for intruding, but as I was in the area, I thought that I might call.'

'That is very civil of you, my lord,' said Lady Thurlby descending the stairs, and giving the earl her hand as he bowed again. 'Allow me to show you into the drawing room, so that I may offer you some refreshment.'

'You are very gracious,' Riseholm responded, following his hostess after she had asked the butler to bring wine. 'Particularly since we barely know one another.'

'Which makes your courtesy in visiting us all the greater,' the countess responded, receiving a gracious inclination of the head by way of reply. 'Is this the first time that you have visited Lincolnshire, Lord Riseholm? Your own estates are in Shropshire, I believe. You must find this countryside rather flat in comparison.'

'As far as I recall,' he answered, taking the seat that she indicated, and crossing his legs, after laying his hat and cane on the floor next to his chair. 'I do not go there very frequently, madam. Unlike your son, I am not a squire by nature.'

The countess's smile did not reach her eyes. 'I know how to be a good hostess, Lord Riseholm,' she said. 'But speak of my son with the slightest disrespect, and I shall show you the door.'

Lavinia looked at the other lady in amazement. Never had she seen her godmother look so haughty!

'I intended no disrespect, I assure you,' Riseholm replied. 'I was merely attempting to point out the differences between your son and myself — differences which I am very well aware show him to great advantage.'

The countess inclined her head. 'I accept

your explanation,' she said, as the butler brought in the wine, together with a jug of lemonade. 'Will you be good enough to pour, my lord?'

'You honour me,' he answered, rising fluidly to his feet and crossing to the sideboard where the butler had placed the tray. 'Wine for you, ma'am, or do you prefer lemonade?'

Lavinia listened to all these politenesses with gathering irritation, and barely managed to accept a glass of lemonade from the earl without snapping at him. The shock of his arrival had been sufficient to push everything else to the back of her mind. Now, she asked herself what could have brought him into the heart of the country. She suspected that he was simply there to torment Isobel in some way. Whatever his reasons, the urgency of her errand became greater with every passing moment, and she was now anxious to be on her way. On the surface, the countess did not appear to be concerned at all; but when Lavinia darted a glance at her as the earl returned to his own place, she frowned and shook her head slightly. She had not forgotten, then.

'And what brings you to this part of the world, Lord Riseholm?' Lady Thurlby asked him. 'My understanding was that you spent most of your time in London.'

'That is so,' Riseholm replied after he had sat down. 'However, a recent letter from an acquaintance reminded me of what I had been missing. Have you been having an agreeable stay, Miss Muir?'

'Yes, very agreeable, thank you,' Lavinia replied, determinedly hiding her impatience.

'My goddaughter is being too kind,' Lady Thurlby interrupted. 'I have been obliged to neglect her for a little when I was called to the bedside of a sick friend.'

'You did not have to leave her here alone, I trust,' murmured the earl, before taking another sip of wine.

'Oh no,' Lady Thurlby answered. 'My neighbour Miss Wheatman came to take my place.'

There was a brief silence before the earl said, 'That was indeed fortunate.' He paused. 'This little fencing match has been entertaining in its way, my lady, but perhaps it is time that I was a little more direct. I believe that you also have a young lady staying here by the name of Isobel Macclesfield, with whom I am acquainted. I would be glad if I could pay my respects.'

'Isobel is not here,' Lavinia said, unable to keep silent any longer.

'No doubt she is off being squired about

the countryside by the young clergyman she is rumoured to be seeing,' he murmured.

'Mr Ames?' exclaimed the countess.

By a strange coincidence, at this moment, the door opened. 'Miss Tasker and Mr Ames,' the butler announced.

'Caroline! Oh, thank goodness,' Lavinia exclaimed involuntarily whilst Lady Thurlby busied herself with introducing Lord Riseholm to the newcomers.

'Mr Ames,' said Lord Riseholm, with a flourishing bow. 'May I congratulate you on your engagement?' The earl's expression was everything that was appropriate to the senti-ments that he was expressing, but his eyes looked cold and empty.

Mr Ames responded by saying 'You are very kind, my lord. I am a fortunate man.'

Lavinia happened to be looking at Riseholm at this moment, and she noticed a strangely blank look cross his face before he said, 'You are indeed. I know the lady slightly, and she is certainly a prize.'

'Why, so do I think so,' answered Mr Ames, glancing warmly at Caroline.

'You are very kind in your sentiments, my lord,' said Caroline. 'But I must confess that I do not recall meeting you before.'

Riseholm glanced from one to the other. 'This is the lady to whom you are engaged?'

he said, frowning slightly.

'It is,' Ames answered.

'You are not, then, engaged to Miss Macclesfield?'

'No indeed,' the clergyman answered hastily. 'Nor was there ever any prospect of my being engaged to her. Miss Tasker and I were betrothed before the young lady arrived in the district.'

The earl looked at him, then began to chuckle. 'Of course you were,' he said.

'Your meaning, my lord?' said Mr Ames, lifting his chin.

'Dear me, I appear to be very maladroit today,' said Riseholm mournfully. 'I do not seem to be able to meet anyone without almost immediately giving them offence. Perhaps I should instantly excuse myself.' He turned to Lady Thurlby. 'Would you kindly have the goodness to inform Miss Maccles-field that I called when she returns? I have taken rooms at the George in Stamford and shall do myself the honour of calling upon her another day. Your servant, ma'am.'

Lavinia looked at the countess. 'Aunt Phyllis?' she said. Lady Thurlby made a gesture of assent. 'Isobel has gone,' she said, turning back to Riseholm.

'Yes, so you told me earlier,' he replied. 'That is why I am now sending her my compliments as I take my leave.'

'No, you don't understand,' said Lavinia urgently. 'She has gone — eloped.'

There was a brief silence, broken only by exclamations from Miss Tasker and Mr Ames. 'Presumably with some gentleman whose identity is unknown to me,' said Lord Riseholm, picking an infinitesimal piece of fluff from his sleeve. 'In that case, you will probably not see Miss Macclesfield in order to pass on my compliments. I will take my leave of you. Pray wish her joy on my behalf.'

'No!' cried Lavinia, hurrying to lay a hand on his arm. 'She will be miserable. Who would not be, if they were called Izzy Twizzle? You must help me to rescue her.'

'Forgive my obtuseness, but ladies do not normally need rescuing when they are eloping,' said the earl, his tone hardening a little. 'I am not her father. It is not my place to drag her home when her choice is made.'

'But it is not made,' Lavinia replied. 'It . . . she . . . ' She thrust Isobel's letter at him. 'You had better read for yourself,' she said.

He took the letter and ran his eye over its contents. His face gave little away, but it seemed to Lavinia as if some of the hardness around his mouth disappeared, particularly as he reached the last paragraph. 'You said that you intended to go after her,' he said, his tone lacking some of its customary languor.

'Yes, I do,' she replied. 'And if you will not help me, I shall go alone.'

'No you won't,' said Caroline. 'We'll come with you, won't we, Timothy?'

'Yes, of course,' replied Ames without hesitation.

'I'll send for the carriage from the stables,' said Lady Thurlby, getting up in order to ring the bell.

'No need,' said Riseholm, stepping between her and the bell-pull. 'I have only driven over from Stamford. My carriage is ready and my team is fresh.'

Before they left, Lady Thurlby said to Lavinia, 'I'll tell Victor where you've gone.'

'Good,' said Lavinia, tying her bonnet ribbons with decision. She had forgotten briefly how angry she was with Lord Thurlby. Now she remembered. 'You can tell him that I have run off with Lord Riseholm.'

Lady Thurlby smiled mischievously as Riseholm's horses pulled the carriage away from the front door and set off at a smart trot.

18

For Benjamin Twizzle, the discovery that Isobel had been conducting an illicit correspondence with Rake Riseholm had been a real piece of luck. The notion of blackmailing Isobel had struck him as being an excellent way of providing himself with the means of getting out of a tight situation.

Isobel's feelings on being exploited in this manner did not greatly concern him. He knew her to be an heiress with a comfortable if not a handsome fortune, and felt sure that she could easily spare something in order to solve his problems. Her protestations that she did not have any money to hand were seen by him to be flimsy excuses. Rich people could always manage to find money if they needed to do so.

Isobel's willingness to flirt with him had convinced him that she did not regard the business of the money with any degree of seriousness. He, too, was very willing to indulge in a flirtation but he never lost sight of the chief object of the exercise. This, of course, was to extract himself from the nightmare situation in which the threat of retribution in the person of Mr Nightshade always seemed to be around the corner.

Just the night before Lord Thurlby returned home with his mother, something very alarming had happened; two of Mr Nightshade's bully boys had actually caught up with Benjamin outside the Horseshoe. They had made it quite clear that their master's patience was not inexhaustible and that he expected to be paid without delay. Just as things were starting to look gloomy, even to one of Mr Twizzle's disposition, he had had the bright idea of mentioning his 'betrothed', the heiress.

'Oh yes, and why didn't you mention this *heiress* before, then?' one of them had asked, nodding to the other who had pinned Benjamin up against the back wall of the inn. The man had released him suddenly, causing him almost to lose his footing.

Twizzle had straightened his cuffs, trying not to show how his hands were shaking. 'I didn't want to drag her into all this,' he had replied with a reasonable performance of carelessness. 'Besides, if her family hear that I'm a gambler, the wedding'll be off and then you'll get nothing at all.'

'Maybe so,' the first man had said after a moment's thought. The two men had held a low-voiced conversation, whilst keeping

Benjamin well in their sights. 'I'll have to ask Mr Nightshade about this,' the same man had said eventually. 'Come here tomorrow evening at this time.'

'And no double-crossing, or you'll be the worse for it,' the other had warned, before the two of them had swaggered away.

After this unsettling encounter, Benjamin had therefore come to his meeting with Isobel at Thurlby Hall determined to get her to part with some money, or at least some jewellery.

To his dismay, when he met her in the gardens that day, she seemed very disturbed and, more importantly, she had no money. 'Nor will I have any more, so it is useless to expect it,' she said, wringing her hands.

'But you must have some jewels,' he protested.

'Well, I do not,' she replied, not entirely truthfully. Most of her jewels, it was true, were in London in Mrs Wilbraham's safe, that lady having refused to release them for fear that her charge would use them as a means to run off with some undesirable character. The only jewels she had with her were the pearls that had belonged to her mother. Not for anything would she reveal the existence of those.

'Then in that case, I will have to disclose

what I know,' he replied, thinking of Mr Nightshade.

'Oh, go on then,' she said wretchedly. 'Disclose what you like, and see if I care. Nobody could possibly think any worse of me than they do now, not even if I were to do something utterly outrageous, like eloping.' She stopped speaking; then, as the words that she had said sunk in, she glanced at him sideways.

'Oh no,' he said backing away.

'Yes,' she replied, pursuing him. 'Just think of the benefits.'

'Which are . . . ?'

'I will be able to lay my hands on a great deal of money straight away,' she answered. 'It comes to me without conditions when I am twenty-one, or when I marry, whichever is the sooner.'

'No conditions at all?' he asked suspiciously. 'You don't even need anyone's consent to inherit?' On one previous occasion, he had come perilously close to getting married, only to find that the young lady in question would forfeit every penny of her estate if she married without her guardian's approval.

'Oh no,' she assured him blithely, quite unaware whether or not this was the truth. 'Just think; you will have all you need.'

'Yes, perhaps I might,' he answered, regarding her suspiciously. 'But what's in it for you?'

'I should like to be a married lady,' she answered with a toss of her head. 'People can't tell you off and bully you if you are married.'

Benjamin Twizzle had not set out that day with the intention of eloping. With Nightshade on his heels, Lord Thurlby's possible wrath to face, and no prospect of any money from any other source, it seemed that it might be the very thing. What was more, the idea of being in a position so that no one would bully him seemed to be very desirable at that moment. 'By Jove, so they can't,' he murmured, his expression lightening. 'But how to do the thing?'

'I have an idea,' she answered after a moment's thought. 'Meet me at the Horseshoe in an hour, and bespeak us a carriage and pair.'

★　★　★

If Lord Thurlby did not feel any more cheerful after his ride, at least the first heat of his anger was gone, to be replaced by a kind of heart-sore weariness. For several years after the girl he had once loved had shown her true colours at Folkingham, he had kept his heart very tightly under wraps. If he were honest, that might have been in part why he had avoided London so determinedly. Others in his position, such as Lord Riseholm, for instance, would no doubt have cultivated the female sex in a cynical way, spreading heartbreak in return. Thurlby had remained on his estate, saving his affection for his mother, his friendship for a select group in the local area, and giving his time to the cultivation of his acres. He had always known that he must marry to continue the family line. Of the kind of woman that he might marry he had not thought a great deal, save that he must be content to think of her occupying his mother's place.

Remembering Lavinia's disastrous visit several years before, he had been very suspicious of her, especially considering the unconventional nature of her arrival. Even while he still disapproved of her, however, he could not help observing how pretty and womanly she had become. As time went on, his respect for her had grown as he had seen her make a friend of an ordinary schoolmistress, and show kindness to an older spinster lady. He had taken pleasure in watching her becoming familiar with his dog, his home and his garden. He had gradually come to realize that his name and his title were of less importance than having her for his own, admitting to himself at last that he wanted her at Thurlby Hall on a permanent basis as his wife.

He had escorted his mother home, full of hope, only to have it destroyed utterly by the discovery that Lavinia's attachment to Rise-holm continued. He had confronted her with this, and she had given him no explanation of her behaviour. Then he had seized her and kissed her in order to punish her.

Furious with her and almost as furious with himself for his lack of restraint, he had thrust her aside and gone for a long ride. He knew that he must get right away from her, otherwise he would be in severe danger of saying or doing something that he might regret. Fool that he was, part of him actually wanted simply to throw himself at her feet and to tell her that he loved her anyway and that none of it mattered, because without her beside him as his countess, life would be dry and meaningless.

As he returned his weary horse to its stable, he spoke a curt word of thanks to his groom — surprising the man by his unusual lack of courtesy — and walked slowly towards the house, his whole posture that of a man twenty years older. He looked around him without pleasure. It was the first time that he could ever remember viewing his home and its surroundings in such a way.

It was only when he was actually standing with his hand on the handle of the side door, ready to go in, that it suddenly occurred to him that Lavinia would still be there. His heart gave a lurch. 'Fool!' he said out loud. 'No doubt she'll be off to be with Riseholm at the first opportunity.' Then he remembered that she had consistently denied corresponding with his rakeship. On the other hand, the landlord, who had no reason to lie to him, had said that all the letters from Mrs Hedges had been for Riseholm, and all the letters that came for the same lady had been franked across the corner. It had been Lavinia who had masqueraded as Mrs Hedges.

His expression hardened again, as he opened the door. Lilly, who had heard his approach long before anyone else, came clattering along the passage, her tail wagging furiously as she jumped up to greet the master who had been gone for so long. He bent to stroke her head and pull her silky ears. All at once, he remembered Lavinia petting the dog not long after her arrival. Lilly had taken to Lavinia at once. He frowned. He had always believed that dogs knew good from bad. Maybe in this, as in so many other things, he had been mistaken.

He walked slowly to his study with Lilly at his heels. He was aware that first he ought to go upstairs and change his dress after his strenuous ride. The way he was feeling, however, he did not much care if he never changed his clothes ever again.

Once inside with the door closed, he poured himself a large glass of brandy and walked over to the desk. There was a piece of paper folded on the blotter, with his name on it, clearly having been written in haste.

Briefly, he hesitated. Was this from Lavinia? Had she gone to Riseholm's arms, leaving him a note informing him in what utter contempt she held him? Telling himself that he was a clot to speculate when all he had to do was to open the paper and read its contents, he picked it up and unfolded it, staring at the words written there, clearly scrawled in haste.

I O U £100. Sorry. Lavinia will explain.
Isobel Macclesfield

His hand went to the drawer where he always kept an amount of money to cover all ordinary occasions. The drawer was slightly opened, the lock forced, and a roll of notes had been taken. Isobel, he thought; it was

Isobel. Suddenly, a lot of things began to become plain. Actions that had seemed utterly out of character when attributed to Lavinia became perfectly comprehensible when laid at Isobel's door.

Putting down his glass, still half full, he strode to the door, quite taking Lilly by surprise. The greyhound had settled down flat on her side on the hearth rug, and only just made it out of the door before her master closed it behind him.

Without a thought for the propriety of his actions, he ran up the main staircase, two at a time, followed by Lilly, who thought this tremendous sport, headed straight for Lavinia's room and knocked on the door, calling out her name at the same time.

'She's not there,' said his mother, coming up behind him.

Thurlby lost a little of his colour. 'Not there?' he said.

She shook her head, sighing. 'Oh Victor, you can be so pig-headed at times.'

'You don't mean that she's gone; she's left?'

Deciding that he deserved to suffer a little for his rash assumptions, her ladyship said, 'That is exactly what I do mean.'

'Because of what I said?' He demanded. 'God, I wish I had cut out my tongue before — '

'The number of times I have heard your father say the same,' Lady Thurlby remarked. She paused, not wanting to tell an untruth. 'Your words and your manner towards her gave her little reason to suppose that you would want her to stay,' she said eventually.

'No, I suppose not,' he agreed. 'But she has been less than candid with me.'

'Some secrets are not ours to share,' she reminded him. 'You would surely not have had her betray a confidence.'

He shook his head. 'No more than I would do so myself.' Then after a short silence, he said, 'Anyone with an ounce of intelligence would have worked out that it was Isobel Macclesfield who was entangled with Rise-holm and not Lavinia.'

'Yes,' his mother agreed. 'Anyone who was not in love.'

After a long silence, he said in subdued tones, 'Mama, the things I said — did I make her cry?'

Lady Thurlby had no intention of betraying her goddaughter over such a matter. 'She said that she hoped you would fall off your horse and into a ditch,' she replied.

After another moment's silence, he said, 'I'm not just pig-headed, am I? I'm an unreasonable bully as well.'

'Yes, you are, although I suppose that if you

realize it at least there is some hope for you. That is, as long as you don't add to your imperfections by being a laggard lover on top of everything. In fact, why are you standing talking to me instead of going after her?'

'You know where she's gone, then?'

'I imagine she's on her way to Gretna Green — with Lord Riseholm,' his mother said placidly.

'What?' roared the earl. Lilly, who had a pronounced aversion to loud noises, immediately slunk behind her ladyship's skirts and looked reproachfully at her master, her tail between her legs.

'Now see what you have done,' said the countess as she stroked the dog soothingly. 'Poor Lilly is shaking.'

'So am I,' he answered, holding on to his temper with difficulty. 'Explain, Mother, for the love of God.'

'What would you do if I said that she had eloped with him?' she asked him curiously.

'Ride after them and kill the bastard, for by heaven he doesn't deserve her,' he answered fiercely.

She smiled. 'Lavinia hasn't eloped with him,' she said. 'They have gone in pursuit of Isobel who has eloped with Benjamin Twizzle.'

'Benjamin Twizzle? Good God, why?' he

exclaimed. 'I thought she barely knew the man. Does the silly chit have any brains at all?'

'Apparently he found out that she was corresponding with Riseholm. He threatened to tell you unless she gave him money.'

'But why go to him rather than to me?' he asked. He had begun his sentence in an indignant tone. By the end of it, his voice had slowed, and his face had turned a dull red.

'I don't suppose she dared,' his mother said frankly. 'She was afraid that you would send her back to London post haste.'

'She was probably right,' he agreed ruefully. 'She needed the money to elope, of course.'

'What money?'

'She broke into my desk,' he told her. 'By God, though, who but Isobel Macclesfield would think to solve her problems by marrying her blackmailer?'

'It is ingenious, you must admit,' said Lady Thurlby. 'But quite unsuitable. Benjamin Twizzle is a sadly unsteady young man, and in any case, Isobel is in love with Lord Riseholm.'

'Who has gone off with Lavinia — *my* Lavinia — quite unchaperoned.' Her ladyship thought about Miss Tasker and Mr Ames, but said nothing. 'No matter that they are in pursuit of another couple, if it becomes known that Lavinia has been in company with his rakeship, her reputation will be blasted beyond repair.' He set off down the passage with hasty strides. 'Don't fear, Mama. I shall bring her back.'

She smiled, holding Lilly's collar to prevent her following her master. 'I know you will, my son,' she said. But she spoke to the empty air.

19

Twizzle eyed Isobel suspiciously as they got into the conveyance that he had ordered at her request. 'If you had enough money to hire this carriage, why didn't you have any to give me?' he asked, frowning.

Very unusually for her, Isobel blushed. 'This is an emergency,' she said. Following her conversation with Twizzle, she had scurried up to her room and had quickly thrust a few necessary provisions into a couple of band boxes.

The next step had taken rather more fortitude. She had caught sight of Lord Thurlby clattering away from the house on horse-back as if all the fiends in Hell were after him. Lavinia had run crying into the garden. Miss Wheatman was out, and she had heard Lady Thurlby's abigail say that she was lying down on her bed, after her early morning start.

Those facts established, she had cautiously made her way into Lord Thurlby's study and had prepared to hunt in his desk for any money that might be there. The desk had been locked, with no key in sight, but a sturdy-looking dagger had been on display on the wall. She thought guiltily of how Lord Thurlby's desk now sported a broken lock from where she had forced it. She had few scruples, but even she had felt uncomfortable about that. She was glad that she had not had very much time to think about what she was doing or her courage might have failed.

She sighed. Her host could not possibly think worse of her than he already did, and in any case, once she was married, she would be able to give him back his money and even, if he were so mean as to demand it, to pay for the repair of the desk. What was more, with her out of the way, Lavinia would be able to tell Thurlby the truth and they would be reconciled. At least some good would come out of the situation. When she thought about the matter in that light, she was really doing them a favour.

'Are you sure that no one will follow us?' Benjamin Twizzle asked his bride-to-be as they trundled along in the hired coach, moving more slowly than either of them would have preferred.

'No. No one,' Isobel answered. 'That is the beauty of it, you see. Nobody cares what happens to me.' She tried to sound airy rather than despondent, but truth to tell, it was rather a depressing thought. Riseholm was far away in London, dancing attendance upon the insipid Miss Egan; Lavinia would be glad to see the back of one who had dragged her into all kinds of misunderstandings; Caroline Tasker would hate her for trying to steal her fiancé; and Lord Thurlby would only come after her in order to have her arrested for stealing his money.

'That's all right, then,' answered Twizzle, supremely unconcerned as to what her feelings might be. The elopement, never part of his plan, had been thrust upon him at the last minute, but he was prepared to make the best of it. They had made good time, and as he looked at the enchantingly beautiful and exceedingly rich Miss Macclesfield, he decided that marriage to an heiress might not be so bad.

He was just engaged in a delightful day-dream, which involved driving up to the door of a fashionable tailor's shop in London in a dashing curricle, entering the establishment, then emerging shortly afterwards in a new suit of clothes which caused every other gentleman to gasp with envy, when the carriage came to a halt, and a voice called out, 'Stand and deliver!'

'Highwaymen!' Isobel exclaimed apprehensively.

Twizzle was just as apprehensive, but for

different reasons. In the voice of the highwayman, he had recognized the tones of his adversary and former gambling partner, Cyrus Nightshade. There was always the chance that Nightshade supplemented his income with a little highway robbery, but somehow Twizzle doubted it. It was far more likely that he had come in pursuit of his debt. Although startled by his appearance, Twizzle was not initially very worried at the arrival of Nightshade. He had, after all, given an assurance that he was to marry an heiress, and here he was doing so. Where was the problem?

Judging that the less that Isobel knew about this the better, Twizzle said boldly 'You may leave this to me, my dear,' and stepped down from the coach, hoping to engage Nightshade in conversation out of earshot. 'Well, fellow? What is this all about?' he said in as high-handed a tone as he could muster.

'I'll tell you what it's about, my young buck,' said Nightshade, his rather sneering voice laced with a slight Midlands accent. 'It's about a certain debt as is owed to one Cyrus Nightshade by one Benjamin Twizzle.'

Looking round, Benjamin saw that his adversary was accompanied by three men, all of whom remained on horseback, whilst Nightshade had dismounted and entrusted

302

his reins to one of his accomplices. He now stood very much at his ease. A blond, tall, heavily built man, he always made Benjamin feel like a mere stripling. 'You'll have your money,' Benjamin insisted, glancing anxiously back at the coach, where Isobel's head could be seen emerging from the window.

'So you say,' answered Nightshade, his thumbs hooked into the armholes of a rather lurid waistcoat, which could be seen beneath his serviceable drab riding coat. 'But the mystery is, why when I'm patiently waiting for my money at our agreed meeting place, you go galloping off with your fancy piece in the opposite direction. I very much resent having to turn out in person, I can tell you.'

'I've told your man,' Benjamin protested. 'I'm engaged to be married to an heiress. Her family has taken exception to me, so now we're fleeing to the border. Once we're married, I'll let you have the money all right and tight.'

Suddenly conscious of a movement behind him, he turned his head to find Isobel walking towards them. She was dressed for travelling in a dark blue carriage dress. Certainly, she looked very attractive as always; but she had made an effort to be inconspicuous, and there was nothing about her that shouted 'wealth'.

'Heiress, eh?' remarked Nightshade with a grin. 'Couldn't she afford to hire a decent carriage and horses?'

'Who is this person?' Isobel asked at her haughtiest.

Nightshade shoved his face very close to hers. 'I tell you who I am, missy. I'm the man who your lover-boy here owes a debt to.'

'And what has that to do with me?' Isobel demanded.

'Why, it seems, missy, that you're the one with the money to pay me.'

'Me?' exclaimed Isobel incredulously.

'Money, or jewels,' explained Nightshade. 'Never say I'm not broad-minded.'

'I haven't got a bean,' retorted Isobel, 'And my guardian keeps my jewels under lock and key.'

There was a short silence. 'It seems to me,' said Mr Nightshade looking from one to the other, 'that one of you is telling lies. Now, which might it be?'

Normally, Benjamin Twizzle had plenty to say. He now found himself in the unusual position of being at something of a loss. His instinct for self-preservation prompted him to declare that his betrothed certainly did have money, although at present she did not carry it upon her person. On the other hand, his sense of chivalry, never very strong, but always buried deep inside, protested that to make her a target for Nightshade's rapacity was hardly fair.

While he was still wondering what to say, Isobel spoke. 'I can see no reason why I should feel obliged to explain my financial circumstances to you, you nasty little man,' she told Nightshade. Then, turning to Benjamin Twizzle, she said, 'Were you really proposing to pay your debts to this man out of *my* money?'

He grinned weakly. 'Well, man and wife — one flesh, don't you know?' he murmured.

'If you suppose that I have the slightest intention of marrying you after this débâcle, then you have another think coming,' Isobel declared. 'I wouldn't marry you if you were the last man on earth!'

'Well, damn it all, that's the outside of enough when I consider how desperate you were to get away,' Twizzle retorted. 'And, if I recall correctly, you were the one who wanted to elope.'

'Only because I could not think of another way out of my difficulties. If there had been any other course of action, I would have taken it, believe you me.'

'There's no need to get so uppity with me. I first met you travelling upon the common stage, remember.'

'Yes, I do remember, and I suppose that I should not be surprised at that for there has never ever been anyone I have met who was as common as you.'

'Well, I like that!' protested Twizzle.

Their conversation was interrupted at this point by the sound of a pistol being fired into the air by Mr Nightshade. Isobel then immediately demanded what he wanted, as it appeared to her that he was poking his nose into matters which were none of his business.

Mr Nightshade was now faced with a dilemma. Three possible courses of action lay before him: one was to escort this ill-assorted couple to the border, make sure that they married and then demand his money. This seemed to him to be fraught with difficulties, one being the length of the journey, during which all kinds of things could go wrong, including the danger of her relatives coming in pursuit. The other major problem was the temper of the young lady, which seemed to indicate that she would struggle vociferously every step of the way, and possibly make such a fuss over the anvil that the blacksmith would refuse to marry them at all.

Another possible course of action, of course, would be to dispense with Mr Twizzle altogether and simply kidnap the heiress for ransom. This, to Mr Nightshade's mind, had one major drawback: he had had an acquaintance who had kidnapped an heiress. That acquaintance was presently hanging in chains on a gibbet, kidnapping being a capital offence. What was more, Nightshade had never heard of the Macclesfield fortune, and he only had Twizzle's word for it that there was one. Their means of flight — a rather shabby hired coach and two horses — did not argue any extraordinary degree of affluence; nor was the reference to travelling on the stage very encouraging. In addition, the young lady had been heard to say that she had no money available. Nightshade's experience of fortunes was that more often than not, they were tied up so securely that it was impossible to get at them, especially if a young lady went against her family's wishes.

There was the third course of action, the least risky to his way of thinking, and this was what he now resolved to take. 'Well this has all been very pleasant, chatting away,' he said. 'But it's time we was on our way. I'm not a vengeful man, so you can have your traps.' He nodded to one of his men, who got into the coach and threw out Benjamin's cloak bag, followed by the two band boxes which comprised all the luggage that Isobel had brought with her.

'What are you doing?' Isobel demanded, as

one of the boxes rolled over, the top came off and some gloves fell out.

'I'm having this coach in settlement of the debt,' said Nightshade. He knew how to shift such a vehicle quickly, no one being the wiser.

'But . . . but you can't do that!' exclaimed Twizzle. 'Everyone'll blame me.'

'My heart bleeds for you,' said Nightshade sarcastically, as he remounted his horse. One of his men had climbed onto the box, having tied his own horse behind the carriage. 'There's a village only a few miles on. I should get walking if I was you. Not a nice place to linger in. Couple like you could easily get set upon by highwaymen.'

Isobel and Twizzle were then obliged to watch helplessly whilst Nightshade and his men galloped laughing into the distance with their booty.

The sound of the retreating coach had only just faded away when a nearby groan alerted them to the presence of the driver. He had been knocked out by one of Nightshade's men and was only just coming round. During careful questioning, he revealed the fact that going on to the next village would be almost twice the walk as to return to the previous one.

Showing remarkable solicitude for the driver, Isobel insisted that he could not possibly carry anything; and since she was obliged to keep an eye upon him, neither could she. That left Mr Twizzle with the task of carrying his own cloak bag and both the bandboxes, which he flatly refused to do.

'Haven't enough arms,' he said frankly. 'Stands to reason.'

'Then you'll just have to leave yours behind,' Isobel told him. 'It's all your fault after all.'

'I wasn't the one who suggested eloping,' he pointed out.

'No, but if you had not become acquainted with that low, criminal person, we would not be stranded now at the side of the road.'

'You can be quite sure that if I had not been in debt to Nightshade, then there is nothing in this wide world that would have persuaded me to elope with you.'

'Well at least we are in agreement about something,' said Isobel firmly. 'You can carry one of my bandboxes as well as your cloak bag.'

'I'll carry the other, miss,' said the driver, looking a little better, although still rather pale. 'It'll give me something else to think about other than the master's horses.'

At this point, it was Benjamin Twizzle's turn to go pale.

★ ★ ★

Lord Riseholm and his party set off from Thurlby Hall at about four o'clock, Caroline and Lavinia facing the front, whilst Lord Riseholm and Mr Ames sat opposite them, their backs to the horses. They paused briefly at the Horseshoe to see what could be discovered about the fleeing couple. Mr Ames, being acquainted with both Miss Macclesfield and Mr Twizzle, took this task upon himself.

'They left just over an hour ago,' he said, as he got back in and took his place in Lord Riseholm's luxurious well-sprung chaise. 'They were heading towards Lincoln. I've told the coachman, my lord.'

'With a pair or a team?' Riseholm asked.

'Just a pair of horses, the landlord said, but quite strengthy beasts.'

Riseholm smiled. 'I doubt they've the stamina of my cattle,' he said. 'We'll catch them, never fear.'

No doubt many would have thought them an oddly assorted party, but in the event, the time passed more quickly than anyone would have supposed. Lord Riseholm had a fine social sense and, hiding whatever anxiety he might have been feeling, made it his business to keep the conversation going. Timothy

Ames had a ready wit, and Caroline was an intelligent young woman, and so between the three of them, they managed to cover a number of topics.

Lavinia was silent for a number of reasons. Most of her thoughts were turned towards Lord Thurlby. Could things ever be put right between them? During the journey, they had passed through Folkingham, and she remembered the moment on the top of the tower when she had tripped and he had almost kissed her. Why had everything had to go so badly wrong since then?

In addition, she was still somewhat annoyed with Lord Riseholm, who undoubtedly bore a good deal of responsibility for the whole situation, having first turned Isobel's head in London, and then compounded his misbehaviour by corresponding with her.

At that moment, had it been possible, she would willingly have thrown Lord Riseholm and Isobel out of the nearest window. Of course, Lord Thurlby himself probably deserved the same fate. For what seemed like the hundredth time, she asked herself why he could not have listened to her and trusted her. She drew a deep breath, and all at once began to feel a little giddy. She visibly swayed in her seat.

Suddenly conscious of having been addressed,

311

she turned to Caroline Tasker. 'Lavinia, when did you last eat?' the schoolmistress asked her. 'I do not count the biscuit that you had with us at noon.'

Too taken by surprise to dissemble, Lavinia answered, 'At breakfast time, I think.'

The earl took out his watch. 'We will stop to eat at the next presentable inn,' he said.

'No, no!' Lavinia objected. 'We must push on. We cannot risk losing them.'

'We will not lose them,' his lordship answered placidly.

'I do not know how you can speak so calmly,' declared Lavinia exasperatedly. 'It is all your — ' She broke off, suddenly conscious of the impropriety of upbraiding a nobleman in his own carriage.

'All my fault?' he suggested. 'Now that I don't admit. Half my fault, perhaps. But then, we are none of us particularly wise when it comes to matters of the heart, are we?' Lavinia blushed and looked away.

It was not very long before they came to a village with an inn of reasonable size, and Lord Riseholm signalled to his coachman to stop. 'We'll dine here,' said the earl. 'It will give the horses a chance to rest, which will mean that we'll be able to take them on for another stage.' He turned to Ames. 'See if you can find out whether they've come through here. I'll bespeak a meal and a private room.'

The arrival of Lord Riseholm's impressive equipage caused something of a stir in such a quiet country place, and in no time, the landlord was at the ready, offering whatever these august visitors might deem necessary to their comfort. 'I've some fine bedchambers, my lord,' said the man eagerly, 'with clean linen, well-aired.'

'You are very obliging,' Riseholm answered. 'We shall, however, be continuing our journey shortly. A good meal served quickly and in privacy is all that I and my companions require.'

'At once, my lord,' the landlord replied, the depth of his bow showing a professional ability to sum up the quality of his guests.

Timothy Ames joined them as they were going into the parlour which the landlord had placed at their disposal. 'They came through here about half an hour ago,' he said. 'We've gained on them. Ought we to lose that advantage?'

The earl waved one hand in dismissal. 'We'll soon regain it,' he replied. 'Remember that they, too, will need to stop for food at some point. We will do ourselves no good if by the time we catch up with them, we are fainting from inanition.'

Lavinia interrupted. 'But what if by the

313

time we catch up with them it is . . . is . . . '
she paused, blushing.

'Too late?' Riseholm suggested conversationally. 'Then I'll kill him. Come now, Miss Muir, have a glass of this wine that the landlord has brought us. I am persuaded that it will lift your spirits.'

Lord Riseholm believed in encouraging good service by offering a *douceur* beforehand, and in less time than seemed possible, they were sitting down to a sustaining meal of chicken pie with a fricassee of cabbage and some potato cakes.

The landlord was just offering to fetch more or, alternatively, to bring some cakes or a suet pudding, when a waiter came in and, with a murmured apology, spoke briefly to the landlord in an undertone. 'Forgive me, my lord,' said their host, 'but some undesirables have come to the door. James will attend you while I send them about their business.'

'Undesirables?' echoed Riseholm. 'How many? Do you need help to eject them?'

'Three, my lord,' answered the waiter. 'They claim they've been set upon by highwaymen.'

'Then you must give them assistance rather than eject them,' Caroline exclaimed. 'To suggest otherwise is . . . is infamous!'

'Don't you worry yourself, miss,' said the landlord, not appearing to take offence at her interjection. 'They're most probably spinning a yarn. I've known some tell that selfsame story of a highwayman as innocent as you please, then in the morning they've gone with no shot paid and most likely something stolen into the bargain. If you'll excuse me, my lord, ladies and gentlemen.'

'Leave the door open,' Riseholm suggested, as the man left the room. 'We'll hear if you need help.'

'Pardon me, sir,' they heard one of the newcomers say, 'but my wife and I have had our carriage stolen by rogues, and our coachman has been set upon. I was wondering whether — '

'Is that a fact?' the landlord interrupted, his tone far from the deferential one that he had used in speaking to Lord Riseholm. 'As it happens, I'm afraid that my inn is full tonight, so I must ask you to move on.'

'My lord — ' the waiter began, only to fall silent as Riseholm raised his hand in a warning gesture. The rest of the party looked at him. They were all thinking the same thing.

'Benjamin Twizzle!' Lavinia exclaimed under her breath, at almost the same time as Timothy Ames.

'Indeed,' purred Riseholm. He rose in a leisurely manner and strolled towards the door.

'Full?' exclaimed Benjamin Twizzle. 'I don't believe you.'

'That's as may be,' the landlord replied. 'But you're a ne'er-do-well if ever I saw one, and if that there doxy is your wife, I'll eat my wife's best Sunday bonnet.'

'How dare you!' Isobel's voice exclaimed.

Riseholm grinned. 'Innocentia, I do believe,' he murmured. He threw open the door. 'Mr Twizzle,' he said, making an elegant bow, 'I do not think that we have met. Your *wife*, on the other hand, is well known to me. I am Riseholm.'

There was a moment's silence as the rest of the group in the parlour came to stand by the open doorway. It had come on to rain a few minutes before, and all the three newcomers looked very tired and bedraggled. Isobel perhaps looked a little worse than the others, since her blue velvet carriage dress had not survived the rain at all well, and nor had her bonnet.

Isobel's hand went to her throat. 'Riseholm,' she breathed. Then, seeing her friend standing by, she exclaimed, 'Lavvy!' her voice breaking on a sob as she took two steps forward. Lavinia hurried to meet her, and without any hesitation put her arms around her dishevelled friend.

Mr Twizzle took a step backwards in consternation. 'The lady appears to be somewhat the worse for wear,' said the earl, staring at him in a way that the young man found extremely unnerving. He paused. 'Perhaps I should inform you, sir, that this lady, far from being *your* wife, is engaged to be married to *me*. It is therefore my privilege as well as my duty to protect her reputation, with which you appear to have been playing ducks and drakes. Well? Do you have any explanation to offer?'

Mr Twizzle had had a very trying day, and given all the circumstances, he really felt that he had done the best that he could. He had managed to escort Miss Macclesfield to safety, for instance, when for two pins he could have left the termagant to fend for herself. Now, the dangerous-looking man who had *not* been in the vicinity when gallantry was called for, stood with his hand resting where his sword hilt should be, clearly threatening violence. It was all too much.

'Be damned to you all!' he exclaimed, and ran out into the inn yard, intending to flee.

A single horseman who had arrived at that very moment blocked his way. 'Benjamin Twizzle!' exclaimed Lord Thurlby, swiftly dismounting and seizing hold of his arm. 'You've a lot to answer for.'

Twizzle's reply was a single word that would have made his father blush right up to his ears.

20

On hearing Thurlby's voice, Lavinia involuntarily took a step towards the door, breathing his name. Riseholm came to take Lavinia's place. 'Go to him,' he said.

Isobel and Riseholm were left facing one another. This was not how she had planned to appear before him next, in a wet gown with a muddy hem and her hair all coming down. With this misfortune, all her ability to flirt or dissemble seemed to have deserted her. 'You can't be engaged to me,' she said, her eyes looking very big in her pale face. 'You're engaged to Miss Egan.'

'I'm no more engaged to Miss Egan than you are to Twizzle out there,' he said. 'Whatever possessed you?'

'It all began when we left London on the stage,' she said with a sigh, clearly intending to embark on a long tale.

'Oh, enough,' he said impatiently, tilting her chin with one finger and kissing her firmly on her mouth. 'Tell me later.'

★   ★   ★

Having first ordered the landlord to make hot drinks for everyone, Timothy Ames went outside to help Thurlby with Benjamin Twizzle who was still struggling. As for Lavinia, the harsh words that she and Thurlby had exchanged were all forgotten. Riseholm had almost challenged Twizzle to a duel, but was now exchanging endearments with Isobel. What if Thurlby felt obliged to fight Twizzle in his place? What violence might be done out there if no one intervened? Regardless of the rain, Lavinia ran into the yard. 'Please, no! You mustn't fight him,' she cried.

On catching sight of her, Thurlby released Twizzle into Ames's care, and covered the ground between them in two strides. 'Lavinia, my darling! Forgive me!' he exclaimed, pulling her against him and kissing her fiercely under the brim of his wide country hat.

'Forgive what?' she asked him as soon as she was able, her eyes shining.

'For keeping you out in the rain, for one thing,' he responded, taking her hand and running with her into the lighted entrance. He handed his wet hat and riding coat to the landlord, but instead of going straight into the parlour to join the others, he drew her along the passage that led towards the back of the inn, and then into the recess beneath the stairs. Once there, he took hold of both her hands and raised them to his lips, one after another. 'My mother told me that I was being pig-headed,' he said. 'I was bound to agree with her. I should say that I also admitted to her that I was an unreasonable bully. Lavinia, I should have listened to you; I should have believed you.'

'Yes; you should,' she agreed, determined not to let him get away with this too lightly.

'What would you say if I promised you that I would greet your every utterance from now on with full attention and absolute deference?' he asked her.

'I don't think I would believe you,' she replied. 'And what's more . . . ' She paused.

'What's more?'

'I think I would find that rather dull,' she said frankly.

He caught her in his arms and, drawing her close to him, kissed her tenderly. 'That's what our first kiss should have been like,' he said remorsefully. 'Instead I handled you with unforgivable roughness, and turned what should have been a pleasure into a punishment. You know why, of course.'

'No I don't,' she responded. 'Tell me.'

'I was horribly jealous,' he admitted. 'Just the thought of you exchanging endearments with Riseholm was more than I could bear.'

'I have never exchanged endearments with Riseholm,' she said.

'I know that now,' he answered. 'I suppose I always did.'

'Nor have I ever received — what was it? — boxes of sweetmeats and palomino ponies,' she added mischievously.

He drew her close to him again, chuckling. 'Would you like to do so?' he asked her.

'Well, maybe just one or two,' she replied, running a hand up the front of his waistcoat.

'I shall attend to it as soon as may be,' he smiled, lowering his head to kiss her again.

In the meantime, Timothy Ames's patient approach had succeeded where Riseholm's insinuations and Thurlby's more open threats had failed, and the vicar had managed to persuade Benjamin Twizzle to come into the inn and to tell his story. Caroline had ministered to the driver who was now dozing by the fire in the tap room, the graze on his head tended by her expert hands whilst he had told her his version what had occurred.

'There's no real harm in him,' the vicar explained to the rest of the party when they were all gathered together in the parlour with the exception of Mr Twizzle. 'He's just a silly young man, desperate to cut a dash in the world but without the means to do so.'

By now, the rain had become increasingly heavy, the inn yard was awash and the company had come to a decision to stay the night.

321

There was no danger of Twizzle's absconding in such atrocious weather, so after he had changed into dry clothing, he had taken refuge in the tap room. Unsurprisingly, he had not wanted to sit in the same room as Isobel or Riseholm, not to mention Thurlby, and the landlord had promised to keep an eye on him.

Thurlby and Lavinia had returned from their spot under the stairs, looking a little bashful, but very happy. Isobel had also changed out of her wet clothes, and she was sitting with Lord Riseholm on a settle next to the fire, her hand in his. Caroline was next to Timothy at the table.

'He was blackmailing me,' Isobel said indignantly.

'He was desperate for money,' Ames explained. 'This villain Nightshade had won money from him, and he had no means to pay it back. He discovered that you, Miss Macclesfield, had a secret that you did not want revealed, and he decided to see if he could make money out of it.'

'All because of a few letters,' Isobel replied. Riseholm chuckled and raised her hand to his lips.

'A pity you had to drag Lavinia into it,' said Thurlby. 'If you'd just given a little thought to someone other than yourself — '

'Hush,' said Lavinia, squeezing his arm. 'It

doesn't matter now.'

Riseholm raised his hooded eyes and looked straight at Thurlby. As the years went by, they would doubtless meet because of the friendship between Lavinia and Isobel; but they were unlikely to become close friends.

'The point is, what to do with the fellow?' asked Ames.

'Have him thrown into prison,' said Isobel.

'It is what he deserves,' Caroline agreed reluctantly. 'He has broken the law after all. Blackmail is against the law, isn't it? And he did run off with Miss Macclesfield.'

'My dear, we must be fair,' the vicar responded. He turned to Riseholm. 'I have no wish to offend you, my lord, but we are not talking about an abduction here. This was an elopement. As we both know, for an elopement to take place, one person generally has to suggest it. I will say no more.'

'Isobel?' said Riseholm.

She had a handkerchief in one hand. Now she began twisting it into a screw. 'I could not see any other way out,' she protested. 'Everyone either hated or disapproved of me. There was no one to help. What else could I do?'

'You could have come to me,' Riseholm suggested.

'Yes, but you were engaged to that insipid Miss Egan.'

323

'I hesitate to contradict a lady, but I was not anything of the kind,' he responded.

'I, too, have been brought up not to contradict a lady,' said Thurlby, 'but I must tell you, Miss Macclesfield that regardless of whether I did or did not approve of your behaviour, I would never have allowed Twizzle to blackmail you.'

Isobel looked up at him. 'I'm sorry for damaging your desk,' she said.

'What's this?' Riseholm asked.

'Twizzle isn't the only law-breaker in this inn,' Thurlby said. 'Tell me, Riseholm, what would you do with someone who broke into your desk and stole a hundred pounds?'

Isobel murmured and buried her head in her lord's shoulder. Riseholm raised an ironic eyebrow. 'Keep my eye on them, in exceedingly close confinement,' he drawled, before kissing the top of her head.

'Nevertheless, Twizzle is a young man with a penchant for bad company, and it would break his father's heart if he were to go to prison one day for lack of guidance,' said Timothy. 'Is there no other way? What he needs is help; a good example; and work to do, for someone who will not let him get away with anything.'

There was a long pause. 'Clearly that can't be me,' said Riseholm, 'for everyone knows that I am an appalling example and I let everybody get away with everything.' He looked down at Isobel.

Thurlby sighed. 'What do you suggest?' he said.

★ ★ ★

After some further conversation, the company retired to bed, the three ladies sharing one room. Thurlby and Ames shared another, Twizzle, anxious to put some distance between himself and the others, bedded down above the stable, and Riseholm slept alone.

Caroline and Lavinia awoke in the morning to find Isobel gone, and in her place a note informing them that she was eloping again, this time with Riseholm. Although the earl had taken her in his own carriage, he had given orders for word to be sent to Thurlby, requesting a conveyance for the rest of the party. For Thurlby and Lavinia, this slight wait was no punishment, and a gentle walk in the countryside, fresh and clean after the rain, provided a welcome opportunity to make further confessions of love, to their mutual delight.

'I think that I began to fall in love with you when you first stepped down from the stagecoach at Stamford,' the earl confessed.

'You confused me because although I was angry with you for behaving recklessly, I couldn't get out of my head what a lovely woman you had become. Then soon I found that I couldn't stop thinking about you.'

'When I was a girl, I was a little infatuated with you,' Lavinia admitted. 'I was so angry with you when you thought the worst of me, but I couldn't stay angry with you for long. Then, at Folkingham when you almost kissed me . . . ' She paused, blushing.

'Well?' he prompted. They had been walking along a little woodland path, her hand tucked in his arm. Now they turned to face one another and he caught hold of her.

'I was so disappointed that you didn't,' she confessed.

'I will do my best never to disappoint you again,' he murmured against her lips.

Epilogue

There could have been no one happier than Lady Thurlby on the morning when her son was united in marriage to Miss Lavinia Muir in Thurlby parish church. The day dawned bright and clear, and the whole village turned out to see the wedding of an exceedingly popular couple.

The ceremony was conducted by The Rev'd Timothy Ames, and the church looked a picture, adorned with flowers arranged by Mrs Ames, whose own marriage had taken place in the next parish only three weeks before, with Miss Lavinia Muir acting as her attendant, as the friends had both agreed.

It had been hoped that Lord and Lady Riseholm would grace the occasion with their presence, but they had not been heard from since their late night elopement.

'We'll soon hear about them cutting a dash in London, no doubt,' said Lavinia one day when she and Thurlby were talking about those who would be coming to the wedding.

'They are welcome to do so,' he responded,

'as long as you don't expect me to do the same.' He paused briefly. 'I hope you won't be disappointed in me, Lavinia,' he went on a little diffidently. 'I know you'll want to go to London from time to time, and I'll be happy to escort you; but essentially I'm a country gentleman.'

'I could never be disappointed in you,' she assured him, giving his arm a little squeeze. 'Unless, of course, I find that Isobel has received more sweetmeats and palomino ponies than have I!'

Lord and Lady Thurlby's wedding breakfast took place in the ballroom at Thurlby Hall, with tables also set out on the south lawn, for the earl's tenants and servants to share his joy. Scurrying between the two was Benjamin Twizzle, who had been made responsible for the arrangements. Part of his salary was being paid to the landlord of the Horseshoe in order to make up for the loss of his horses and carriage.

'He makes me laugh,' Lady Thurlby told her son and daughter-in-law at the wedding breakfast, when they asked her if she would be lonely without them whilst they were on their honeymoon. 'And with Miss Wheatman to keep me company, I shall be very well cared for. Unless, of course, you would like to take her with you. Should the weather be inclement, I'm sure that she would have some helpful suggestions as to what to do.'

'Oh, I don't think that that will be necessary,' the earl replied, smiling down into his wife's eyes.

We do hope that you have enjoyed reading this large print book.

Did you know that all of our titles are available for purchase?

We publish a wide range of high quality large print books including:
Romances, Mysteries, Classics General Fiction Non Fiction and Westerns

Special interest titles available in large print are:
The Little Oxford Dictionary Music Book Song Book Hymn Book Service Book

Also available from us courtesy of Oxford University Press:
Young Readers' Dictionary (large print edition) Young Readers' Thesaurus (large print edition)

For further information or a free brochure, please contact us at:
Ulverscroft Large Print Books Ltd., The Green, Bradgate Road, Anstey, Leicester, LE7 7FU, England. Tel: (00 44) 0116 236 4325 Fax: (00 44) 0116 234 0205

Other titles published by
The House of Ulverscroft:

THEODORA IN LOVE

Ann Barker

After her father's death Theodora Buckleigh's new adopted family want to give her a London season. But though she is a pretty girl, Theodora has limped from birth, and dreads exposure to the social round. She takes evasive action, accepting an invitation from Dorothy Wordsworth to stay with her and her poet brother, William, in Dorset. Here she will find love, danger and intrigue. Might Coleridge and the others be engaged in treason? Can Theodora's chaperone, Alex Kydd, rescue her from this dangerous company; and even if he does, could there ever be any more between them than friendship?

JILTED

Ann Barker

When Eustacia Hope is jilted at the altar, her parents send her to stay with her godmother Lady Agatha Rayner, a clergyman's widow. Her mother warns her to shun Lady Agatha's brother, the notorious Lord Ashbourne and his son Lord Ilam. And she soon discovers that her godmother isn't all she seems either. Then Eustacia meets Lord Ilam and the two are attracted to one another. But it is only after the arrival of Eustacia's estranged fiance and the unexpected appearance of Lord Ashbourne that matters can be resolved in a way that is satisfactory to all parties.

CLERKENWELL CONSPIRACY

Ann Barker

When Captain Scorer died in action, his wife Eve was obliged to seek refuge with her cousin Julia. Treated as a poor relation and pursued by Julia's admirer, Eve is thankful when escape is offered through the bequest of a bookshop in Clerkenwell. She has no knowledge that Colonel Jason 'Blazes' Ballantyne, her husband's commanding officer, has been ordered by William Pitt to make enquiries concerning a codebook that has been left in the bookshop by French spies. When certain incidents and rumours convince Jason that Eve has a dubious reputation, it doesn't prevent attraction flaring between them . . .

LADY OF LINCOLN

Ann Barker

For Emily Whittaker living in Lincoln, the closest thing to romance is her lukewarm relationship with Dr Boyle. But a new friendship with Nathalie Fanshawe brings interest to her life. Then Canon Trimmer and his family move into the cathedral close. When Mrs Trimmer's brother, Sir Gareth Blades visits them, he seems a romantic figure, and apparently attracted to Emily. But she finds a mysterious side to Sir Gareth with the arrival of Annis Hughes, not to mention his connection with Mrs Fanshawe . . . Is Sir Gareth really a gallant gentleman or would Emily be better off settling for Dr Boyle after all?

THE OTHER MISS FROBISHER

Ann Barker

Elfrida Frobisher leaves her country backwater and her suitor to chaperon Prudence, her eighteen-year-old niece, in London. Unfortunately, Prudence has apparently developed an attachment for an unsuitable man, which she fosters behind her aunt's back. Attempting to foil her niece's schemes and prevent a scandal, Elfrida only succeeds in finding herself involved with the eligible Rufus Tyler in a scandal of her own! Fleeing London seems the only solution — but Prudence has another plan . . . Elfrida yearns for her quiet rural existence, but it takes a mad dash in pursuit of her niece before she realises where her heart truly lies.

THE ADVENTURESS

Ann Barker

Florence Browne lives in poverty with her miserly father, but seeking adventure, she goes to Bath under the assumed name Lady Firenza Le Grey. But there, she meets a man calling himself Sir Vittorio Le Grey, who accuses her of being an adventuress. When her previous suitor, Gilbert Stapleton, visits Bath, Florence is plagued by doubts. Is Sir Vittorio the wicked Italian he appears to be? Are Mr Stapleton's professions of love sincere? And how can she accept an offer of marriage from anyone while she is still living a lie?